The Healing Train

D1520899

a novel by
Kim Cano

For my husband.

I'm glad I beat cancer so I can keep growing old with you.

Chapter 1

Sarah's mother reached for her hand and gave it a gentle squeeze. "You okay?" Beverly asked.

Sarah gazed out the train window. She was definitely not okay. As a healthy eater who didn't take medication and walked ten thousand steps per day, she still couldn't believe they were going to Chicago for her first chemotherapy treatment rather than a day of shopping and fun. To make matters worse, she had a super aggressive kind of breast cancer called triple-negative, which meant Sarah agreed to put one of the most powerful chemotherapy drugs ever created into her body. A medication named AC, or what many called The Red Devil.

"I'm okay," Sarah told her mother because her mother needed her to be okay—as did her husband, daughter, and brother. No matter how on edge she felt—how absolutely terrified—she would need to be okay for them.

Beverly turned toward her. "I still can't get over how crazy this is. I mean, you never smoked. You rarely drink. You buy organic food and take all those expensive supplements. And no one in the family has had cancer. It doesn't make sense."

It didn't make sense to Sarah either. She and her

husband, Jeff, tried to live a healthy lifestyle. Although organic groceries cost more, they had figured they were making an investment in themselves. A pay now or pay later type of thing.

"These things just happen," Sarah said. She wished there was a logical explanation, but oftentimes, there wasn't. Some people became recipients of unlucky prizes on the wheel of life.

After reading about diagnosis mistakes, Sarah made sure that two pathologists at two different hospitals examined the biopsied tissue. Both had come to the same conclusion. It was cancer. That was no mistake.

As the train rumbled toward its next stop, Sarah's phone pinged. She pulled it from her purse and saw a text from her daughter Heather.

"Thinking of you."

Heather had wanted to come to Sarah's first chemo treatment, but Sarah didn't want her to miss school. College was important, and Heather was in her third year and doing well. Sarah didn't want her illness to interfere with her daughter obtaining her business degree.

Sarah texted a row of hearts back, hoping Heather wouldn't spend valuable study time worrying about her. It was bad enough that her husband was so upset. When she'd made Jeff breakfast this morning, he didn't eat it. Instead, he'd rushed out the door after giving her a kiss and wishing her luck, claiming he was running late for work. Jeff never missed breakfast, whether he was running late or not. He ate two scrambled eggs with toast and coffee every day, while Sarah, who worked from home doing Facebook ads for small businesses, had her first meal at noon. The look in Jeff's eyes had said it all before he left. He was terrified to go on the journey they were about to embark on together.

The train conductor announced the next stop.

"We're almost there," Beverly mentioned after putting her phone away.

She'd probably been texting Sarah's brother or stepdad as everyone wanted to know what was happening. Sarah appreciated their concern but disliked being the center of attention, especially for something as horrible as this.

Passengers rose in advance of the final stop downtown and began lining up at the train's door, each appearing eager to get off first. Sarah and Beverly had come to the appointment early and weren't in a hurry, so they stayed seated, allowing others to leave before them. Sarah had taken an earlier train on purpose because, although Beverly was in good health at seventy-five years old, Sarah didn't want to push her to walk too quickly and chance a fall.

A sea of people moved toward the escalators, Sarah and Beverly part of the wave. The crush of humanity suffocated Sarah, who tried to avoid crowds whenever possible because being with large groups of people made her anxious. Working from home and rarely interacting with others probably didn't help.

Sarah and Beverly hopped into one of the cabs lined up outside the train station. Shortly afterward, a plethora of luxury stores appeared on the Magnificent Mile. Beautiful women with shopping bags walked down the street. They looked happy and like they were having fun. Suddenly, Sarah wanted to jump from the cab and join them. She wanted to escape reality and make a new friend. Instead, the cab driver turned the corner, and they were at the hospital. It was time to do what she had to do, whether she liked it or not.

Beverly paid the cab driver. "I'll get this one," she told Sarah. "You can get the one on the way back."

Sarah nodded, appreciating her mother's help. Choosing treatment at this hospital meant spending more on trains, cabs, and meals away from home than she would've usually spent. But after Jeff learned his health insurance covered this institution, he decided to spare no expense in saving Sarah's life. They had been together for thirty years, and in that time, they'd always gotten along well and rarely fought. She promised him she would do everything in her power to survive for him and Heather.

Now it was time to start.

Beverly reached for Sarah's hand as they entered the hospital. A security guard gave them passes to access the fourth floor, then they took the elevator up, and Sarah checked in for her appointment.

After sitting down, Sarah noticed most of the women in the waiting area were bald or had scarves wrapped around their heads. Instinctively, she ran her fingers through her long blonde hair. She'd considered cutting it shorter when she turned fifty. She hadn't because her daughter claimed she could still pull off her current style. Dr. Zimmerman told her it would begin to fall out shortly after her second treatment. She said many patients got a pixie haircut or shaved their heads before it happened, so they were in control of the loss. She also gave Sarah information on wigs.

A nurse called Sarah's name. She and Beverly rose, followed the young woman down a corridor of hospital rooms, and entered the one on the right. Sarah sat on the edge of the bed, waiting for instruction. Her mom sat on a nearby comfy chair.

The nurse smiled at Sarah. "We take blood first and check all your numbers before we start."

Sarah nodded and unbuttoned her shirt. A week before, she had a chemotherapy port put into her chest. Dr. Zimmerman had said it would save the veins in her arms and that it was safer for the kind of chemo she was going to receive. Sarah hadn't liked the idea of having a foreign object stuck into her body but gave in after weighing the pros and cons. She now had a round plastic device the size of a nickel below her collarbone. Attached to it was a small tube that ran into the jugular vein in her neck.

"This may feel odd the first time it happens," the nurse warned.

Sarah closed her eyes as the woman approached with the needle. She felt it prick her skin and then press into the port, putting slight pressure on her chest. Sarah had always hated needles. Hated them with a passion. She used to get worked up about the butterfly needle they used to draw blood at her annual exam. This experience was worse than that, and it was definitely odd. It was like being a human voodoo doll.

The nurse got the needed vials and left the room. Sarah made eye contact with Beverly. She could tell her mother wanted to know how it went. "It wasn't too bad," she fibbed. "The first time is weird like the nurse said."

Beverly's raised shoulders relaxed as she let out a deep sigh. Sarah felt terrible that this experience was as stressful for her mother as it was for her. She could understand, though, being a mother herself. If she were here with Heather, she'd be out of her mind with worry. The calm Beverly portrayed would be impossible for Sarah to attain.

Sarah gazed out the window at Lake Michigan. "It's a pretty view."

Beverly nodded in agreement. "It is. I love the details of all the old buildings. Unfortunately, they don't make them like that anymore."

The nurse returned, bringing their focus back to her. "Let me tell you more about the medications we'll be giving you while we wait for the bloodwork results."

Sarah and Beverly hung on her every word. First, they'd give her fluids, then something to prevent nausea, and then they'd start the chemo. Afterward, they'd give her a medication to increase white blood cells, which wouldn't be delivered via the port but by a pager-like device attached to the back of her upper arm.

The nurse showed her the device. "This is called Neulasta. A needle inside pricks your arm after it's applied, and then we tape it so it's secure. The medication gets delivered twenty-four hours after your chemo session ends. You'll hear a beeping sound before it's released.

Remove the device from the skin when it's empty. When it goes below this line." She indicated where to look and then turned to Beverly. "It may be easier for you to pull this off your daughter's arm. Loosen the tape first and pull it straight out, like this," she said, demonstrating how to do it. "You don't want to pull it up or down because the needle will dig into the skin and cause bleeding."

"Pull it straight out," Beverly repeated, ensuring she'd understood.

Another needle, Sarah noted. She'd thought the port would eliminate additional pricks, but of course, it would just lessen the overall amount.

"One more thing," the nurse said. "Don't put your cell phone near the device. Doing so can interfere with the release of the medication, and if that happens, you'll have to come back, and we'll have to give you another one."

"No phones near Neulasta," Sarah repeated.

Beverly and Sarah exchanged a look. They seemed on the same page and understood everything the young lady had said.

The nurse continued after setting the gadget down. "Now, I'd like to discuss what to do and not do after receiving this chemotherapy."

Dr. Zimmerman's assistant had reviewed this with Sarah, and she had purchased everything she had said she'd need in advance but figured it couldn't hurt to hear the information again.

"Since your bodily fluids won't be safe for others to come in contact with for the next two months, you'll need disinfectant wipes and special gloves to clean the toilet seat each time you use the bathroom. The blue gloves we use here aren't sufficient. They need to be chemo-rated. The kind the police use when interacting with dangerous substances like fentanyl."

Sarah nodded. "My husband bought them online last week."

"Good." The nurse paused before continuing. "Ideally, you'd have your own bathroom, so you don't have to share with anyone else, but if that's not possible, you have to do this. Follow the same cleaning protocol if you vomit. Of course, we'll give you anti-nausea pills to manage those symptoms, but take them at the first sign of nausea. Don't wait until you're ill because they'll take longer to work."

"Okay," Sarah said, hoping she wouldn't need to take them.

"Also, your tears and saliva shouldn't interact with anyone. You should sneeze into a tissue and promptly dispose of it in a garbage can with a lid, then wash your hands afterward. Make sure to have tissues with you wherever you go. And never sneeze into the air while doing AC chemo as the droplets will fall to the ground and could negatively affect your pets."

The thought of Sarah's tabby cat Walter being harmed was unthinkable. She'd make sure never to sneeze into the air.

"And on that note, don't forget to have someone else care for your pets. No cleaning kitty litter or picking up dog poop. It's not good for your immune system. Plus, we don't recommend kissing your pet's fur."

"Got it," Sarah said. Heather had already agreed to be Walter's housekeeper while she got well. It would be tough not to kiss Walter, as she'd been in the habit of kissing him on the top of his head many times per day.

Sarah mentally reviewed all the rules as the nurse left the room. She hoped she wouldn't forget anything and wished she had taken notes.

"It's a lot to remember," Beverly said. "But I highlighted that info in the treatment booklet, so it's easy to find. Heather and I reviewed it, so we should know what to do between the three of us."

Sarah nodded. Just then, the nurse returned with a clear bag of medication.

"Let's get you started on fluids and the steroid," the nurse said. She hung the bag onto what looked like a tall silver coat rack with rolling wheels. Except this coat rack was plugged into the wall. Sarah watched the nurse attach the tubing line to the port in her chest. When the drip started, she felt nothing, which was a pleasant surprise. The nurse showed Sarah which button to press if she needed anything before leaving, and then Sarah smiled at Beverly, letting her know everything was fine. She felt awful that her mother was at the hospital battling cancer with her instead of taking that highly anticipated riverboat cruise through Europe with her spouse. Sarah had tried to convince Beverly not to cancel the trip, but her mom said there was no way she could leave Sarah and have fun. And putting chemo off until she returned from the cruise wasn't an option because Sarah's cancer was too aggressive.

A loud beeping sound repeated a little while later, making the nurse return. This time, she had a bag filled with red fluid in her hands. The sight of it filled Sarah with fear.

"Some people say looking away makes it easier," the nurse said as she got ready to start.

Sarah did as instructed, focusing on her mom's caring face instead of the chemotherapy drug. Like the previous infusion, it was painless. After reading several breast cancer blogs online, she learned that would be the case and was grateful the information had been correct.

As she took deep breaths to remain calm, her phone vibrated. She eyed the screen and noticed it was a call from her father. They hadn't spoken in years. What on earth could he want?

Chapter 2

Heather and Jeff were in the kitchen when Beverly dropped Sarah off at home. Heather smiled brightly when she saw her mother, while Jeff seemed to be waiting for a reaction from Sarah before deciding how to respond.

Exhausted, Sarah managed a wan smile as she set her purse on the counter. Heather rushed to her and gave her a hug. Jeff watched the interaction closely, giving Sarah an empathetic look and acknowledging how she really felt.

Jeff ran a hand through his wavy brown hair, something he did when he was nervous. "Caleb dropped off beef stew for dinner, and Heather and I made you some green juice."

Heather's boyfriend Caleb was a cook at a local family restaurant. Sarah thought it was sweet that he had gone out of his way to make them dinner when they were all stressed out and pressed for time. The green juice didn't look appealing, but she didn't want to disappoint Heather, who had read about the elixir's positive effects on cancer patients. Sarah had agreed to drink the vegetable concoction and do chemo as her oncologist had said it was fine. So far, there was no sign of nausea. The medication the nurse had given her was doing the trick. She wasn't all that hungry but figured she'd eat now so she could lay down afterward and rest.

"I'll try the juice first," Sarah said with manufactured enthusiasm. The plan was to get it out of the way so she could enjoy her meal.

"Excellent!" Heather said as she headed to the cabinet and reached for a glass.

Her husband and daughter were buzzing with energy. A combination of fear, worry, and hope, Sarah supposed. She sat at the kitchen table and waited as Heather poured all three of them a serving of juice. Sarah had assumed she would be the only one stuck drinking it and found their solidarity considerate in what was likely to be an unpleasant experience at best.

Heather's blue eyes sparkled as she handed Sarah her portion. Sarah lifted the glass and took a sip. The green juice tasted like lawn clippings with a hint of lemon. Not something Sarah liked, but it was tolerable, so she continued drinking it, forcing herself to swallow every last drop. Jeff's face wrinkled with displeasure as he forced himself to do the same.

Heather chugged hers like it was a chocolate shake and set her glass on the counter. "The juice goes right to your cells," she exclaimed. "It's better than eating vegetables because your body can use it ASAP. No time is wasted digesting all the fiber."

Sarah had read some of the information Heather had emailed to her. It was all about how eating more veggies and drinking freshly made juice alkalized the body, making it inhospitable for cancer cells. To Sarah's knowledge, no clinical trials had been conducted on the subject. When she had mentioned that to Jeff, he had pointed out that it wouldn't make sense to run clinical trials on food because there was no money in it. He had said they only ran trials on drugs that could be sold for big bucks. Sarah wasn't sure if that was true or not. All she knew was she would do chemo, eat veggies, and drink juice. She'd throw everything in her arsenal at the disease, hoping to be cured.

Caleb's beef stew was tasty, with tender cuts of meat and potatoes and carrots that were cooked just right. Sarah had been warned that soon everything she ate would taste like cardboard. A side effect of chemo, which was expected and would resolve when treatment ended. Unpleasant but nothing to worry about, Dr. Zimmerman had said.

Jeff rinsed the dishes and loaded them in the dishwasher when they finished their meal.

As Sarah rose from the table, Heather asked, "Do you need anything?"

"No, thanks," Sarah said. "You guys have already been a really big help."

Heather nodded and then disappeared into her room. Sarah didn't want her daughter to spend too much time taking care of her. She wanted her to focus on her homework and graduate from college. She was supposed to take care of her child. Not the other way around.

Sarah went to the restroom, washed her face, and brushed her teeth. As she changed out of her clothes to put on comfy pajamas, she looked at herself undressed in the mirror, noting her perfectly even but slightly sagging breasts. They had been perkier before but had dropped with age. She used to get upset because they didn't look as good as they once had. Now she loved them simply because they existed. She couldn't imagine losing one and how she would emotionally deal with that. Reconstruction options were available, Dr. Zimmerman had said. They would set up a consultation with a plastic surgeon so she could learn more about them and make a choice. But Sarah didn't want a new breast. She wanted to keep the one she had. She told herself not to worry about it as she reached for the hairbrush and started brushing her hair. She had to get through five months of chemo first. Surgery would be afterward when the cancerous lymph nodes in her underarm had hopefully shrunk. Removing underarm lymph nodes could negatively affect the use of a person's arm. That's why shrinking them with chemotherapy before surgery was crucial.

Sarah shuddered as she considered losing her hair, her breast, and the use of her left arm. She stared at her reflection and realized what she hadn't been able to accept—that she could die from this. Triple-negative breast cancer is the deadliest kind of breast cancer. The kind they tell you not to google online. Of course, Sarah had researched it and read all the grim statistics. But she planned to beat the odds and ignore those life expectancy results.

Sarah gathered a box of tissues and a small cleaning bucket to put next to her bed in case she got sick and couldn't get to the bathroom in time. She made sure the gloves and disinfectant wipes were close to the toilet as they only had two bathrooms, one in their bedroom, which she and Jeff shared, and one next to Heather's room, which Sarah and Jeff didn't use. As Sarah entered her bedroom, she found Walter curled up on her bed. He lifted his head as she approached. His green eyes held her gaze, seeming to understand everything she felt without words or meows.

"Hey, sweetie," Sarah said as she put the tissues on the nightstand. She would normally pet and kiss him but refrained, fearing it could harm him. Instead, she climbed under the blankets and dimmed the light. Walter inched closer, burrowing next to her legs. He purred even though she hadn't petted him, which made her feel less guilty about not being able to give him the attention he deserved.

Sarah mentally reviewed her to-do list after closing her eyes. All her cancer-related tasks were done, and client emails could be handled in the morning. Luckily, there were only a few of those. She still hadn't listened to her father's voicemail because she didn't have the energy for that kind of drama. Plus, she needed to keep the phone as far away as possible from the device on her right arm. When it had finished delivering the medicine, she'd feel comfortable using the phone again.

Jeff came into the bedroom. He undressed, turned off the light, and climbed into bed.

"Are you okay?" he asked in the dark.

Sarah wasn't sure but felt the best answer was yes, so that's what she said.

"You're not in pain, are you?"

"No. There were a couple of needle pokes, but the chemotherapy infusion doesn't hurt."

Sarah heard Jeff exhale loudly. "That's good." He rolled over and faced her. "I wish I could've been there."

"Me too," Sarah replied.

Jeff had used up all his remaining vacation days taking her to previous doctor appointments. She had assured him he didn't need to come to the biopsy or PET scan, but he wouldn't hear of it. He had been worried and wanted to know what the doctors said as they said it instead of hearing it after the fact. Since both of them had always been healthy, neither had expected something as serious as cancer to occur. Sarah was grateful that her mother was retired and available to go to appointments with her downtown. She could take the train to the hospital herself, but it was easier to have someone along for support.

Jeff gave Sarah a quick kiss on the cheek instead of the lips because of AC chemo. Usually, he turned over and fell asleep afterward. Tonight, he snuggled up to her, wrapped his arms around her, and held her close. Light snores came within a few minutes; although extremely tired, Sarah was wide awake. It felt good to have her husband so close. They still had date nights now and again, but as the years passed, they were fewer and farther between. When they were younger, they had been able to work full-time, cook and clean, raise their daughter, and still have an active sex life while making time to see family and friends. But time seemed to move faster now, and they couldn't do as much as they once had in a single day.

When Sarah had complained of being tired all the time, Jeff had said he was tired too and had joked that they were getting old. Fatigue was the only sign of cancer Sarah had received. One that was easy to dismiss as nothing more than needing better quality sleep.

A slight wave of nausea came, and Sarah tensed, wondering if she should reach for the bucket or run to the restroom. Not wanting to disturb her husband, she remained calm and took a few deep breaths. Thankfully, the nausea abated in a few minutes. She hoped it would stay gone for the rest of the night. As she lay there, she thought of the chemotherapy drugs. She feared them and had previously thought of them as poison. Now she wanted to see them as friends. An image of a miniature red devil holding a pitchfork came to mind. He stomped through her cells, stabbing at cancerous ones and leaving healthy ones alone. Visualizing him going about his work helped Sarah relax. She liked to have control over things, and since the cancer diagnosis, she felt totally out of control. Vowing to let him handle the problem, she finally drifted off, her husband still holding her, making her feel safe. She slept for over twelve hours, not waking up until noon the next day.

Sarah padded to the kitchen and saw a cast iron pan on the stove with a lid. She lifted it and looked inside, finding scrambled eggs. Jeff must've made double the portion and left some for her. Although she wasn't hungry, Dr. Zimmerman had said how important it was to eat, so she turned on the flame to heat the food. She rubbed her eyes and headed to the coffee maker. Copious amounts of caffeine were needed if she was going to get any work done today. Walter appeared and sniffed his bowl. Jeff had already given him soft food in the morning, but he tended to beg for dry nuggets whenever someone stepped into the kitchen. If humans were eating, he wanted to eat, too. Sarah found his dry food container and poured him a small amount before making a piece of toast to go with her eggs. When she had finished eating, she went to the restroom. The red urine in the toilet frightened her until she remembered that was supposed to happen. She closed the lid and flushed, then sanitized the area as instructed before washing her hands and drying them on a towel just for her to use.

On the way out of the bathroom, Sarah felt a tickle inside her nose. She realized she had to sneeze and rushed back to grab a wad of toilet paper, balling it up just in time. She disposed of it afterward and rewashed her hands. "This could get crazy," she muttered before grabbing a box of tissues from the linen closet and taking it to her desk.

Sarah opened her laptop. She handled client emails before logging into Facebook to check their ad accounts. Most of the metrics looked good. Their cost per click was low, engagement was decent, and only a few ads needed minor tweaks. She yawned and checked the time, noting she'd only been up for two hours. Just then, a beeping noise got her attention. She glanced around, unsure where it was coming from, then realized it was the device attached to her arm. Walter had been sleeping in a sunny spot on the sofa but jumped up and ran toward Sarah when he heard the sound.

"It's just medicine." She turned her arm and pointed at the gadget. Walter eyed it with suspicion and looked as if he was going to swat at the foreign object, but thankfully, he chose to leave it alone.

Sarah reached out to pet him, thinking she had been overly cautious the day before. The nurse told her not to kiss her cat; she never said she couldn't rub his fur. After they had reconnected, Walter returned to the sunny spot on the sofa while Sarah browsed chemo scarves online. She wasn't particularly good at tying scarves and found a light tan bucket hat that seemed easier to wear and matched pretty much everything. She ordered it, knowing she'd need it soon. Then she reached for her phone since it was safe to use.

There was a text from her brother Mike. He hoped she was doing well and said he'd stop by after work tomorrow with dinner so she wouldn't have to cook. Sarah replied, thanking him and saying she'd see him then. Her father's voicemail was all that was left to check. She had run out of excuses for not listening to it and figured she might as well do it now.

Sarah pressed the button to hear the message. "Hey, Sarah. It's your father. I heard about the cancer diagnosis and want to talk to you. Please give me a call when you can."

Sarah had no idea who could've told him she was ill. Her mother hadn't talked to him in ages, and she didn't think her brother had spoken to him since she got sick. It didn't matter who had told him, she supposed. He knew now, and she would have to call him back. Not today, of course, because she was too busy. But she would get it over with at some point soon.

The doorbell rang, and she went to answer it. Beverly and her stepdad Richard were on the front porch. She opened the door and let them in.

"I'm here to take that thing off your arm," Beverly said.

Richard lifted a large brown bag and smiled. "I've got food!"

Sarah smiled back at him, thinking she could get used to people bringing dinner every night.

Her mother set her purse down and took the bag of food from Richard. She turned to Sarah. "Let me heat the oven so it's ready when we're done. That way, all you have to do is reheat this, and it will be ready when Heather and Jeff get home."

Sarah nodded, happy she was there to help.

"How are you doing?" Richard asked.

"Hanging in there," Sarah replied.

Richard and Beverly had met when Sarah was thirty years old. He had never tried to act like her father but was definitely a father figure.

"That's all you can do," he said. "I know you're not a fan of doctors and medication, but you're kind of stuck dealing with both for a while."

Beverly reappeared, grabbed her purse, then used her finger to gesture for Sarah to follow her to the restroom.

"Let me put on my reading glasses so I can see better." Beverly dug them from her bag and washed her hands afterward, using the hand towel Sarah handed her—the one for everyone else.

Sarah took off her top and let her mom slowly remove the tape that held the Neulasta device to her arm.

"I'm going to pull it off on the count of three. One. Two. Three."

A slight pain was all Sarah felt as it came off. Her mom put a Band-Aid on her arm, and Sarah threw the device in the garbage can and closed the lid.

"I'm glad we only have to do that every two weeks," Beverly said.

"Four times total," Sarah added. "Only three left to go."

Beverly studied her daughter closely. "How are you feeling?"

"Super tired. I thought I was tired before, but this is next-level fatigue."

"And there's something else," Beverly said.

Sarah had no idea how her mother knew these types of things. She seemed to have some kind of sixth sense when it came to anything involving her kids' well-being.

"Dad called," Sarah blurted. She figured she might as well tell her because she'd find out anyway. "Somehow, he heard I was ill, and now he wants me to call him."

"Figures," Beverly huffed. "He never made time for you or your brother, and now he feels guilty because you're sick."

Suddenly, it all became crystal clear. Her seventy-nine-year-old father worried the daughter he never really knew could die before he did, and he didn't want that weighing on his conscience.

An idea on how to best handle the situation came to mind, and Sarah planned to implement it soon. She knew just what to do to make this problem go away.

Chapter 3

Mike showed up the next day with dinner as promised. He didn't cook much, but when he did, every meal he made tasted great. As he put the tray of baked chicken and rice on the kitchen counter, Sarah noticed the whites of his eyes were bloodshot, most likely from the joint he had smoked before he arrived.

"Heard the old man called. What the hell did he want?"

Sarah smirked. "He wants to talk to me because I'm sick."

Mike let out a sarcastic chuckle. "What a douche." He paused before adding, "Seriously, what a fucking piece of shit."

Some people disliked her brother's constant use of swear words, but not Sarah. She admired his ability to use so many of them in a sentence and felt if there were an expletive championship, he'd surely win.

Sarah headed to the living room and sat on the couch. Mike followed, sitting opposite her in a leather club chair.

"Remember when you made all that lemonade and sold it for fifty cents a glass? Mom and I were there. Where the fuck was he?"

Sarah had to think back to being ten years old. "Shanghai, I think. At a conference."

Her father had been a salesperson for an international corporation. They sent him all around the world, and in return, he made great money, most of which he invested wisely. The surplus went toward wining and dining women other than his wife.

The mention of the lemonade stand reminded Sarah that she had planned to show her father how much she had earned that day, but when he didn't show up or ask about the event, she spent the money on a new box of crayons and several packs of bubble gum. She pushed the memory from her mind and pulled her legs onto the sofa. "How about that football game you won in high school? Where was he then?"

Mike tilted his head to the side. "San Diego, I think. At an important sales meeting. He couldn't reschedule it to make it to the game."

Sarah remembered the heartbreaking expression on her brother's face when he'd scored a touchdown and looked up into the stands. His smile faded when he realized his dad had never shown.

They could do this for hours. They had both experienced an endless stream of this kind of disappointment with their dad. Throughout her life, Sarah had learned to tuck each hurt away and distance herself from the problem. Her brother, on the other hand, would start a fight with their father and give him a piece of his mind, letting him know how he felt about how he behaved. Neither approach improved the situation, but

Sarah felt her technique was preferable because it used less energy and time.

"How do you think Dad found out I have cancer?"

Mike shook his head. "I have no clue."

Sarah tapped her fingers on the arm of the sofa and stared into space. She'd asked Jeff and Heather if they had spoken to him, but neither of them had, and Beverly hadn't talked to him in years. Sarah frowned, wondering who could have told him.

"Let's not talk about that moron," Mike said. "Tell me how you're doing."

Her brother had looked like he might faint when she told him the diagnosis. And whenever they discussed her upcoming treatment, she could tell it made him nervous. So he would ask the same questions over and over, and she would provide the same answers to ease his mind.

"I haven't barfed yet," Sarah joked.

Mike smiled. "That's awesome."

Sarah wanted to have a nice family dinner tonight and not talk about her symptoms, so she switched the subject. "Jeff and Heather will be home soon. Why don't I start heating up the food?"

Sarah went to the kitchen and preheated the oven as Mike got comfy in a dining room chair.

"How is Donna?" Sarah asked as she brought silverware to the table.

"Not good."

Her brother had the world's worst luck with women. Like most of the females he dated, Donna had issues, but she was a nice person, and Sarah had high hopes that

Donna and Mike's relationship would last.

"What happened?" Sarah asked.

"Remember the transmission issues with her car? Well, I had that fixed, and more stuff broke, so I suggested she buy something more reliable."

Sarah eyed her brother warily. "You didn't."

"I had to," Mike countered. "How else could she get to work?"

As a service manager at a car dealership, Mike got an employee discount on vehicle purchases. He had used it once to get his ex-girlfriend an SUV, co-signing for her because her credit score was low. Unfortunately, the woman stopped paying for it after they broke up, and he had to sell it before it got repossessed and use his savings to cover the loss. He'd already paid for Donna's transmission. Sarah had no idea why he would do this again.

"So, if you helped Donna get a car, how come she's not doing well?"

Mike sighed. "Because the car got totaled yesterday. Donna's fine, but the car is toast."

Mike drove a twenty-year-old truck. Sarah wished he'd get something new instead of buying vehicles for women he hadn't been dating for long. It would be different if he were doing it for his wife. But her brother had never been married. His relationships always ended in catastrophe instead of producing wedding bells and the additional grandchildren her mother had so hoped to have.

But Sarah was the younger sister. It wasn't her place to give her older brother advice. Despite his negative experiences with women, he remained optimistic about finding "the one." Donna had earned a good wage as a toll booth attendant, but unfortunately, she'd recently lost that position due to automation. She'd retrained to become a hairdresser and was trying to build up a clientele. Sarah was just about to ask how her new job was going when Heather came home.

"Hey, Uncle Mike. Long time no see." Heather came over and leaned over his chair to give her uncle a quick side hug. She'd been at school the last time Mike was over. They could rarely sync their schedules, it seemed. That's why Sarah was happy everyone could be together tonight. Heather turned to her mother. "Dad is on his way. He should be here in a half hour."

The oven beeped, and Sarah put the food inside before joining Heather and Mike in the other room. She listened to them chat about how college was going and smiled, enjoying the normalcy of the moment, which wasn't about her health, for once.

Jeff walked in and kissed Sarah on the cheek. He said hello to Mike, and everyone gathered around the table.

Heather turned to Mike. "Do you want some green juice?"

"Funk that," Mike said, wearing a playful expression.

When Heather was a toddler, Sarah had asked her brother to refrain from using the F word in her presence because children were prone to repeating things they had heard. Mike had obliged, but as Heather got a little older, he'd modified the phrase "fuck that" to "funk that," claiming it was an expletive workaround and not technically swearing. Heather had found it funny and proceeded to use the line at school, earning a detention from her eighth-grade English teacher.

Jeff grinned at Sarah. No doubt he was thinking the same thing she was thinking, remembering that parent-teacher conference with Mrs. Roberts. Her thin, pursed lips hadn't softened as they told her about the scenario with Uncle Mike. She had looked down at them from beneath her bifocals, clearly annoyed that she had to waste time on something like this. To make matters worse, the phrase had caught on with many of Heather's friends. It had gone viral! Mike had found it hysterical, of course. But it was Jeff and Sarah who had to do damage control.

Heather put three glasses of green juice on the table. One for everyone but Mike.

Mike eyed them. "You know, I think I will try one. Why the F not?"

Heather smiled, then returned to the fridge to pour him a glass of his own. After handing it to him, she said, "You'll like it. Seriously, it tastes good."

Mike was a junk food aficionado but had begun eating salads for lunch since Sarah got sick. Everyone in their circle had upped their game on the food front, making small positive changes without going overboard. They dug into the main course, and Sarah listened to Jeff and Mike discuss the possible origins of a new noise in the dash of their car. She excused herself in the middle of the conversation to use the restroom. When she returned after finishing the cleaning routine, they'd moved on to talking about a new flooring product at Jeff's work. Mike had been keen to replace the old carpet in his condo with wood floors. Sarah listened to Jeff describe the pricing and benefits of the available options, and although she was having a good time, she was getting sleepy and yawned.

Jeff looked her way and, shortly afterward, took his empty plate to the sink and rinsed it off. They used to have some form of dessert when they had company but stopped since cancer came to town. When Sarah had the PET scan, the tech explained how the test located cancer in the body. First, they injected a radioactive sugary substance into her vein, then the machine scanned her, and the areas that "lit up" were cancer. Sarah had asked why the sugary dye made the cancerous areas glow and was horrified to learn it was because cancer cells love sugar. There was no scientific proof that sugar consumption caused cancer, but when she considered how the PET scan worked, it was enough to scare Sarah straight. Since then, she ate a piece of fruit when a dessert craving hit. Sure, it still had sugar, but at least it wasn't a candy bar or slice of cake. Although she'd done many things to stay healthy, she'd always had a sweet tooth. It had been her only vice. Dr. Zimmerman told her not to beat herself up over things she'd eaten in the past. Instead, she suggested a healthy, balanced diet from now on. Still, Sarah wished she could go back and not eat all those desserts. Maybe things would've turned out differently. Maybe she wouldn't have gotten sick.

Heather rose from her seat, bringing Sarah's attention

back to the group. Her daughter took Mike's empty plate from him and put it on top of her own before taking it to the sink. Then Sarah got up to bring hers to the sink too.

"Everything was delicious," Sarah told Mike when she returned to the table. "Thanks so much."

"You're welcome." Her brother stood. "I should probably get going so you can rest."

Mike said goodbye to everyone before Sarah walked him to the front door.

"Kick cancer to the curb," he said on his way out. "And let me know what happens with the old man."

"Will do." Sarah shut the door. She felt a wave of lethargy that could only be cured by sleeping and, ultimately, handling that issue soon. Even though it was only nine, she headed upstairs to get ready for bed.

Jeff usually turned in by ten but called it a night at nine for her sake. He climbed into bed and turned on his side to see Sarah. "How are you doing?"

"It's like the nurse said. I'll feel worse as the weekend approaches." Sarah's bones had started hurting, which was a common side effect of Neulasta. She took several pills with breakfast daily to reduce treatment symptoms. So far, the medication had worked well for nausea but didn't do much for bone pain.

"What does it feel like?" Jeff asked.

Sarah wasn't sure if he wanted to know what cancer felt like or how she felt a few days after receiving chemo, so she described both. "My underarm lymph nodes are swollen and a little painful, but my breast doesn't hurt." She tried to think of the best way to explain her current state. "The chemo after-effects feel like…" She trailed off, wondering how much she should share. Jeff had fallen to his knees and sobbed when he learned she had cancer. She wanted to answer his question honestly but didn't want to upset him again. "It feels like I've been poisoned," she admitted. "Like an atomic bomb went off inside of my body."

Jeff's eyes widened.

"But that means the medicine is working. It's sweeping through my system and killing those cancer cells, the ones in my breast and underarm, and the ones that may be floating around undetected but getting ideas on becoming something more."

"Why don't they have better treatment options?" Jeff asked, sounding frustrated. "Why do they have to inject you with that crap?"

"Because it's all they have," Sarah replied. Emotion unexpectedly bubbled to the surface, and she sat up, hoping she wouldn't cry. Jeff reached out to hold her, but she pulled away. "My tears can't touch you. Remember? It's not safe."

Sarah managed to get a tissue off the nightstand just in time. She blotted her eyes and blew her nose.

Jeff watched her with the same defeated expression she'd seen too many times in the last few months. "I can't even comfort you when you need me most."

"You can," Sarah said. "Just give me a few minutes to throw this out and wash my face and hands."

She rushed to the restroom and did just that. They'd both gone through several bouts of breakdowns before coming to terms with the diagnosis and the long road ahead. She thought she'd cried all the necessary tears and had no idea where the new tears came from anymore.

Jeff took her in his arms when she returned. "You're going to make it," he said softly. "We're going to get through this. It's just going to be tough."

Sarah closed her eyes, hoping he was right. Her neck and shoulder muscles relaxed as he rubbed her back. She and Jeff had made it through many challenges, but this was the biggest one they'd faced. In the past, he'd let Sarah take the lead on all of them, agreeing with her ideas and doing his part to help overcome each one. This was the first time since they'd been together that he had decided to steer the ship. Jeff had located the best hospital and doctor and began coordinating things when Sarah had been too overwhelmed to handle it herself. Although Sarah had always loved her husband, she appreciated this new and improved version more.

"They say low stress is important for healing," Jeff added. "That's why I'm worried about this situation with your dad."

Sarah pulled out of his embrace and said, "I'm handling that, so no need to worry."

Jeff didn't look convinced.

"I'll take care of it tomorrow," Sarah promised.

Jeff kissed the top of her forehead. "Okay."

Later that evening, Sarah couldn't sleep. She went to her computer and tried to draft an email to her dad. She thanked him for his concern but told him that she was fine, that he'd heard a false rumor of her cancer diagnosis.

She would say whatever it took to make him go away. She wrote and rewrote the same paragraph dozens of times. Finally, she pressed delete.

"Funk that!" she said, closing her laptop. "I don't owe him anything."

Chapter 4

Saturday was a blur of long naps and funny movies. Jeff and Heather had created a comedy watch list for the next few months. Heather chose more recent films, while Jeff opted to revisit favorites he and Sarah had enjoyed. Both movies were entertaining, and more importantly, they made Sarah forget her problems for a while.

During the last film, she lifted her head from the sofa pillow and saw her husband and daughter laughing hysterically. Heather snorted and slapped the top of her thigh with her right hand. Jeff set the bowl of popcorn on the coffee table before howling and doubling over, holding his gut. Walter slept on the carpet next to them, oblivious to it all. Sarah watched them, thinking this was what she'd miss after she was gone. Then she dismissed the thought, preferring to remember this day. She would save it for a time when she was feeling low and needed a pleasant memory.

Caleb brought spinach lasagna for dinner. Although Caleb's cooking was excellent, all the meals Sarah ate had started tasting like sawdust, just as Dr. Zimmerman had told her they would, and the food had begun staying in her system too long. The nurses had warned that chemo could cause diarrhea or constipation, but Sarah hadn't been worried because she had been regular all her life. Now she sat in the restroom, struggling to go. She'd taken the medication the nurses had said she might need, hoping it would work right away, but it hadn't helped much.

Everything she had once taken for granted was quickly changing. Food was no longer tasty. Elimination had become a chore. Fatigue was her constant companion, along with bone pain that worsened daily. Before cancer, Sarah could walk for miles at a time with ease. Now she struggled to make it up the stairs.

Five months of chemo. That was what she had to do.

It was only the first week.

Sarah had no idea how she would make it through.

Jeff went to the grocery store on Sunday, and Heather spent the day with Caleb. Sarah reached for a novel she'd bought before getting sick, sank into the leather club chair, and opened the book. After reading the first paragraph, she stopped, unable to understand what it said. She shook her head, refocused her eyes, and read it again. The words were in English, but it felt like she was reading a language she couldn't comprehend. Finally, frustrated and a little confused, she attempted to begin the book again. It was starting to make a little more sense, but it was such an effort to figure out what was going on in the story she finally gave up.

Sarah went to the bedroom, climbed under the blankets, and pulled out her phone. Jeff had said to call or text if she needed anything while he was out. Having difficulty reading hardly seemed like an emergency.

Besides, Jeff wouldn't be able to help with that problem anyway. The doctor had mentioned she might experience something called chemo brain. A bit of forgetfulness and foggy thinking here and there that would dissipate when treatment ended.

No one had said she would struggle to read. That seemed a bit more serious than forgetfulness and foggy thinking. Sarah took a deep breath and reminded herself this was all part of the healing journey. She opened the audiobook app on her phone and decided to listen to a book instead. Jeff had bought her a subscription for Christmas, and she had a few monthly credits that had accumulated, so she scrolled through the bestsellers and made a choice.

Walter jumped onto the bed as the story began. For some reason, her cat liked audiobooks. He always came around when they were on. Sarah gazed at Walter as the narrator spoke, his eyes open and head slightly tilted as if he understood the plot. Sarah smiled, enjoying their time alone. How lucky she and Jeff had been to adopt such a beautiful kitten several years ago.

It was nighttime when Sarah woke. The book had ended while she slept. She made a mental note to start it over again soon, and then checked the time and realized she had missed dinner. She padded to the restroom, did her business, completed the special cleaning routine, then searched the house for Jeff. She found him in the garage putting together the drone he'd bought. Sarah didn't understand men's fascination with such gadgets but loved the smile it brought to her husband's face.

Jeff looked up when he saw his wife.

"Don't stop," Sarah said. "I just wanted to say hi, and then I'm going to heat up some food."

"I can come with you," he said.

"No. Please stay here and keep having fun."

Jeff looked unsure about what to do. Finally, he said, "If you say so."

As Sarah ate a tasteless sandwich, Heather came home.

"How are you feeling?" her daughter asked as she sat down.

Sarah forced down the current mouthful. "I'm hanging in there," she said, which was technically true. She'd chosen not to tell her family that she had struggled to read earlier. Why worry them any more than they already were?

Heather appraised her, seeming satisfied with that answer. "I just found out that one of my teachers had breast cancer ten years ago. She's better now, with implants and a full head of hair."

The mention of hair reminded Sarah that hers would start falling out after the second session. She heard losing large clumps could be traumatic. "I'm glad your teacher is doing well." Sarah paused, made a decision, and said, "Speaking of hair, we should call Grandma and pick a day to shave my head."

Heather's eyes widened. "Okay. Sure. Let's do that. When do you want to have it done?"

Shaving her head was the last thing Sarah wanted to do. It had taken years to grow long, beautiful hair, but if she was going to lose it, it was better to do it all at once instead of slowly clogging the drain and having an expensive plumbing issue down the road.

"How about this Friday?" Sarah suggested. The doctor said chemo side effects would improve as she got closer to the next treatment, and she could expect one or two decent days before it started all over again.

"Friday works for me. Let me call Grandma and check with her."

Shortly afterward, Heather told Sarah that she and Beverly would shave her head on Friday night. Sarah put it on her calendar, which was silly because there was no chance she would forget.

Sarah went into the bathroom and began brushing her hair in front of the mirror.

It's just hair, she thought. *I'm still me, with or without it.*

Jeff was there when she came out. "I just heard," he said.

Sarah sighed, the reality of it hitting her hard. Before her diagnosis, Sarah had considered switching to a shoulder-length haircut, thinking perhaps she was getting too old for bra-length waves. She had wanted a little less hair so it would be easier to manage. She didn't want to be bald.

"You'll look beautiful no matter what," he assured her. "Plus, that cute little hat you ordered is coming soon. You said it matches everything."

Sarah nodded in agreement. "It does."

"It will grow back," Jeff reminded.

Sarah put her chin up. "I know." She reached for his hand, and they walked to the bedroom. "Tell me about the drone," she said, desperate to change the subject.

Jeff's face lit up as he described all the cool things it did. Sarah listened closely, enjoying the transformation of the middle-aged man she loved into a boy who had just received a long-wished-for toy. She was like that when she scored a great deal on a handbag or new pair of shoes. Of course, she would never again be her giggling teenage self, but a good bargain could raise her excitement level.

Sarah's treatment symptoms improved toward the end of the second week, just as the doctor had promised. So on Friday, she washed and styled her hair, then took a selfie to commemorate this day. Soon, everyone would be over and eating the pizza Sarah had ordered. Having them there would force her to find the courage to go through with her plan.

The pizza delivery guy showed up right after Beverly and Richard arrived. Jeff and Heather put slices on paper plates and made sure everyone had something to drink, and as the group ate, Sarah looked at her stepdad's partially bald head. Richard had a full head of hair when he met her mom, but like so many men, he'd been a victim of male pattern baldness. Before tonight, Sarah hadn't considered how hair loss may have affected him. He'd always joked about it, frequently poking fun at him himself. Sarah wondered if losing his hair bothered him more than he put on but knew he'd never admit to it if asked.

As the meal came to an end, Sarah took a few deep breaths and reminded herself the hair was coming out either way. She could cut it tonight, or it could fall out in clumps after the next chemo session. Within a week or two, it would be gone no matter what.

After Heather cleared the table, Sarah pulled Jeff aside. "Do you want to be a part of this?" she asked.

"No. This should be a girl bonding event for you, Heather, and your mom." He kissed her on the top of her head before heading to the living room and turning on the TV. Richard walked past and made eye contact with Sarah. He gave her a compassionate look before joining Jeff on the sofa, where they got comfortable watching the sports channel.

"Are you ready to do this?" her mom asked.

Sarah shook her head. "Not really, but I kind of have no choice."

Beverly gave her daughter a hug. "C'mon," she said. "Let's get this over with."

Heather was already in the bathroom. She'd pulled out a pair of scissors and an electric razor and set fresh towels on top of the sink. "Let me grab a folding chair," she said, "so you don't have to sit on the toilet."

"Good idea," Beverly agreed.

Sarah took the recently washed bathmat off the floor and draped it over the side of the tub so it wouldn't get dirty. Shortly afterward, Heather returned and put the folding chair in the center of the room. The three women stood there, unsure how to proceed.

"I've done some reading," Heather began, "And I heard it's easier to cut most of the hair off before shaving it."

Sarah nodded. "That makes sense."

Heather added, "We also have options for the hair. We could throw it away, keep it in case you want a wig made of your hair, or we can donate it so another cancer patient can have a wig. If you want to go the wig route, they recommend putting the hair into tiny rubber bands before cutting it. I bought some just in case."

The price of human hair wigs was astronomical, especially those of Sarah's length. "Let's donate it," Sarah said. "I'd prefer to wear the bucket hat during treatment and try a new hairstyle when it grows back."

Heather nodded, then pulled the package of rubber bands from the medicine cabinet and set them on the counter as Sarah sat in the chair facing the mirror. Beverly wordlessly gathered a small lock of hair and tightened a rubber band around it. Heather followed her lead and did the same. Soon, Sarah resembled Medusa. It looked like a sea of snakes had sprouted from her scalp. She would probably laugh at how silly she looked if she wasn't about to lose all her beloved hair.

When they had finished, Sarah asked. "Who wants to cut the first clump?"

Beverly and Heather eyed each other. No one volunteered to go first.

"Mom, why don't you start?" Sarah asked.

"Okay." Beverly reached for the scissors. After she opened them, she stopped. "Sorry," she said. "I'm a little nervous."

Sarah managed to smile. "I think we all are."

Beverly took a deep breath and exhaled loudly before

positioning the scissors an inch from Sarah's skull. She snipped and set the rubber banded lock of hair on top of the towel. Before cutting a second piece, she made eye contact with Sarah as though she needed to get the go-ahead before continuing.

"Why don't you do one side, and I can do the other?" Heather suggested.

Sarah closed her eyes and listened to her mother cut off lock after lock on the right side of her head. No one spoke as it happened. The metallic snipping was the only sound. When it eventually stopped, Sarah opened her eyes and saw her mother and daughter studying her reflection in the mirror.

"It's weird," Sarah said. "It's like one side is me, and the other is someone else."

No one commented.

"It's your turn, sweetie," Sarah said, her tone more pleading than she would have liked. What had started as a symbolic ritual had become a moment she was desperate to be over and done with.

Beverly handed Heather the scissors, and she cut the first lock without hesitation. Sarah didn't close her eyes this time, preferring to watch her daughter work. Heather's brow furrowed as she completed the task in a methodical fashion, her hands steady as she snipped. Little by little, Sarah watched herself become more of that new person. That spikey-haired fighter who would beat cancer and live.

When Heather had finished, she asked, "Do you want to do the same thing with shaving? Grandma does one side, and I do the other?"

Losing that last inch of hair suddenly became more than Sarah could take. "I'd rather keep it like this."

No one stated the obvious, that it would start falling out next week, and that keeping it didn't make sense. Instead, her mom and daughter told her it was a wise decision before putting the hair into two large freezer bags and leaving the room so she could be alone. Sarah locked the bathroom door and looked in the mirror after they'd left. As soon as tears began to spill, she turned on the bathroom fan so her family wouldn't hear her grieving the loss of her former self. When she stopped crying, she undressed and hopped into the shower, wanting to freshen up before facing them again.

They were waiting for her in the living room. Each assured her that she still looked good with short hair, and then everyone left, opting to give her space. Jeff offered to give her a shoulder massage, and she decided to take him up on that.

As she went to the bedroom to join her husband, the doorbell rang. Sarah turned around, assuming her mom had forgotten her reading glasses again.

When she opened the door, there stood her dad.

Chapter 5

"Can I come in?" Norman asked.

Her father's presence rendered Sarah temporarily speechless. She hadn't known he was in town. After an uncomfortably long pause, she recovered and said, "Sure," before stepping aside and watching him walk into the house.

Her dad had aged since she'd seen him last. His face had more wrinkles, and his hair had turned pure white. He seemed to be surveying her appearance as well, with a look of fear and disbelief in his eyes.

Norman didn't say anything, so Sarah spoke first. "Sorry I didn't call. I've been meaning to, but I've been super busy." She had no idea why she was apologizing, let alone making excuses for her behavior. She'd had no intention of calling her father but didn't have the nerve to say it to his face.

"I understand," he said. "You've got a lot going on."

Jeff entered the room and looked from Norman to Sarah. He made sure to get a nod of approval before saying hello to Norman and then quickly made himself scarce. Afterward, Sarah offered her father a glass of water, and he accepted, so she went to the kitchen to get it for him.

Norman studied a framed photo of Heather as Sarah returned. "She's so grown up," he commented.

"That she is," Sarah agreed, handing him the drink. "And in college."

"Is she home?"

"She was here earlier but went out with her boyfriend."

"Oh," her father replied.

Sarah sat in the leather chair and gestured for Norman to sit on the sofa. He took a sip of water and set his glass on a coaster. As he turned ever so slightly to the side, Sarah was reminded that she and her father had the same straight nose. Heather had inherited it as well. At least one good thing came out of being related to him.

Sarah waited for Norman to continue small talk or say whatever he had to say.

He made eye contact with her. "Linda's sister is friends with a hairdresser who works at the salon you go to. That's how I heard the news."

Linda was her dad's second wife. After Beverly divorced him, he'd been able to date as many women as he liked without having to hide it from her, and eventually, he'd met Linda, a woman Sarah's age, and tied the knot fifteen years ago.

Norman continued. "It's so shocking to hear you have…you know."

"Breast cancer?"

Norman nodded. "No one in the family has it."

"True," Sarah replied. "But these things can just happen, I guess."

Her dad's eyes were filled with sadness—the kind of manufactured pity appropriate for someone's father to display. Sarah wondered how long they would continue pretending he cared about anyone but himself. She'd give him an hour tops. Then she'd politely explain that she was exhausted and had to go to bed.

"So, how does the doctor plan to cure you?" he asked.

Apparently, they were going to chat like they had a real relationship. He thought he could waltz into her life uninvited and feign fatherhood, and somehow, that would be okay. Choosing to play along for the allotted time, Sarah explained Dr. Zimmerman's treatment plan, keeping an eye on the clock as she spoke.

"When is the next chemo session?" he asked.

"Tuesday," Sarah responded, hoping they could wrap things up soon.

Norman leaned forward. "I'd like to take you to that visit."

Sarah felt her jaw drop and her eyes go wide. How dare he try to get involved? She wanted to cuss him out the way her brother had always done but chose to minimize the interaction instead. "You don't have to do that," she told him. "Mom is taking me to my appointments."

"I know I don't have to do it," Norman replied. "I want to."

Even through the inevitable fog setting in after a long and emotionally brutal evening, Sarah couldn't help clenching her jaw in agitation. "Look. It was nice of you to come out of your way to see me and offer to help, but you should go back to North Carolina and do something fun with Linda. Don't worry about me. I'll be fine."

Norman sat up straight. "I can't go back to North Carolina."

"Why not?"

"Because Linda and I just got divorced, and she got the house."

Sarah sighed. She and her brother had always known this day could come. They didn't care about it much, but they'd discussed it, wondering when their age gap would become too large.

"I'm sorry to hear that," Sarah said. This new information was a conversation curveball. She wasn't sure what to say next.

"I heard about you as I was moving out of the house," Norman explained, "and I took it as a sign that I should come back here and rent an apartment so I could help."

He'd rented an apartment nearby to help the daughter he never cared to know. The notion of him doing such a thing was absurd. It was akin to aliens invading from Mars.

"What do you say, Sarah? Will you give me a chance?" her father asked.

Sarah had given him a lifetime of chances, and he'd only managed to show up to about one percent of those. She had no intention of restarting now.

"Let me take you to that next treatment," he said when she didn't respond.

Norman had been in sales all his life. Sarah knew he wouldn't stop trying to overcome her objections until she threw him out of her house or said yes. They stared at each other for a full minute, no one saying a word, neither looking away.

"One treatment," Sarah agreed, caving from sheer fatigue.

"Excellent!"

Norman smiled and stood. Sarah thought he might reach out to shake her hand and seal the deal. But instead, he stepped forward, lightly patted her upper back, then asked her for all the details and wrote them on a piece of paper before leaving.

As Sarah shut the door, Jeff appeared. "I heard most of the conversation," he said. "Sorry to eavesdrop, but I wanted to make sure he wasn't upsetting you."

Her father's visit had been an unwelcome intrusion on what was already a very long and emotionally overwhelming day. "I'm okay," Sarah said. "But I'll take you up on that massage if it's still available."

Jeff reached for her hand and led her to the bedroom. They hadn't had a date night in a long time, and even though getting a massage wasn't exactly a date, Sarah was grateful Heather was staying overnight at her boyfriend's place, and they'd have time alone.

Sarah removed her clothes and set them aside before lying on the bed. She made a cradle for her face with a pile of pillows and got comfy, making sure she could breathe. Jeff got the lavender massage oil from the bathroom and went to work. They didn't talk about her father or newly short hair as he rubbed her back. He just let her relax and unwind. Usually, she would give him a massage afterward. Each would get twenty minutes. A quick tune-up, they'd joke. Now Sarah was unable to return the favor and hoped she would be able to find a way to make it up to him soon. She fell asleep as he rubbed her back, visualizing everything they would do once she was well again.

On Saturday, Mike called, eager to hear how Sarah was doing after the haircut.

"It's not the most attractive style," Sarah said. "But at least I got it over with. Plus, my hat arrives today, so I'm covered. Literally!"

Mike chuckled. "Not sure if I'm supposed to mention this or if it's a surprise, but Mom got you some scarves from the website where you bought the hat. They're already wrapped. You just put them on your head, and you're good to go."

"Cool," Sarah replied, making a mental note not to mention that her brother had told her about them when she received the gift.

"Have you heard anything else from the old man?" her brother asked.

"Actually, I saw him."

"WHAAATTTT?" Mike shrieked.

Sarah told him what happened, leaving nothing out, then waited for the inevitable.

"So, the motherfucker is all washed up, and now he wants to play Daddy. Unfuckingbelievable. He's got a lot of balls showing up like that. He put you in the position where you couldn't say no."

Her brother could say no, though. He could say no in

fantastic fashion. The kind of no Sarah could only dream of saying. That was the difference between the two of them. He never held back. Sarah tended toward polite banter and dodged confrontation when it arose. Mike could have called her out on this behavior, asking why she had no guts, but he didn't because he was a good brother.

"I'll let him take me to one visit," Sarah said. "That should be enough."

"How do you think Mom's going to feel about this?"

Sarah hadn't considered how this might make her mother feel. She was going out of her way to take her to all these appointments, cutting her hair and buying her headscarves, and bringing food for dinner once weekly. Beverly was also in charge of removing Neulasta the day after chemo.

Oh, no, Sarah thought. *What have I done?*

The bucket hat arrived shortly after Sarah hung up with her brother, and she tried it on, wanting to focus on anything except what she would say to her mom. Jeff had planned to run to the grocery store, and Sarah decided to join him. They always shopped together before she got sick, and Sarah actually missed the weekly task. Why, she didn't know.

After showering and putting on jeans and a tee shirt, Sarah donned her hat. She added a few last-minute things to the grocery list and found her daughter in the kitchen. "Do I look weird?" she asked her.

Heather looked her up and down. "No. Why?"

"Because I'm wearing a hat in the middle of summer."

"Plenty of people wear hats to protect them from the sun."

Sarah considered her logic and found it reasonable, then went to the garage and hopped into the car with Jeff. They rolled the windows down on the way there, enjoying the fresh air as they drove. But when they entered the grocery store, Sarah realized she was the only person wearing a hat like hers. A few men wore baseball caps, but there weren't any women wearing hats because there was no need for sun protection inside the store. Suddenly embarrassed, Sarah focused on her list. She examined fruits and vegetables closely before adding them to her cart as Jeff waited at the deli counter to order lunchmeat. Most patrons were busy doing the same, and she and Jeff made short work of completing the task in record time.

A teenage girl with arm tattoos scanned their food. "I like your hat," she told Sarah.

The compliment took Sarah by surprise. "Thank you," she said, brightening a bit.

"My grandma had one like that. Cancer, right?"

Heat rose in Sarah's cheeks. "Yes," she replied, wishing she could disappear.

Sarah glanced behind her and found an older woman staring at her, a look of compassion in her eyes. Sarah nodded at her and turned away. She wanted to get out of this store, and she wanted to do it quickly.

Jeff opened the car door so she could climb in while he loaded the bags into the trunk. When he'd returned the cart, he hopped in and reached for her hand. "At least the kid gave you a compliment."

"True," Sarah said, realizing he could never understand because he was a man.

Men judged each other in different ways. It was nice to have good looks, but most gave more weight to things like net worth, type of house owned, and brand of car driven. Women also liked to excel in those areas, but a woman's looks were very important to her. She wouldn't want to be told her style reminded someone of their cancer-riddled grandmother.

As Sarah buckled her seatbelt, she realized she'd have to develop thicker skin. This was her style now. She didn't have to like it, but she had to accept it and not let it get her down. Luckily, she worked from home, so she wouldn't have too many interactions like that going forward. In that respect, she was lucky. She would remember that whenever she started to feel sorry for herself.

After dinner, Beverly sent a text, saying she had a present for her and would stop by. Sarah knew her brother would have already told her everything that went down with her dad. And she was grateful. That way, she wouldn't have to tell the whole story again. Sarah didn't know if her mother would chastise her for not standing up to Norman or if she would let it slide since the circumstances were so strange. Sarah would accept either result. She only hoped her mom wasn't hurt that she'd let someone take her place at the upcoming appointment.

Jeff answered the door this time. Sarah trailed at a safe distance behind him and smiled when she saw it was her mom.

Beverly held up a gift bag stuffed with pink tissue. "I got you something."

"What is it?" Sarah asked.

Beverly handed Sarah the bag. "You'll have to open it and see."

Sarah set it on the counter and removed the tissue. Then she pulled out three super soft jersey knit chemo scarves. A light gray one, a pink paisley one, and a floral one the color of fall hues. "I like how they're sewn together on one side, so I don't have to try and figure out how to tie them." Sarah chose the light gray one and slipped it on. "This will be nice to wear around the house too."

Beverly eyed Jeff. "He sent me the link to the site where you got the hat, and I had a feeling you'd like these."

"I love them," Sarah said before reaching out to hug her mom.

Jeff excused himself to use the restroom. After he left, Sarah said, "I'm sure you heard about what happened with Dad."

"I did," Beverly replied. "It's a shame his marriage didn't work out, as no one wants to end up alone, especially this late in life." She paused, then added, "And I think it's nice that he wants to help. I just worry that he'll disappoint you."

Sarah smiled at her mother. "Doesn't matter. I have you."

Chapter 6

Sarah showered and donned the pink paisley headscarf for her second chemo treatment, digging its Boho vibe. Although she wasn't bald, she liked decorating the top of her head to match her clothes. It wasn't exactly high fashion, but it added a bit of fun to a bad situation.

As she gathered her things and waited for Norman to arrive, she remembered Jeff's advice the previous night. "All of this is about you getting well," he'd said. "If anything happens that makes you angry or stressed out, say something. Don't let your father make you upset."

Jeff had never gotten involved in their rocky relationship. When she and her brother ranted about the past, he'd listen without giving an opinion. If asked for his, he'd often say he couldn't comment because he wasn't there when things had gone wrong. Jeff tended to see the good in people, though, probably because he had a set of normal, loving parents that had always treated him well. Unfortunately, they lived in Florida now, and he didn't see them as often as he'd like, but they talked on the phone every week and made sure to visit each other once or twice per year. Sarah always enjoyed spending time with them. Both were warm and friendly, just like their son. Sometimes she envied Jeff for having the childhood she and her brother deserved but sadly lost.

The phone rang, and Sarah answered it, learning her dad was waiting outside. She put her phone in her purse and said a quick goodbye to Walter as she ran out the door. After climbing into her father's car and saying hello, she showed him how to get to the train station and told him where to park. She paid for the parking space, and then they waited for the train to arrive. As they stood side by side on the platform, Sarah wondered what they would talk about all day. She'd only seen her father a few times in the last decade, and each visit had been brief.

"At least it's a sunny day," Norman mentioned, squinting at the sky.

"We've had great luck in that department," she replied. Discussing the weather was always a safe bet. Sarah wished they could stay on the subject for as long as possible. The next eight hours would be ideal.

Other passengers gathered on the platform, some staring at Sarah for longer than people had looked at her before. It was that extra few seconds it took to see the scarf and let everything click. Once that occurred, they averted their gaze.

A few minutes later, the train arrived. Everyone boarded, and instead of sitting on the seat next to Sarah, as her mother had, Norman folded the seat in front of them over so he could sit opposite her, and they'd be face to face.

"Tell me about that business you started," Norman began.

He'd clearly spent time thinking of discussion topics in

advance. Sarah thought about how to best describe what she did. "It's an online marketing company. I create targeted ads on social media to help my clients generate business."

"So, it's sales. That's great," Norman said, looking proud.

"It's more technology than sales." Sarah wasn't a salesperson. They weren't alike in any way, no matter how hard he tried to put them on common ground. And no amount of looking proud gave him any right to be since he had nothing to do with her success. "But the ads help my clients make more money."

Norman nodded. "It's a new world now. People can buy things on the computer without leaving their houses. They can attend meetings from home." He peered out the window. "Things were different in my day. We had to meet clients in person. Build relationships, as they used to say."

Sarah supposed she had the advantage of building business relationships from the comfort of her couch, which afforded her the luxury of spending more time with her family. She compared Norman's situation to hers and still didn't think it was a good enough reason to abandon his family. If Sarah had a job like his, she'd learn to balance everything to succeed at both. Her career wouldn't be the most important part of her life.

The train's conductor approached for their tickets. Sarah had bought them using the app on her phone. She lifted her cell and tapped the screen, and instead of moving on, the man said, "I know where you're going."

Sarah studied him. "You do?"

"Yep. You're going to the cancer center downtown."

Sarah was surprised that he knew her destination. Hearing him say such a thing could've been weird, but this man had a kind face.

The conductor continued. "I've been working here for twenty years, and in that time, I've seen lots of people doing what you're doing now."

The conductor had piqued Norman's interest. He turned toward the man, seeming eager to hear more. Sarah listened closely, wondering what he'd say next.

"They cured my uncle of colon cancer, and he's doing well. Just came back from a beach vacation in Mexico."

"That's great!" Sarah said.

"The treatment is tough, but you'll get through it, and after that, you'll fear nothing. One of the women I met on the train even went skydiving afterward."

Sarah chuckled. "I don't think I'll jump from a plane, but I hope to go on vacation when I feel better."

The conductor smiled at her before moving on.

"Thanks for sharing that," Sarah said. "Say hello to your uncle for us."

"Will do," he replied. "You two have a good day."

Sarah and Norman faced each other after the man was gone.

"That was a pleasant surprise," Norman said.

"It was," Sarah agreed.

Sarah looked out the window, wondering how many of the cancer patients the conductor had met had survived. They'd all been like her once, riding the train to the hospital, hoping they would be one of the lucky ones who beat the odds. She had no idea why someone who'd fought so hard to save their life would risk it by skydiving. But maybe what the conductor said was true, that fear dissolves when treatment ends.

"Where would you like to go when you get well?" Norman asked.

Sarah tilted her head as she formulated a reply. "I'd like to go to Sedona, Arizona. I heard it's really pretty there. Plus, they have vortexes. Places throughout the town known for healing energy."

"I've heard of those," Norman said. "I think it was in a documentary on the Southwest." He paused, then added, "Too bad you couldn't go there now."

"I'd love to, but I can't stop treatment and take a trip."

The conversation flowed naturally between Sarah and her father. If Sarah didn't know better, she'd almost believe they were getting along. Norman was skilled in the art of communication, though, and it showed. He'd learned to chat with just about anyone, win their trust, and close the sale. But all the smooth talk in the world wouldn't make up for years of abandonment. They wouldn't be buddy-buddy just because he had decided that's what he wanted now. Sarah would remember that as they spent the day together. She'd be friendly but careful not to let her guard down.

They approached the town they'd lived in when Sarah was a kid. Norman noticed and said, "Hey, that's the old apartment."

Sarah had seen the building on her first train ride

downtown. She had chosen to turn away from it then but glanced at it now. "Remember when I learned to ride a bike out front? How I fell off it and scratched my knee?"

Norman seemed to be searching for the memory and coming up blank. "I don't think I was there for that."

No, you weren't, Sarah thought. Mike had been the one to teach her how to ride a bike. Her brother had cheered her on as she pedaled down the block, and after she wiped out, he'd taken her to Beverly to have the wound cleaned and bandaged before urging her to try again.

The discussion stalled. Perhaps Norman was trying to recall a time he had been there for something important so he could mention it, but too much time passed, allowing the banter to burn out. Sarah pulled her phone from her purse and checked her email, deleting junk messages and scanning for important messages that needed handling. Luckily, she had none of those. Norman gazed out the window and remained quiet until it was time to get off the train.

After taking a cab to the cancer center and checking in, Sarah's name was called. A nurse took her to a chair and accessed her port, drawing blood so they could check her numbers before chemo started. She returned to the waiting room, where her father was seated, and they called her name again. This time, to meet with her oncologist.

"I'd like to come with you if you don't mind," Norman said.

"She's going to do a breast exam, but I can see if they will let you in afterward."

Norman nodded. Thankfully, he didn't push back.

After changing, Dr. Zimmerman came in, wearing a bright, genuine smile. Sarah explained that her father wanted to come in after the breast exam, and Dr. Zimmerman said she'd have a nurse get him when they were done.

Once Sarah had put her top back on, Norman was led into the room and offered a chair. He and Dr. Zimmerman exchanged pleasantries, and then the oncologist turned her attention to Sarah, having plenty of patients and no time to waste. "I see you've cut your hair. That's a brave step."

"Thanks," Sarah said.

Dr. Zimmerman sat down, focusing on Sarah, with her body positioned to include Norman in their chat. "You'll lose the remaining hair shortly after today's treatment. I recommend a drain catcher for the bathroom."

"Okay," Sarah said, realizing she should've bought one when she decided on the pixie cut.

"Tell me how you're doing. Are there any symptoms not being managed with the medication you have?"

Sarah described what she'd experienced so far. Her doctor didn't break eye contact as she listened to her speak.

"Okay, so remember that chemo symptoms are cumulative. With each treatment, they may get worse, so you'll need to take something for constipation. We want you to have normal bowel movements. Also, you'll need to purchase a special mouthwash or make one of your own because you may develop blisters in your mouth and throat. I'll post the recipe in my notes."

Sarah glanced at Norman. He seemed to hang on every word her oncologist spoke.

Dr. Zimmerman continued. "I recommend Claritin for the bone pain. It helps reduce the inflammation caused by the histamines in Neulasta. Give that a try this time, and if it doesn't help, let me know." She paused before adding, "As far as the memory issues, they're annoying but temporary. You can use sticky notes to remind yourself of things you need to remember and do crossword puzzles to keep your mind sharp."

Sarah had never done a crossword puzzle but figured she'd give it a shot. As she talked with Dr. Zimmerman, she noticed she was only a little older than her, with wavy brown shoulder-length hair. Sarah liked the style.

"We're going to fix this," her oncologist said. "If you have any problems before your next treatment, feel free to call or send a message in your chart." Dr. Zimmerman stood. She turned to Norman. "It was nice to meet you. I always like it when a patient has family support." Before Norman could reply, her doctor turned to Sarah and said, "Good luck. I'll see you in two weeks."

A moment later, she was out the door, and a nurse appeared and asked Norman to return to the waiting room as she took Sarah to the infusion center. Sarah had a private room for the first chemo session but was put into a group setting for treatment today.

The nurse led Sarah to a room with oversized gray reclining chairs spaced several feet apart. One chair was available, and Sarah sat in it, briefly making eye contact with the other women before another nurse came and introduced herself.

After fluids were started, Sarah heard a bell ringing, followed by clapping and cheers. Sarah turned to the black woman sitting beside her and asked, "What's going on?"

"You get to ring the bell on the last day of chemo."

Sarah craned her neck, trying to get a look at the person who had finished the program, but she couldn't see her because she was surrounded by hospital staff. She turned back to her neighbor and introduced herself.

"I'm Nancy," the woman replied. Nancy lifted a cup of water from the tray beside her chair and took a sip. "What kind of breast cancer do you have?"

"Triple-negative."

"Me too," Nancy said as if she discovered they were the same astrological sign. "You're the first person I've met here that has what I've got."

Sarah immediately felt a kinship and was eager to continue their conversation when Nancy's machine beeped, and a nurse arrived, saying Nancy's chemo session was over. Sarah's good fortune of meeting her had ended as quickly as it began.

"Do you come back in two weeks?" Nancy asked as she got ready to leave.

"I do."

Nancy smiled. "Maybe I'll see you then."

Sarah hoped she would see Nancy again so they could chat. They had something in common. It was a shame their appointments hadn't aligned. Sarah closed her eyes after Nancy left and woke to the sound of her machine beeping. She was surprised she had slept through her treatment, but it was easy to do without someone to talk to.

Norman rose from his chair when he saw Sarah coming. He offered her his arm to steady her when she wobbled, and Sarah accepted it, too tired to put up a fight. They took the cab to the train station and were fortunate that their train was about to leave soon. After boarding, Norman was unusually quiet as he watched the city go by.

"I used to live not far from here as a kid," he mentioned as they reached the outskirts of town.

Sarah had never thought of her father's childhood. "Yeah, where about?"

"In a run-down unit a few miles away." He continued staring out the window, almost as if looking into the past. "My parents were very poor. Not because they weren't smart. They were. But they were alcoholics who fought constantly, and my dad couldn't hold a job."

That sounded terrible to Sarah. It also explained why she had never seen her father with a drink in his hand.

Norman made eye contact with her. "Luckily, a neighbor looked out for me. He'd bring me food from time to time so that I wouldn't starve to death. He was different than my parents. He provided for his family. He didn't let them down. I vowed to be like him when I had a family of my own."

This new information shocked Sarah. She wasn't sure what to say. As she processed what she'd just heard, she realized that while she'd felt abandoned by her father, he'd never left her for alcohol, and she'd never wanted for anything—except, of course, a father. She wondered if he ever looked back and realized that his vow came at the price of having a meaningful relationship with his daughter. Maybe that was why he was with her now.

Chapter 7

The bedroom door creaked on its hinges. Heather peeked in, and when she made eye contact with Sarah, she smiled and approached the bed.

"I made an omelet big enough for two. Do you feel well enough to eat?" Heather asked.

Sarah didn't want to disappoint her daughter, who didn't have class today. "I'm not too hungry, but I'll give it a shot." She climbed out of bed, feeling heavier, although she had lost weight.

Mother and daughter padded to the kitchen, trailed by Walter, who never missed an opportunity to eat a meal or snack. Heather poured a few nuggets of dry food into Walter's bowl so he wouldn't feel left out, then put their food on plates and brought them to the table.

Sarah took a bite of her omelet and clutched her throat after swallowing it.

"Are you okay?" Heather asked.

"The inside of my mouth hurts. It feels like I swallowed broken glass." Sarah reached for her orange juice and drank a large gulp, which burned like acid on the way down. "That made it worse," she cried.

Heather seemed confused as to how she could help. "Let me get you some cold water," she said before rushing back to the kitchen.

Sarah remembered that Dr. Zimmerman had said she might develop mouth sores next. She sipped the cool water Heather had given her, which helped a little, and said, "My doctor mentioned this could happen. She gave me a recipe for a mouthwash."

"I'll make it right now," Heather said, rising from her chair.

"No. Please, let's finish our food, and then we can make it together."

Heather seemed to wrestle with her decision before sitting down and resuming her meal. Sarah felt bad that new symptoms had coincided with the meal her daughter had made. She would've liked it if this morning could've been a positive experience. But instead, it had already gone wrong. Sarah chewed her food thoroughly, hoping to make it as small as possible so it would hurt less on the way down.

"I hate that this is happening to you," Heather said after a long, quiet lull. So far, she had been the picture of positivity since learning about her mother's diagnosis.

Sarah reached across the table and squeezed her daughter's hand. "I hate it, too, and sometimes I wonder why and get frustrated, but then I realize that none of that helps." Sarah hated how hard this was on her family. Her condition had created chaos in the lives of everyone she loved, and she wished there was some way to curtail their stress. "I appreciate you making this for me. I really do."

Sarah's heart deflated at the sight of tears welling in

Heather's eyes as she nodded wordlessly. Sarah let go of her daughter's hand and said, "Let's put these dishes in the dishwasher and make the mouthwash."

Heather's voice sounded small as she replied, "Okay."

Sarah gathered the baking soda, salt, and water, and Heather grabbed a travel coffee mug with a lid from the cupboard. After combining the ingredients, Heather shook the cup a few times, making sure they were mixed well. Then she handed it to her mother so she could use it right away.

After Sarah brushed her teeth and used the mouthwash, she found Heather sitting on the floor petting Walter. She joined them, and then Walter rolled over and showed off his belly, happy to be the center of attention.

"How's your mouth?" Heather asked.

"Still sore, but I know it will get better if I use the mouthwash several times per day." At least, that was what Sarah hoped.

Heather grabbed Walter's favorite cat toy, the one with a rainbow of feathers attached to a wand. She began swishing it back and forth, and Walter pounced on it, then did a backflip. Both women laughed. These were the moments Sarah treasured most. She hoped she would live to see many more in the years to come.

Heather set the toy aside after Walter lost interest. "How was your day with Grandpa?"

Sarah considered how to respond. If she were having this discussion with her brother, they would probably focus on the negatives because that was their thing. But

Heather didn't know her grandfather, and Sarah saw no reason to bring her daughter down. "It was decent. Better than expected." She could tell Heather wanted more than that, so she tried to figure out what to say. "We managed to keep a conversation going."

Heather examined her mother before asking, "How come you guys aren't close? Did you have a fight?"

Sarah wasn't sure she could explain their relationship to her daughter. "We didn't have a fight. But we were never close, and as time passed, we grew apart and didn't stay in touch."

"That's sad," Heather said. "I'm so glad you're reconnecting now."

Heather's optimism was so like her father's. Part of it was probably genetic; part could be that they both came from families with two parents who were always around.

Sitting on the floor hurt Sarah's lower back, so she got up and moved to the couch. "How's Caleb doing? I haven't seen him in a while."

"He's been busy with work and school. The latest cooking class is Mexican food. You wouldn't believe how many different styles there are. Each region has different dishes."

"Huh, I didn't know that," Sarah said. "But it makes sense. The United States is a big country, and the food is different everywhere you go." Walter jumped on the sofa and curled into a ball next to Sarah. She reached out to pet him and said, "Tell Caleb he's welcome to come over any time. He doesn't have to stop visiting you because I'm ill."

Heather nodded, and Sarah made a mental note to invite Caleb over soon. He and Heather had been dating for over a year, and she didn't want her condition to interfere with their relationship or cause it to fizzle out. He was a polite guy who was most likely trying to give their family space. But if the two of them became even more serious, he could eventually become a part of their family.

Sarah had to finish some work, so she went to her desk and checked her clients' ads. She made a few changes to some of them, responded to emails, and afterward, took a nap.

A beeping sound woke her, and she grabbed her phone to turn off the alarm. When she discovered she hadn't set one, she realized the sound was coming from the back of her arm. That meant her mom would be here soon to remove the device, so she got up, brushed her teeth, and used the mouthwash she and Heather had made earlier.

Beverly was there when Sarah came out of the bathroom. She hadn't heard the doorbell ring but assumed Heather had let her in. Beverly's eyebrows knit together in concern. "I heard about the mouth sores."

"Yeah," Sarah said. "They're not fun."

They re-entered the bathroom so Beverly could remove the device from the back of Sarah's arm.

Sarah turned to face her mother afterward, and as she did, Beverly smiled. "Your hair looks cute this way. Very few people could pull off that look."

"Thanks," Sarah said, absently reaching to pull at the

ends beside her ear. The pixie cut wasn't her style, but at least she still had some hair on her head.

Something had been on Sarah's mind since she and her dad had taken the train downtown. She figured she might as well bring it up to her mom. "What do you know about Dad's parents?"

The question didn't seem to surprise Beverly. Perhaps she'd expected they'd talk about Norman today. "They were terrible," she said, shaking her head. "Your father rarely brought me around them, and when he did, boy, was that a mistake." Beverly crossed her arms and leaned against the bathroom door, seeming to reminisce before continuing. "They both drank a lot, and there was drama every time we were around them. Either they'd fight in front of us, making us wish we hadn't come over, or they'd ask your father for money."

"That's awful!" Sarah remembered Norman mentioning that his dad hadn't been a good provider when he was a kid. She couldn't imagine having that kind of childhood and then growing up and dealing with more of the same. "So, what happened? Did Dad give them money?"

"He helped them out early on, but he stopped spending on them once we got married and started a family. When the money flow ended, so did their relationship. Eventually, your father stopped visiting them, and then they passed away."

Norman didn't have to help his parents financially, especially after they had proven they wouldn't help themselves. He had been generous, and that surprised

Sarah. "What about aunts or uncles? Was he close to any of them?" Norman had been an only child, but Sarah assumed he had other family members in his life.

"He had a mean uncle. He would tell your father he was a loser who wouldn't amount to anything."

"Good grief!" Sarah exclaimed. "Seems like Dad couldn't catch a break."

After saying the words aloud, she realized she had afforded her father kindness. She hesitated, wondering if she should take the words back, but then decided they were warranted, considering what she had just learned.

Heather opened the bathroom door. "What's going on in here? Am I missing anything good?"

Beverly replied. "We just finished taking off the medical device. Now, I can help you make dinner."

Although no one asked for Sarah's help, she joined them, rinsing off veggies and getting them ready for her daughter to chop. Sarah listened to Beverly pepper Heather with questions about school as the three of them prepared the meal. Heather answered each with enthusiasm. Their family had always been close, and although they didn't see cousins, aunts, and uncles frequently, they gathered for major holidays and always managed to have fun. It was a shame her father had never had that experience with his family. And then, when he began one of his own, he was never around. Perhaps Norman didn't know how to properly be a part of a family because he'd never experienced being in one himself.

After dinner, Beverly went home, and Heather went to

visit Caleb. Sarah did her best to stay awake as Jeff explained the latest manufacturing snafu at work. She nodded and responded in all the right places during their conversation, but the next thing she knew, she was waking up the following morning. She had no memory of going to bed, let alone drifting off to sleep. Jeff had left breakfast on the stove with a note stuck to the kitchen counter. *I love you and will see you tonight!*

Sarah picked at the food, still unable to eat without feeling like she had swallowed broken glass. The Claritin wasn't doing much for the bone pain, either. She abandoned her meal and went to check on her clients' ads.

She gasped. "No," she breathed, scrolling for the toggle she was sure she'd turned on. "No, no, no," she pleaded, but it was useless. Her biggest client's top-performing ad had been turned off. She didn't remember making the mistake, but she was the only one who accessed the account, so there was no one else to blame. Sarah turned it back on and double-checked every ad in every account, making sure she hadn't blundered anything else. Her clients loved her because she achieved results. She hadn't told any of them about her illness, and although she was sure they'd be compassionate and understand, it didn't mean performance could drop.

She rolled her neck from side to side, trying to loosen the muscles that had tightened while she worked. Struggling to read a novel was one thing. Chemo brain fog causing business trouble was something else.

Sarah rose and paced the room until her eyes landed

back on Jeff's sticky note from breakfast. That was it. She could use Jeff's sticky notes to leave reminders for herself in case another bout of cognitive dysfunction occurred. She'd known she would lose her hair and breast, but her mind? When she considered the value of the three of them, she realized the latter mattered most. Her hair would grow back after treatment, and if she was interested, a plastic surgeon could create a new breast. But she only had one brain and needed to care for it as best she could. That was top priority and would come before anything else.

Sarah remembered that Dr. Zimmerman had suggested doing crossword puzzles to stay sharp. Sarah had initially discounted the tip, assuming it was a waste of time. Now she returned to her computer and ordered several, eager to start. Between the sticky notes and the puzzles, she'd be fine. At least, that's what she hoped as she lay down to rest.

After a long nap, Sarah needed a shower. She hadn't taken one the day before and was feeling pretty grungy today. She ensured the stainless-steel hair catcher was over the bathtub drain before turning on the water, then stepped in and lathered up. The pulsing hot spray helped her relax. She stood under it longer than usual before getting out, wrapping a towel around her head, and donning her spa-like terry-cloth robe. Instead of rushing to get dressed, she decided to pamper her skin, which seemed to have aged considerably since her first chemo session. She used an exfoliating scrub on her face, followed by a chamomile toner and rich day cream that made her face glow. Next, she applied a scented body moisturizer, then took the towel off her head. A clump of hair fell to the floor, making Sarah gasp.

She looked in the mirror and saw a large bald spot on the right side of her scalp. Tears came quickly, and she sank to the floor and sobbed, grateful she was home alone. She appreciated Jeff and Heather comforting her on this journey, but sometimes it felt good to process things on her own. The level of grief surfacing was unexpected. She'd mentally prepared for this and thought she'd be ready for it when it occurred. Sarah reached for a tissue and blew her nose, realizing that maybe she couldn't anticipate each hurdle and formulate a plan to deal with it in advance. She could try but would still be on this roller coaster of emotion. A ride she couldn't get off. Feeling out of control was a thing she disliked more than anything, and she wished there was a way to make it stop.

After taking a few deep breaths, Sarah knew what she had to do. She got up and found the hair clippers, and after verifying it was on the correct setting, she slowly slid the shaver against her head, working from front to back. Her heart hammered in her chest as she completed the first strip, and she had to set the clippers down afterward to wipe sweat from the palm of her hand.

You can do this, she thought, trying to find the courage to finish the job.

Sarah grabbed the clippers and started the next row, following the same path. Then she did a third row and paused to examine herself in the mirror, thinking she looked like a creature from a science fiction flick.

Before her nerves sent her into hyperventilation, Sarah padded to the refrigerator and took a cold beer out of the fridge. She rarely drank alcohol but decided to make an exception today. The first sip was to celebrate her small accomplishment. The next was because she was thirsty and hadn't realized it before. She found her phone as she continued drinking the bottle and thumbed through photos of her and Jeff. They looked good together and had managed to age well. Of course, they weren't as attractive as they had been when they first met, but the years had been kind to them until now.

Sarah knew Jeff would love her no matter what, but she wished he hadn't been put in this position. It wasn't fair to him to have a wife who was less than the person he had planned to be married to for the rest of his life. In sickness and in health were words people repeated but never really gave much thought. However, the phrase had real meaning now that they were going through this together. She hoped that their marriage could make it through this difficult time.

Newly determined and fortified by liquid courage, Sarah returned to the restroom and continued shaving her head.

She was a wife, a mother, a sister, and a daughter.

Today, she had found the strength to become a fierce cancer warrior.

Chapter 8

Mike sat at the kitchen table with Sarah, tapping his pencil as he studied his crossword puzzle. He'd bought an adult version full of swear words and slang.

"I could do fuckface horizontally, but then asshat won't fit in the vertical spot."

Sarah had been thinking about which word could work in her puzzle but burst out laughing when she heard what he said.

Mike grinned. "Or maybe fucksicle would be better?"

That word didn't have the same number of letters as the original word. Her brother was obviously making this up as he went along.

Sarah set her pencil down, too foggy to work on her puzzle anymore. "You want to go for a walk?" she asked.

"Sure. Let me take a leak and grab a smoke first."

Sarah put on her sneakers and donned her bucket hat as Mike used the restroom. When he'd finished, they went outside and stood on the back porch, which dirty from the last few winters and needed a power washing soon.

Mike pulled half of a joint and lighter from his pocket, then lit the joint and took a drag. "Want some?" he asked after exhaling a plume of skunk-scented smoke.

Sarah shook her head. "No, thanks."

She wasn't against using marijuana, which was no different than alcohol, in her opinion. But she had no desire to do more drugs than she was currently taking, mainly because she didn't want to incur new, unwanted side effects. Mike had told her the history of marijuana recently, including his theory that the pharmaceutical industry had demonized it to make more money for themselves. It was legal in Illinois now, and he often frequented the shops selling a myriad of cannabis products. Sarah had gone with him to the opening of the first one in their town and was surprised by the dizzying array of marijuana varieties to choose from, each with custom names.

As Mike took another puff, Sarah asked, "How is Donna doing?"

"She's alright."

When her brother gave two-word answers to questions, things were definitely not alright.

"What's going on?" Sarah asked.

Mike stubbed out the remainder of his joint and put it in his pocket. "She's getting clingy. She thinks we should live together."

Sarah thought Mike really liked Donna and wasn't sure why that was a bad idea. Instead of asking him why he was against it, they set out on their walk. She knew he'd elaborate if she gave him a chance to explain.

"She's a good person," Mike continued. "And I like spending time with her. It's just that I don't see us together long-term."

Sarah didn't know why he'd put his credit on the line to help her with a car if they weren't taking things to the next level. But men did all kinds of things that didn't make sense, and she had stopped trying to figure out the logic behind their actions long ago.

They entered the trail near Sarah's house, a wooded area with several miles of paved paths, and she continued the conversation. "What kind of woman would you like to marry?"

Mike flinched. "Marry? Who said anything about getting married?"

Sarah looked up at him. "You know what I mean."

"I know," he replied. "I'm just messing with you."

An attractive young blonde with a black Labrador walked toward them. She nodded politely as they passed.

"Someone like her works," Mike said.

Sarah chuckled. Unlike their father, Mike had never dated anyone outside his age group. Sarah wondered why if that was the kind of girl he liked. "So, why don't you ask her out?"

Mike laughed. "Because a girl like that wants to get married and start a family. I'm too old for that shit."

At fifty-eight, her brother wasn't too old for marriage or kids, but Sarah didn't belabor that fact. He'd had plenty of opportunities to settle down and start a family through the years, but it never happened. Each relationship failed, and there was always a valid reason for its demise. One woman turned out to be a compulsive shoplifter and got arrested for stealing a designer sweater from a department store. Mike was blindsided by her behavior and felt he had never really known her. Another woman had mental problems that medication couldn't solve. Mike had stayed with her for several years, hoping things would improve, but her issues became too much for him to handle, and they eventually went their separate ways.

As they rounded the bend on the trail, Sarah asked, "Who is your ideal partner?"

Mike sighed. "I don't know."

Sarah wasn't letting him off so easily. "If you had to describe who you're looking for on a dating site, what would you say?"

Mike took his time before answering. "I'd like an independent woman. Someone smart with a career that she enjoys. Maybe she's been married before and has a family, so she doesn't want to have kids with me." He paused, then added, "Plus, she has to be hot."

Sarah smiled at her brother. He seemed to know precisely the kind of woman he wanted but just hadn't found her yet. Luckily, Mike worked with the public and met new people every day. His dream girl could show up at the dealership, needing repairs on her car. He would just have to engage this damsel in compelling conversation and ask her on a date. Sarah had no doubt he would be successful if given the opportunity.

Mike stopped to tie his shoelace. "Has the old man called since you guys went to chemo?"

Sarah shook her head. "Nope."

Mike stood. "Maybe he's going back to North Carolina? He's done his bit and is ready to roll?"

"Maybe," Sarah said. "I honestly don't care."

As they continued walking, Sarah wasn't sure if that was true. On the one hand, having a father taking her to cancer treatment was nice. On the other hand, his mere presence this late in their relationship infuriated her, and she wished he'd leave her alone once and for all.

Sarah noticed a bench up ahead and headed toward it. She used to be able to walk for miles per day but could only go for a short while now before huffing and puffing and needing to take a break. Her phone vibrated in her pocket after sitting down. She pulled it out and saw that a voicemail from Norman had arrived.

"Speak of the devil," Sarah said, showing her brother the phone.

Mike snickered. "Let's listen to the message and see what the fuck he wants."

Sarah obliged, turning up the volume before pressing play.

"Hey, Sarah. It's your dad. I hope you're doing all right." There was a pause, then he added, "I know you're resting, but if you have energy and would like to come over for lunch one day this week, that would be great. Bring Heather if she's available."

Sarah eyed Mike after the message ended. Her brother rolled his eyes and shook his head simultaneously. "He wants to play 'Grandpa' now. One day of Dad duty in the last decade, and he thinks he qualifies for a promotion."

Sarah saved the message, unsure if she wanted to meet her father for lunch, let alone bring Heather. Norman certainly wasn't qualified for any level of parenting, but he was giving it a shot. He was wandering into unfamiliar territory and trying to find his way. If he was anyone but her dad, Sarah would say he deserved a second chance.

She stood abruptly, ready to continue their walk—especially if it meant changing topics.

"What are you going to do?" Mike asked.

Sarah put her phone in her pocket. "Of course, I'm not interested." And she wasn't. Except that she had a feeling she'd be accepting his invite, nonetheless.

Mike mentioned a TV show he had just started watching, and they continued light banter for the rest of their walk, which lifted Sarah's spirits and kept her mind off her problems for a while.

She took a much-needed nap after Mike left, sleeping heavily and dreamlessly until Jeff kissed her on the forehead to let her know he was home from work. He looked handsome, sitting on the edge of the bed in his khaki pants and blue plaid shirt. Somehow, he managed to make business casual seductive. If Sarah weren't sick, she'd pull him close and show him how much he meant to her. She missed him and hoped they could reconnect after she finished AC chemo, as feeling like a walking nuclear reactor with dangerous bodily fluids wasn't sexy or fun.

"My parents ordered us pizza," Jeff said. "It's on the way."

He'd recently mentioned that her parents-in-law wished they could cook something and bring it over. But that was out of the question since they were in Florida, so sending dinner was the next best thing.

Jeff rose from the bed. "Caleb is coming over too. Is that alright?"

Sarah nodded. "Of course!"

She got up, eager to freshen up before Heather's boyfriend arrived. She brushed her teeth and donned her chemo scarf. Sometimes she sported her bald head around the house because it was too warm to wear anything, but she felt funny doing that with Caleb around.

The pizza delivery guy pulled into the driveway shortly after Caleb arrived, and then everyone gathered around the table, eating off paper plates. Sarah sat next to Jeff, watching Heather and Caleb interact. She offered him a glass of her famous green juice, and he graciously accepted, telling her it tasted great. It was hard to believe her baby was all grown up and had a serious boyfriend—a nice guy with goals who treated her right.

Before biting into his second slice of pizza, Caleb eyed Jeff and said, "That's cool that your parents sent food." He turned to Sarah. "I can cook you guys a weekly dinner from now on. Just let me know what you'd like to eat."

Sarah was about to tell Caleb not to go to all that trouble when Jeff replied, "Thanks. We really appreciate that."

Sarah watched as her daughter smiled broadly and gave Caleb a sideways glance. Caleb seemed pleased that they'd accepted his offer. Sarah felt the tension melt from her shoulders. Every little bit helped during this difficult time.

During their meal, Jeff called his mom and thanked her for the food. Then, he passed the phone to Sarah, who did the same and let her know that she was doing okay and that she hoped to see her as soon as she got well.

As the pizza box emptied, Caleb told Sarah, "I heard your dad moved here to help you with your cancer treatment. That's so nice."

Sarah had been chewing her food but stopped mid-bite. She reached for her glass of water to wash it down while thinking of how to reply. Clearly, Caleb wasn't in the loop on all things Norman. If he had been, he wouldn't have committed the faux pas he was currently committing after knocking it out of the park all night.

"Yes, it's nice," Sarah said, realizing any other answer would seem rude. "We aren't close," she clarified, "so it's been a little strange but still nice, I guess."

Sarah could tell this was the first time Caleb had heard this information. His pleasant smile froze with the apparent blunder. Sarah was trying to think of something to reassure him that he hadn't said the wrong thing when Heather said, "Grandpa lives out of state, but he got divorced recently and came here when he heard Mom was ill."

Caleb nodded. Heather had saved him, and he didn't seem keen to say anything more about Norman once he'd been redeemed. Sarah was glad. She was tired of talking about her father and wanted to finish her meal in peace.

To her surprise, Heather asked, "How is Grandpa? Have you heard from him lately?"

Sarah didn't know if Norman had Heather's phone number. She didn't think so, but if he did manage to get it, had he contacted her as well? "Actually," she said, "he called earlier today and left a message inviting us over for lunch."

From the corner of her eye, Sarah noticed Jeff's shoulder and jaw muscles tense. He'd become extra protective since she'd been ill and frequently reminded her that stress needed to be kept to a minimum to beat this disease.

"What day are we going?" Heather asked.

Sarah stalled. If she said they wouldn't meet Norman for lunch, she'd look terrible in front of Caleb. He'd probably think she was cruel and insensitive and wonder what was wrong with her. "I don't know," Sarah replied, wishing her daughter hadn't asked.

Heather frowned. "I'll bet he's lonely in that apartment all by himself."

Sarah had no idea how Norman was becoming the sweet old man who just wanted to help. Sure, it was sad that he and Linda had split, but with the large age gap and his penchant for womanizing, it was no surprise. Maybe his relationship with Linda had been a repeat of his first marriage, and she was moving on, just as her mother had. Sarah couldn't blame Linda for that.

Heather wore a mopey, puppy dog expression. Caleb placed an empathetic hand on hers. Both were normal reactions to the situation, but Norman wasn't normal. He was the very definition of self-absorbed. He always had been, and he always would be. And even if he had changed, she had no obligation to forgive him. So either way, their concern was unwarranted and shouldn't apply to him.

Part of this was Sarah's fault. She had thought it best not to tell her daughter negative things about her grandfather or childhood. There was no benefit in tarnishing Norman's name since he wasn't involved in their lives. But now that the past had come to the present, she wished she had told Heather some of the things she and her brother had repeatedly experienced growing up. If she knew how Norman really was, she wouldn't be worried that he was old and all alone.

If Mike were here, he'd solve this problem with a litany of F-bombs. Norman would gain no traction with Heather and Caleb. Instead, her brother would have the two of them laughing hysterically while setting the story straight.

But then, it hit her. Sarah looked Heather in the eyes and said, "Honey, if you're worried about Grandpa, we'll meet him for lunch."

Heather smiled. Sarah's kind, caring daughter probably thought she was making a difference in the life of an older man. She hated to burst her daughter's bubble, but in this case, it was better to show than tell. She'd give Norman all the figurative rope he wanted and watch as he used it to hang himself.

Chapter 9

Heather skipped to the car even though it was a muggy summer day. Her level of enthusiasm about the two of them meeting Norman for lunch broke Sarah's heart. She could remember being that way as a kid, eager to spend time with her dad, only to be let down because the experience never materialized. She would brush the disappointment aside by playing with her dolls or coloring pictures. Her brother would get into trouble with his friends. Nothing serious, but the kind of mayhem expected of angst-filled boys.

"I'll drive," Heather said, pulling the car keys from her slouchy, tan leather bag.

Sarah hadn't felt confident behind the wheel since chemo started, so she was relieved when Heather offered to drive. Her daughter punched Norman's address into her phone's GPS, and fifteen minutes later, they arrived at a hotel—the kind of place that offers furnished units for people in between homes. This wasn't what Sarah had imagined when her father had said he lived in an apartment across town. But it made sense. He'd be around for a while to help, and then he'd return to North Carolina and probably buy a condo. Something small that would be easy for a single person to clean.

Norman greeted them with a big smile. "Look at you!" he said to Heather. He opened his arms, and his granddaughter stepped into his embrace on cue. Norman hugged her tightly. Sarah watched the interaction, reminding herself not to make too much of it.

They entered the hotel room, which looked like a studio apartment. It had a small but stylish kitchen with white cabinets and stainless-steel appliances, a round dining table with four chairs, a queen-sized bed off to the side, and a bathroom nearby. It had everything a person needed without feeling like home. Then again, Norman had spent so many years of his life traveling for business that maybe he found this environment comfortable.

"I ordered Chinese food." Norman stepped into the kitchen and opened the fridge. "What would you two like to drink? I've got Coke or bottled water."

"I'll have Coke," Heather said.

Mindful of her sugar intake, Sarah chose water. Norman did the same.

The group sat at the kitchen table. Sarah opened her bottle of water and took a sip, waiting for her father to start a conversation. He'd been the one to suggest they come over, so she knew he would have prepared for this meeting in advance.

"How are you feeling?" he finally asked her.

Although Sarah had been gargling with the special mouthwash, swallowing food still hurt. Her bones still ached even though she took Claritin, and her constipation had dramatically increased since her last chemo session. When she could defecate, it felt like glass particles coming out of her backside, and often, there was blood in her stool. "I'm doing okay," Sarah replied, since her bowel problems didn't exactly make for polite dinner conversation. Some things were better left unsaid.

Norman nodded at her generic response. He looked as if he was going to ask her more questions, but the food arrived, and Sarah was saved by the doorbell.

Everyone opened their container of orange chicken with rice and dug in. Thankfully, the meal had a soft texture. There were no sharp edges that could hurt Sarah's throat. The fortune cookie that came with each serving was another matter. Eating it would be next to impossible, but Sarah still wanted to read her fortune and planned to open it after she got home.

Norman made eye contact with Heather. "I hear you're in college now."

Heather smiled brightly. "I am. It's really fun."

Sarah listened to them discuss her classes as she ate. Norman seemed genuinely interested in what Heather told him. He asked his granddaughter questions that couldn't be responded to with yes or no replies, and Heather answered each question in detail, munching on her meal when it was his turn to speak. Their conversation made a memory surface from a time when Norman was actually home. Sarah had just started telling her father about the book report she was working on when he received an important phone call from work. He'd gone into the other room to talk and closed the door, then grabbed his coat and took off afterward without even saying goodbye.

Sarah sipped her water, her eyes shifting from Norman to Heather, watching the current scene with distrust. The two of them chatted easily, like they had known each other for years. Norman hadn't seen Heather since she was a kid. They were basically strangers. If Sarah hadn't told Heather that Norman was her grandfather, she'd walk past him on the street, completely oblivious that any relation existed.

Now they were forming a connection. It was doomed to fail, of course, but poor Heather had no clue. Sarah began feeling guilty that she had allowed her daughter to be a part of this situation. She'd willingly led her to the emotional slaughterhouse.

As she mentally scolded herself, Norman asked her a question. She glanced up absently and asked, "What's that?"

"How's the food taste?" he repeated.

Sarah swallowed the bite she'd been chewing before saying, "Good." She didn't mention how everything she ate tasted bland. That was something people in her family knew. She had no interest in sharing that information with her dad. The desire to be close to her father had dissipated long ago. There was no point in pretending it had returned just because he had. But she'd be polite and fulfill her role until he went home.

Heather opened her cookie and read the fortune out loud. "Financial prosperity is coming your way." Her daughter held up the strip of paper and grinned. "Maybe I should play the lottery this week?"

Sarah smiled at her daughter. "You definitely should."

The plastic around Norman's cookie crinkled as his hand shook from the effort of opening it. Finally, he was able to extract it and break it open. "A new life begins with a new home." Norman's jaw dropped as he eyed Heather. "This is amazing. And accurate."

Heather set her fortune on the table. "How so?"

Norman glanced at Sarah, then turned his attention back to Heather. "I was thinking of buying a place in Illinois."

"That's a great idea!" Heather said.

Sarah had been holding her cookie, assuming they'd ask her to open it next. Instead, she slipped the package into her pocket, alarmed by the news.

Norman put his elbow on the table and rested his chin in the palm of his hand. "I figure it's best to start over here after the divorce."

Heather leaned toward her grandfather. "I heard about that. I'm so sorry."

Norman looked dejected and sighed. "Thanks."

Heather put her elbow on the table and rested her chin in the palm of her hand, mirroring Norman. "What went wrong? If you don't mind me asking."

Sarah was surprised her daughter had been so forward. It wasn't any of her business, but maybe she thought talking about it would bring them closer. Sarah took a sip of her bottled water, waiting for her father to spin a reply that wouldn't paint him in an unfavorable light.

"It's kind of embarrassing," Norman said.

"It's okay," Sarah chimed in. "We're all adults."

Norman looked unsure, like he wasn't going to tell

them what happened. Finally, he caved. "She cheated on me with a friend of mine. A client turned friend. Someone younger."

"That's horrible!" Heather said.

And utterly predictable, Sarah thought.

Norman glanced at Sarah, but she couldn't bring herself to console him after he'd repeatedly done the same thing to her mom. There were limits to her diplomacy. Being good-natured and respectful was one thing. It was another to pretend he was someone he wasn't and rewrite the past. If he was looking for Sarah's sympathy, he was setting himself up for disappointment.

He turned back to Heather. "Linda and I got along so well. I still don't understand why she did what she did."

Heather's puppy dog face returned. "That's heartbreaking, Grandpa. But things will get better. You'll see."

Sarah couldn't believe her ears. She was already calling him Grandpa!

Norman sniffed, then his eyes turned glassy. "I hope so. It's harder to start over at my age. But at least I have kids here."

"And a grandkid," Heather added with a warm smile.

Norman's tale of woe had lured Heather in, and she was under his spell. Sarah would have to keep a close eye on their interactions going forward, so she could be there for her daughter when he inevitably let her down. With any luck, Heather would be too busy with school and Caleb to be a big part of Norman's life. Or maybe Norman would change his mind about buying a place and staying in Illinois.

Norman smiled back at Heather, then gathered the empty food containers and threw them in the trash. When he returned, he sidled up to Sarah. "I can take you to your next treatment."

"Thanks," Sarah replied, "but Mom is going with me. We're meeting with the plastic surgeon to discuss options for a new breast."

Norman's face grew several shades whiter. Sarah could tell the subject made him squeamish. She hoped it would throw him so off-guard he'd stop offering to help.

"I'll take you to the next one then," he said.

Sarah was trying to figure out a way to say no when she met Heather's gaze. The pleading look in her daughter's eyes told her she'd have to say yes. After doing so, she was eager to leave, partly because she was tired and partly because she was tired of being with her dad. Tired of being constantly on edge.

Sarah eyed her daughter. "We should get going."

"Sure thing," Heather said, rising from her chair. She looked Norman's way. "Thanks so much for lunch. Why don't I give you my phone number?"

"Good idea," Norman replied.

He scuttled to the kitchen and pulled a pen and paper from a drawer. Sarah frowned as they exchanged phone numbers. No good could come of it, but she was in no position to intervene.

They said their goodbyes, and then she and Heather drove home.

At a stoplight, Heather glanced at her. "That went

well. Don't you think?"

"It did," Sarah reluctantly agreed.

When they got home, Heather said she had some homework to finish, and Sarah went to her room so she could rest. She climbed under the blankets next to Walter, who was sleeping on the bed, paws outstretched, snoring lightly. Sarah closed her eyes, frustrated that things had not gone as planned. Instead of Norman revealing his true nature, he'd charmed the heck out of Heather. Where was this guy when Sarah needed a father? What kind of game was he trying to play?

Sarah's temples throbbed as her anger level rose. She took several deep breaths to calm down, reminding herself she didn't need additional stress. The exhalations must've been loud enough to wake Walter because he inched closer and snuggled up to her hip. Sarah reached out to pet him. He was twelve pounds of pure goodness. Never hurting anyone's feelings. Never letting anyone down. She yawned, thinking the world would be better if people were more like cats. That was the last thought Sarah had before taking a much-needed nap.

A crunching sound woke Sarah. Disoriented, she rubbed her eyes, trying to figure out what she had heard as there were nothing but soft blankets around her. Moving again proved it was close by. That's when she remembered the fortune cookie. She pulled it from her pocket and saw all the broken pieces, which didn't upset her because she hadn't planned on eating it anyway.

She went to the kitchen, opened the package over the sink, then read her fortune aloud.

"Love heals all wounds."

It was a lovely saying. Too bad it wasn't true.

If it was, she wouldn't be going through everything she was going through.

Chapter 10

"Implants are the most popular choice." The plastic surgeon pulled a silicone breast from his desk drawer and handed it to Sarah.

She held it, and it felt natural. She handed it to her mom, who held it for a moment before giving it back to the surgeon.

"Are silicone implants dangerous?" Sarah asked. "I heard some of them leaked and caused another kind of cancer."

The surgeon reopened his desk drawer and pulled out another implant. "That was this kind. No one uses them since they've been recalled."

"Recalled?" Beverly asked. "Does that mean people had to have them replaced?"

The surgeon nodded grimly as he put the implant back in the drawer.

The thought of putting a foreign object into her body, one that could be recalled later for causing the very disease she was fighting, didn't sound good to Sarah.

"Ninety percent of our patients choose the silicone implant," the surgeon continued. "The ones we use are completely safe."

Until they discover they aren't, Sarah thought.

"How does it work," Sarah asked, "if I choose an implant?"

The surgeon leaned toward her. "We work with your breast surgeon. If the cancer is only in your breast, an implant can be put in during the mastectomy. You wake up after surgery with a new breast. If cancer has spread elsewhere, like the lymph nodes, and you need radiation after the mastectomy, we put in a tissue expander. It's like a placeholder for the implant, which we will put in after you've finished radiation treatments."

Since the cancer was in Sarah's underarm lymph nodes, she wasn't a candidate for the first option. She mulled that over. "That means another surgery, right?"

The surgeon nodded. "Correct. And since you're only having the left breast done, they may not match perfectly. The real one will hang lower. It will have a more natural teardrop shape. If you want them to be more alike, we could add a small implant to the top of the right breast. That would give it a fuller, rounder appearance, like the implant. We can also add a nipple after you've healed from the implant surgery."

Sarah mentally reviewed what he'd said to make sure she understood. First, there was the mastectomy with the tissue expander. Then she'd have a second surgery where he'd swap the tissue expander for the implant, and she'd have to let him cut into her healthy breast and add an implant so it would match the fake one. Plus, she'd have to return to have a nipple added to the left breast.

Overwhelmed, Sarah turned to her mom. It was evident by the look on Beverly's face that she was thinking what Sarah was thinking. Way too many surgeries. Especially after going through treatment and being tired from the cancer fight.

Sarah turned back to the surgeon. "What are my other options?"

"We can do a flap surgery. We take tissue and blood vessels from the abdomen and use them to create a new breast. The great thing about this type of reconstruction is that the new breast looks like your remaining real breast. It will grow and shrink as you gain and lose weight, unlike the implant. The negative is that you'll have a scar across the abdomen by the panty line. And it takes longer to recover from this type of surgery because you'll have an incision in two places. But unlike the implant, it won't have to be replaced in ten years."

"Wait," Sarah said. "The implant has to be replaced?"

"Yes."

Sarah had lost count of how many surgeries would occur with an implant. And although she liked the flap surgery's end result, she wasn't comfortable with having someone cut into her abdomen, remove a portion of it, and use it to create a breast. She also wasn't keen to have an additional scar and a longer recovery, which she took as code for being in a lot more pain.

The plastic surgeon gave her an empathetic look. "It's a lot to think about. You don't have to decide today." He rose from his chair. "You can also choose to have no reconstruction. You can have a mastectomy and get a prosthetic breast. It looks just like the silicone breast, but instead of being inside your body, it fits into a pocketed bra."

He handed Sarah a folder containing information about the options they discussed and told her to contact his office if she had further questions. Sarah thanked him, and then she and Beverly wordlessly walked to the coffee shop inside the hospital to order a latte. Sarah was too stressed out to have anything to eat or drink.

After the women found a table, Sarah set the folder down and stared at it in disbelief. None of the options the plastic surgeon mentioned sounded good. But she had to choose one of them because keeping her breast wasn't something she could do.

Beverly shook her head, a pained look on her face. "I can't believe you're in this situation. I mean, how do you choose?"

"I don't know." Sarah stared into the distance, feeling numb. Nurses scurried past, some on their way back to work after lunch; some just starting their shift. Patients of all ages ambled through the hospital walkway, looking like shell-shocked zombies, each doing their best to make it through the day. An older woman in a wheelchair made eye contact with Sarah as she passed. They held each other's gaze for only a few moments, forming what felt like a powerful connection. Then, just like that, the woman was gone.

After taking a deep breath, Sarah reminded herself that

even though she had the most aggressive form of breast cancer, she was at the top hospital with the best doctors and surgeons. She tried to be grateful that there were choices available in today's world. All she had to do was research the three options and determine which was best for her.

Sarah clasped her hands together and set them on top of the folder before saying, "I'll have to go online and read the pros and cons of each option. The surgeon told us the basics, but I'd like to do a deep dive into all the data, and then I'd like to ask other breast cancer patients what they chose and find out if they're happy with the results."

"Good idea," Beverly said. "When it comes to this, the more research, the better."

Having an action plan calmed Sarah down a bit. She wasn't exactly relaxed, but her anxiety level was to a point where she was no longer freaking out and could head to her oncology appointment. Beverly stayed in the waiting room to read her book while Sarah met with Dr. Zimmerman and told her the constipation had worsened and that the Claritin hadn't worked well.

"I'd like you to take more stool softeners and drink lots of water going forward. I can prescribe a pain killer that may help better than Claritin, but because it's a low-dose narcotic, it may cause more constipation."

Sarah groaned. "I think I'll pass on the constipation-increasing painkiller."

Dr. Zimmerman nodded, then Sarah got dressed and headed to the treatment room. She smiled when she noticed that Nancy was there. The nurse put her in the chair next to her.

"How's it going?" Nancy asked.

"I just had my first meeting with the plastic surgeon. Needless to say, I'm a little spooked."

Nancy nodded. "That'll do it to you."

The nurse verified Sarah's name and birthdate, then accessed her port and started her on fluids. When she left, Sarah turned back to Nancy. "Do you mind if I ask which reconstruction option you chose?"

"I did the flap surgery."

Sarah was confused by Nancy's use of the past tense. She thought all triple-negative patients had chemo first and surgery afterward. "Are you happy with the results?"

Nancy hesitated. "I was happy with how it turned out because it looked like my other breast. Not a perfect match, but close. The only negative is that flap surgery can only be done once. I had it done ten years ago, and now that the cancer is back, I can't have it done again, so I'm not sure what I'm going to do."

Sarah was speechless. She had assumed Nancy was getting her first set of treatments. She had no idea this was her second go around with the disease.

Nancy let out a frustrated sigh and continued. "I can either go flat or do the implant. If I do the implant, it won't match the other breast. One will be perky and young. The other..." she chuckled, "Well, the other, not so much."

Sarah nodded, fully understanding what she meant. It was hard enough to make this choice the first time, but having to make it a second, let alone being limited to two completely different-shaped breasts or no breast at all? Sarah's position was bad, but she found Nancy's unimaginable.

Nancy reached for her bottled water and took a sip. "I know a few people who got implants. Some are happy with them; some haven't had the best luck."

Sarah raised an eyebrow. "What do you mean?"

"One woman got an infection afterward and was hospitalized. She eventually had to get the implant removed. Another lady had a bunch of pain that wouldn't go away. She ended up with scar tissue that got hard and kept tightening around the implant. She couldn't take it anymore and had them take the implant out." Nancy leaned toward Sarah and murmured, "Plus, I heard you don't feel anything. No sensation like your real breast. It's basically just for show."

Sarah's eyes widened as recognition hit. Unfortunately, the implant surgery seemed to have a lot of complications. Sure, there were happy patients, but the horror stories were hard to ignore.

Nancy's nurse arrived to check on her. As they chatted, Sarah tucked all the breast reconstruction data into a mental file to review later and thought about how the person sitting beside her had a breast cancer recurrence. That was one of Sarah's biggest fears. She tried not to think of it because she still had to beat the disease. Worrying about it coming back didn't help her current situation.

Sarah watched Nancy joke back and forth with her

nurse and admired her upbeat attitude in the face of despair. Her odds probably weren't good, but she was here, doing whatever it took to survive. Suddenly, Sarah wanted to know everything about Nancy to emulate her positive personality traits.

When the nurse left, Sarah asked, "Have you been with Dr. Zimmerman all this time?"

"Yep. Ten years and counting."

A well-dressed woman in her seventies rose from her treatment chair, slung her designer purse over her shoulder, and waved at Nancy as she walked past.

Nancy waved back, and when the lady was out of earshot, Nancy whispered, "She's on medication to extend her life so that she can have more time with her family."

Sarah watched the woman leave. As the door closed behind her, Sarah wondered if she would ever see her again. Earlier, she had been overwhelmed by her plastic surgery options. Now, she realized that those choices, although difficult, were of far less importance than the primary goal of staying alive.

Sarah turned back to Nancy. "Do you have family nearby?"

"I do. I have a son in college, studying to become a doctor."

"Oh, my goodness! You must be so proud."

Nancy nodded. "I am. Especially because his father, who I'm no longer married to, was such a loser."

Sarah had no idea how Nancy could afford medical bills and medical school and hoped her son received a scholarship of some sort.

"How about you?" Nancy asked. "Do you have family nearby?"

"I do," Sarah said. "I'm married, with a daughter in college. And my mom is out in the waiting room."

Nancy smiled and said, "That's nice."

There was a pause in the conversation, and as Sarah was thinking of what to say next, Nancy added, "My mom used to take me to treatments when she was alive. She and my sister would take turns."

"So now it's just your sister?" Sarah asked.

"Now it's just me."

Sarah wasn't sure what that meant. Luckily, Nancy didn't keep her waiting long.

"My sister and I don't talk anymore."

"I'm sorry to hear that," Sarah said. "It's a shame to fight and drift apart, especially now."

Sarah winced, kicking herself for going too far. She held her breath, waiting for Nancy to respond.

"We never had a fight," Nancy said. "That's the funny part."

Sarah scrunched her brow. "I don't get it."

"My sister ghosted me when the cancer came back."

"Ghosted you?" Sarah asked, wondering why Nancy's sister would choose to ignore her.

"Cancer ghosting. It's a thing. You haven't heard of it?"

Sarah was stunned. "No. I can't say that I have."

"Well, consider yourself lucky because it happens to a lot of cancer patients. A friend or family member will disappear from your life with no explanation."

Once again, Nancy had rendered Sarah speechless, wondering how on earth a loved one could turn away in a time of crisis like this. Jeff would never ghost her like that. Neither would Heather. Mike, maybe? No. No way. And her father didn't count since he'd ghosted her most of her life.

"You can google it," Nancy added. "There are websites with plenty of stories like mine."

Sarah added it to her mental research list. "Why do you think it happens?"

Nancy rubbed her chin with her forefinger in thought. "Maybe they're scared? They think you're going to die and can't bear to see it?"

Sarah could see the logic behind that theory, but it didn't seem to match Nancy and her sister's scenario. "But didn't you say your sister used to bring you to treatments?"

Nancy nodded. "She did. She was super supportive for the longest time. She even threw a party once I was cancer-free. But now that it's back, she stopped calling and doesn't return my calls."

Maybe Nancy's sister had decided she was already gone, or maybe she just couldn't go through all this again. Either way, Sarah vowed that no matter how long Nancy lived, she would always be her friend.

Chapter 11

The air conditioning wasn't working on the train they took home. And, of course, their car was packed with people.

Beverly sat opposite Sarah, looking at the information the plastic surgeon had given them. "It's too warm to read," she complained, closing the folder and using it to fan herself.

"It feels like we're in a sauna," Sarah griped.

Frustrated, Sarah removed her bucket hat and wiped the sweat from her forehead with the back of her hand. She never took it off in public because she was too self-conscious, but today, she was too hot to care.

Sarah closed her eyes, exhausted by the day's events. A few minutes later, she sensed someone staring at her. She opened her eyes and found a businessman doing just that. She waited for the usual mortification to strike, but it didn't. In fact, it didn't bother her at all. She knew it wasn't personal. It was natural for people to feel fear when they saw her because she reminded them of death.

Sarah couldn't control what other people thought. Most ruminated on the minute details of life, never appreciating today. Perhaps seeing her bald head would put things into perspective. It would shake them out of autopilot, and their mood would improve.

Beverly reopened the folder and began reading. Apparently, the sweltering heat wasn't going to get in the way of what she wanted to do. Sarah watched her study the paperwork with laser-like focus. Sarah would do the same after a good night's sleep. Then she and her mother could have a more in-depth discussion about the reconstruction options, and hopefully, the decision would be easier to make.

Sarah wondered if Nancy's mom had helped her choose a decade before. If she were still alive, she'd take Nancy to treatments and probably give her other daughter a piece of her mind for abandoning her sister when she needed her most.

Beverly looked up from her reading material and smiled at her daughter. "We're almost home," she said in a soothing tone.

Sarah nodded and closed her eyes, eager to get to their stop. She felt safe knowing there was no chance her mom would ghost her because her mother loved her with all her heart.

After they walked in the door, Beverly kissed her on the cheek before saying goodbye, and then Sarah changed into pajamas and climbed into bed. She woke the following day to Walter meowing, which meant he wanted to play or have a snack. Sarah was surprised that Jeff had let her sleep and miss dinner. But she was glad he did because she had needed that many hours of rest to feel human again.

Sarah played with Walter for a few minutes and then

ate breakfast before working on her clients' ads. Jeff had sent her an email mentioning he'd be home early. She looked forward to seeing him. For some reason, yesterday had felt like an entire week.

Walter curled up next to Sarah on the sofa as she perused the pages the plastic surgeon had given her. She read the pros and cons of each option, keeping in mind what Nancy had said. Once she finished reading everything in the folder, she went online to find out what women who'd had each procedure thought.

Plenty of people were satisfied with their implants. The happiest had a bilateral mastectomy with implants on both sides, which created a more balanced look. Sarah also read horror stories like the ones Nancy had mentioned, where women who had fought so hard to battle cancer had to have surgery after surgery to fix problems that occurred from trying to recreate what they'd lost. Many women who'd had flap surgery liked getting a tummy tuck and new breasts from one procedure, saying it was a win-win. Others said it was difficult to walk afterward because it caused core weakness, and they regretted ever having it done. All patients mentioned breast reconstruction gave them self-confidence. It made them feel whole again. That's what Sarah wanted. But which option would get her there?

All that was left to research was no reconstruction. The benefits were faster healing and fewer surgeries. Choosing this path put less stress on the body, which had already been through a tremendous amount of stress. Logically, this option was the clear winner. However, emotionally, it seemed the worst choice.

Sarah opted to forget about it for a while. Instead, she typed cancer ghosting into her browser's search bar, then clicked on the first of many links and began reading. Post after post described friends and family who had disappeared from a cancer patient's life. One woman used to go to dinner with her girlfriends on Friday nights. She had been included after the cancer diagnosis, but when she threw up in the restaurant bathroom after starting chemo, she hadn't been invited since.

Sarah tried to remember the last time she had been out with girlfriends. Sadly, it was years ago when she worked at the ad agency. She and her co-workers would go to lunch together. Occasionally, they'd do dinner, but most were too busy to visit much more. Sarah lost touch with them after starting her own business and working from home. They had tried to meet a few times, but someone always canceled for one reason or another, and eventually, both sides stopped trying to connect. Sarah felt bad about it all of a sudden but didn't think contacting them now made sense.

Instead of dwelling on friendships that had fizzled out, Sarah read the next post. It was a lengthy one about a lady who had been excluded from gatherings on her husband's side of the family. She said they treated her like cancer was contagious and she had the plague. Sarah read all the reader comments, some decrying the in-law's ignorance; others offering words of support. The story made her think of Jeff's parents. She had always liked them, and they had always liked her. Their kindness was genuine. In that regard, Sarah was fortunate.

Reflecting on family made Sarah think of her dad. Norman had ghosted her for ages, but he was back now, trying to be a parent.

Perhaps, she could be easier on him?

She would try. That's the best she could do.

Sarah returned her attention to the online posts. Her breath caught as she read about a man who had divorced his wife while she was dying of breast cancer. She glanced at a framed photo of her and Jeff. He would never do such a thing. At least, she didn't think he would.

A few moments later, she heard the garage door open. Jeff was home early, as promised, making Sarah happy and uneasy at the same time. He wasn't the guy in the blog post, but for some reason, Sarah felt cold and shaky.

Jeff entered the bedroom. "How are you feeling?" he asked before kissing her cheek and sitting down.

"Okay," she fibbed, not wanting to be the perpetual bearer of bad news. She wanted to tell him the truth. She was tired, overwhelmed, and thoroughly spooked by the posts she'd read. But Jeff worked so hard and was under so much stress. He deserved a break from her problems and fluctuating emotions.

Jeff's smile relieved Sarah of her lie—totally worth it. He kicked off his shoes and climbed into bed, putting several pillows behind his head for support. "How did things go with the plastic surgeon?"

Sarah explained each reconstruction option in detail, describing the pros and cons, then shared the stories she'd heard from Nancy and patient information she'd read online. Jeff held Sarah's gaze as she spoke, and she watched his expression change gradually from curious to a furrowed brow, which morphed into wide eyes and a dropped jaw. Then, he was quiet for a long time, which meant he was processing all the data and forming a conclusion.

"This is bullshit!" He slammed his hand on the nightstand. "Total bullshit!"

Jeff rose and started pacing the room, his face turning beet red. "You've got to suffer enough with chemo. Now they want you to suffer more?" He stopped and faced Sarah. "It's unacceptable."

It was unacceptable, but there was no one to complain to about it or other options available. She and Beverly had figured that out earlier. Jeff, who was usually mild-mannered and not prone to angry outbursts, was realizing it now. She couldn't blame him for getting upset. Breast cancer was a difficult situation that seemed to get more complicated as time passed.

Jeff continued pacing the room, arms flailing as he muttered obscenities that would've made Mike proud. The vein in his forehead bulged as he huffed. Eventually, he ran out of steam and collapsed in the chair beside the bed. "I guess I was under the impression you'd have the surgery to remove the cancer, and you'd wake up with a new breast that looked just like the other breast."

Sarah had been under a similar impression. "Turns out it's a bit more involved."

Jeff shook his head and frowned. He enjoyed solving problems and usually gave great advice, but Sarah could tell he was stumped on this one.

"I've been thinking," Sarah said, "that no reconstruction with the prosthetic breast is the choice with the fewest surgeries. I would look like the women who had reconstruction while wearing clothes, but when I'm undressed…" Sarah visualized a scarred, flat chest on one side of her body, with a healthy breast by its side. It was a frightening image. Just thinking of it made her shudder.

"When you're undressed, you'll look like someone who won a battle," Jeff said, with an air of what seemed like awe. "A warrior princess."

Sarah met his gaze, which was soft and full of love. "But what about us?" she asked, worried that her future self would disgust him. "How could we sleep together if I look like that?"

Jeff got up and joined her on the bed. "I want to be with you no matter what you look like. Young. Old. Long hair. Bald." He took her hand in his. "One breast is better than no breast. We have to think of the positives."

He was saying all the right things. Sarah had no doubt he meant them, but how would he feel when he saw her looking that way? Would he still be attracted to her?

As if reading her mind, Jeff added, "If they have bras that hold the prosthetic breast, I'm sure they have lingerie."

Sarah nodded, assuming there would be lingerie for women in her situation. She could even use a needle and thread to retrofit some of her favorite nighties so they wouldn't go to waste. She inhaled deeply and let out a resigned sigh. "It could work," Sarah admitted. "I don't like it, but it could work."

As Jeff wrapped her in his arms, she realized how lucky she was to have a husband who loved her unconditionally. If she were single, she would've chosen implants or flap surgery. She doubted this would be her choice. Sure, she could meet someone and start a relationship after a mastectomy with no reconstruction, but the chances of that happening seemed slim, not because men were superficial and couldn't see beyond a woman's appearance, but because she would lack the self-esteem to even give them a chance.

"You made the right choice," Jeff whispered into her ear.

Sarah hadn't realized she'd made one until a few moments ago. She had hoped Jeff would know what she should do, but his reaction proved he was just as torn as she and Beverly were, and in the end, Sarah was the one who had to decide.

After Jeff released her, she said, "Remember that hiker who got his arm stuck between those rocks? He hoped someone would rescue him, but they didn't, and he had to cut off his arm to survive."

"That was so awful."

Sarah pictured the man doing the unthinkable. "He was so brave. No surgeons. No anesthesia. Just a pocketknife and the will to live."

There was always someone worse off. Someone who lost a part of themselves and had to learn to live without it. The hiker had lost an arm. Soldiers often lost their legs.

Sarah could lose a breast if she had to, so she could stay with her family and enjoy the rest of her life.

Heather poked her head into the room. Sarah hadn't even heard her come home. "Sorry to interrupt," she said. "But I wanted to invite Grandpa to dinner." She made eye contact with Sarah. "Is that okay?"

Sarah's mouth instinctively began to form a "no," when she recalled her plan to take it easier on him. "That's fine."

Jeff kissed her on the cheek before saying he was going to help Heather with dinner. Shortly after he left, Walter entered the room and jumped onto the bed. He rubbed up against Sarah and began purring when she started petting him. Suddenly, things seemed like they were going to be okay. She'd made a surgical decision. No one in her family was ghosting her. And Jeff wasn't a horrible husband like the guy in the blog post online.

Walter shot straight up when the device on the back of Sarah's arm started beeping. The sound alone seemed enough to propel him into the air. He scurried to safety after he landed, anxious to be away from the noise. It was then that Sarah remembered her mom was coming over to remove it. She had also told Heather it was okay to invite Norman for dinner. Her parents hadn't seen each other in a long time, which was by design. As long as Beverly was on time, that unwelcome little family reunion wouldn't happen tonight, either. The problem she was supposed to be there now.

Come on, Mom. Hurry up.

Half an hour passed. She texted her mom to tell her

not to worry about it—that she'd have Heather or Jeff take it off. When Beverly didn't respond to the text, Sarah called and left a voicemail. Her mother didn't check texts as often as most people but always answered her phone. But, of course, today would be the day when she wasn't doing either.

Sarah wondered where her mother was and wished she could reach her before it was too late. As it got closer to dinnertime, Sarah called her stepdad.

"Pick up. Pick up," Sarah repeated, but Richard didn't answer his phone.

Frustrated, Sarah gave up. She had tried her best. Now she would move on and deal with the consequences. With any luck, her mother and father's paths wouldn't cross.

There was a knock at the door. By the time Sarah made it to the living room, Heather was already taking a large bowl of salad from Norman. Her father smiled and waved when he saw Sarah. She smiled back through gritted teeth, realizing this happy scene would turn into a nightmare very soon.

Jeff brought napkins and silverware to the table. He greeted Norman, thanked him for bringing the salad, and offered him a chair.

"Don't mind if I do," Norman said, then took his seat just as the doorbell rang.

Chapter 12

"Norman," Beverly said flatly when she spotted him at the table.

"Beverly," Norman countered in a similar tone.

Time seemed to stop as they appraised each other like gunslingers about to start a fight in the Wild West. Although Sarah hadn't had a chance to tell Heather that Grandma and Grandpa hadn't seen each other in years, it was evident by her wide-eyed, frozen expression that she was quickly catching on.

"You look well," Norman offered.

"So do you," Beverly politely replied.

An awkward silence ensued, one that Sarah desperately wanted to fill. "Are you ready to remove this?" she asked her mother, pointing to her arm.

"I sure am," Beverly said before nodding at Norman and following Sarah down the hall.

Once they were safely in the bathroom, Sarah locked the door and turned on the fan so no one could hear their conversation.

"I tried to warn you," Sarah whispered. "I texted. I called."

"My phone was off because I was at the salon." She

turned her head from side to side.

"I love those highlights," Sarah said in an attempt to smooth things over.

Beverly told her to stand still as she removed the device with a practiced hand. Sarah stood there, waiting for the impending scolding that she'd put her mother in this position, but it never came.

"Richard and I are going out for a fancy steak dinner tonight," Beverly said when she was done. "He went to the barber while I was at the salon." She smiled. "We both needed to do some primping for our date tonight."

Sarah felt bad that the side trip to her house had put a damper on their special day. But from how Beverly was behaving, it seemed she wouldn't let anyone or anything ruin it. Least of all, an ex like Norman. And the last thing her mother needed to hear was her reconstruction choice, so she kept her mouth shut about it for now. Instead, she smiled and said, "Have a good time."

"I will." Beverly hugged her and turned off the fan. "Give me a call tomorrow if you feel like talking."

"Sure thing," Sarah said.

They walked back into the living room, where Beverly said goodbye to everyone and offered a little wave as she left.

Sarah waited for someone to comment on the discomfort of the previous moments. Instead, Jeff started a conversation with Norman about his drone. They chatted easily as the group dug into the salad her father had brought. Sarah thought the drone was silly, but the fake bird saved the day. Long live the drone!

"We can take it for a spin after dinner if you like," Jeff told Norman.

Norman grinned. "I'd love to." Her father seemed to share the same level of enthusiasm Jeff had for the toy.

Sarah listened to Norman and Jeff talk as they ate. They touched on so many subjects: Jeff's work, minor issues he had with subordinates he managed, the current state of the economy and how it affected the flooring industry. Heather didn't check her phone during dinner as she usually did. She just ate and allowed the space for her father and grandfather to chat. Sarah felt a surge of pride for her daughter's manners. She and Jeff had lucked out with that kid.

Right after having the thought, Heather looked up from her plate and beamed at her mom. It was moments like this that Sarah wanted to keep experiencing. These seemingly inconsequential slivers of time that filled her heart with joy. Just then, it occurred to her that Norman was a part of one of these moments.

Heather helped clear the table when everyone had finished eating. From the kitchen, she called out, "Who's ready for my famous green juice?"

Norman grimaced, probably at the prospect of drinking something green, but he managed a weak smile and said, "I am."

Sarah wasn't crazy about the concoction but always reminded herself that it was meant to heal her and that, more importantly, her daughter made it with love.

Heather brought the glasses of green juice to the table. Jeff chugged his, as was his custom. Sarah sipped hers, visualizing its vitamins and minerals bringing her good health as it rolled over her tongue.

Norman took his glass from her, eyeing the green juice with distrust. He looked from Heather to Sarah, then from Sarah to Jeff. When Jeff nodded, Norman lifted the glass to his lips and tossed it back in two gulps. Afterward, his face contorted and began to turn a shade almost as green as the juice. "It tastes terrible!" he croaked.

Everyone but Norman burst into laughter. Then Norman joined in. Heather howled, and Jeff slapped his knee as he tried to catch his breath. Sarah laughed so hard it brought tears to her eyes. She wiped them away as Norman set the glass on the table. He met her gaze and smiled.

"Let's fly that drone," Jeff said to Norman, rising from his chair.

Norman rose, too, without so much as a second glance at the green juice. Sarah sat for a moment, watching them walk out the door together. Before she could stop it, she felt the nagging twinge of missing him.

Everyone headed to the backyard. Although Sarah was having a good time, she was getting tired and chose to sit on the porch while Heather, Jeff, and Norman huddled around the drone. The three of them chatted for a bit, then they fanned out, and the metal bird took to the sky. Norman used his hand to shield his eyes from the setting sun so he could watch the drone swoop from left to right, buzzing as it went. Heather jumped up and down, excited. Sarah couldn't understand why everyone was so thrilled with the toy but was glad they were enjoying themselves.

Sarah closed her eyes and took a deep breath. She would keep trying to be the new and improved version of herself. Less judgmental. More go with the flow. Instead of focusing on the past, she'd enjoy the here and now. She exhaled just as the drone flew overhead. She opened her eyes and saw Jeff grinning at her.

She smiled back and waved. "It's getting dark!"

The members of all three generations groaned in the dusky yard. Jeff fetched the drone and headed to the garage with Heather. Sarah knew this would mean time alone with her father—maybe Jeff had even intended it that way—but she didn't mind it so much. Letting go was relieving her of so much resentment. Or maybe she was just too tired to care.

Norman seemed tired, too, from how he trudged up the porch steps. Sarah pushed herself up from her seat and went to walk him into the house, just in case he needed an arm to lean on.

"I'm available to take you to your next treatment," Norman told Sarah as they entered the kitchen.

"Sounds good," Sarah said. "I'll text you the details." She paused, then added, "Thanks for coming tonight."

"Thanks for having me," Norman replied.

Sarah considered hugging her father goodbye but opted not to. That was too big a step for today. Heather rushed in and did it for her. Jeff came in last and reached for Norman's hand to shake.

"You want some juice to go?" Jeff joked.

Norman laughed. "No, thanks."

Everyone said their goodbyes, and Sarah watched her father leave before shutting the door. It had been a long day, with many highs and lows, and now she was ready for bed.

Sarah padded to her room and found Walter already curled up and snoozing. She joined him and was out the moment her head hit the pillow. She hadn't even removed her chemo scarf before lying down.

She slept late the next day. She took a shower before working on her clients' ads and then called her mother.

"How was the steak?" Sarah asked.

"Delicious. It was pink in the center and crusted with peppercorns. I wish I could make it that way at home." Sarah thought her mother would ask how the evening went with Norman. But instead, she asked, "How are you doing with the research? Have you figured out what you're going to do?"

"It was a tough decision," Sarah replied, "but I weighed the pros and cons of all three and chose to have no reconstruction with the prosthetic breast."

Her mom was silent. Perhaps, that wasn't the choice she expected her daughter to make. "That's a good plan, honey. Get well, and you can always do an implant in the future if you change your mind."

Sarah doubted she'd change her mind, but it was good to know she could if she wanted to be cut open again. "Maybe there will be a medical breakthrough where breasts can grow back. That would be a major miracle, but with the way technology advances, you never know."

"They can clone animals. I don't see why not."

Maybe it would happen for the next generation of breast cancer patients. Some brilliant people were working in the field. If it could be done, they'd find a way.

"What did Jeff say?" Beverly asked.

"He didn't like any of the options and was upset because he doesn't want me to suffer more." Sarah considered telling Beverly the intimate details she and Jeff had discussed but held back. Some things were best kept private. She didn't want to know about Beverly and Richard's sex life and assumed her mother felt the same about her and Jeff.

"He's been under so much pressure to remain calm and stay strong," Beverly said. "It's got to be difficult, not knowing what will happen."

Beverly never went there. She never hinted that Sarah might not make it, but the truth was, it was a possibility, one that probably made Jeff sick with worry every day.

"Sometimes I forget that everyone who loves me is going through this too. I'm scared. They're scared."

"It won't last forever, honey. When you get better, no one will be afraid."

Sarah hated that everyone she loved was worried about her. It wasn't fair that they had to go through this. Then again, life wasn't fair.

Sarah switched the subject. "How's Mike? I haven't heard from him in a while."

"He's been a bit depressed. He and Donna broke up because he wouldn't let her move in with him."

"I'm surprised he didn't tell me." Sarah had a feeling they would part ways, but she didn't expect her brother to be sad over it.

"He didn't want to bother you with his problems while you're doing chemo."

Sarah frowned. Not only were her loved ones worried about her as she went through cancer treatment, but they didn't want to tell her about their problems for fear it would cause additional stress. "I'm gonna call him."

"Call him, but remember, you didn't hear this from me," Beverly said.

Sarah reassured her mother that she knew how to handle it before finishing their conversation and saying goodbye. Afterward, she searched through her phone's contacts and called Mike.

Chapter 13

Mike mentioned leaving work early to have his teeth cleaned and said he could stop by afterward. Sarah took him up on his offer, eager to catch up on what was happening in each other's lives. As Sarah added a few stray dishes to the dishwasher, she realized she hadn't visited the dentist in a while. Dr. Zimmerman had said having a cleaning during treatment wasn't recommended, so she would have to come back to her teeth after she finished chemo.

When Mike arrived, he said, "I had a cavity filled. Do I sound normal, or do I sound like I've taken way too many drugs?"

His reference to dental anesthetics made Sarah chuckle. "You sound normal."

Mike looked tired. She didn't know if it was from his dental appointment, the breakup with Donna, or both.

Her brother sat on the couch. "Mom told me about the plastic surgery options. All of them suck and sound scary."

"They do," Sarah replied. "But I picked one."

Mike didn't ask her to elaborate on her decision, so Sarah didn't divulge which one she'd made. "So, how are you doing?"

"I'm staying the course." It was another version of *I'm hanging in there*. She didn't want to use the latter too frequently and have it sound repetitive. Staying the course at least sounded fresh.

Mike nodded. "Good. And how's the old man? Is he driving you nuts?"

Sarah considered his question carefully before replying. "Oddly enough, he's been okay. In fact, Heather invited him to dinner last night, and we actually had fun."

Mike's eyebrow rose. "What do you mean you had fun?"

"We were smiling and laughing."

"Shut the fuck up."

"I'm serious," Sarah said. "I know it sounds crazy, but it's true."

Mike shook his head. He obviously found it difficult to believe. "That's cool that you had a good time, but remember, tigers don't change their stripes."

His warning was clear. Norman would always be Norman, and she shouldn't expect anything different, even if he occasionally tried to act like a real dad. Sarah would take it visit by visit, and if their relationship reverted to how it had been before, she wouldn't be surprised.

Sarah had been expecting Mike to mention the meeting between Beverly and Norman. Their mother must not have told him. Maybe it wasn't as big a deal as Sarah had thought it would be, or maybe Beverly was taking it all in stride because Sarah was ill, and Norman had returned to help.

"Are you thirsty?" Sarah asked her brother.

"Yeah, I'll have water."

They headed to the kitchen, and after Sarah poured her brother a glass of water, she asked about Donna.

Mike took the glass from her and set it down without drinking any. "We broke up."

"Why?" Sarah asked.

"Because I wouldn't let her move in. She said she didn't want to waste time on a relationship that's going nowhere."

Sarah could see why Donna might feel that way but didn't say so aloud. "And you're okay with how it ended?"

Mike shrugged. "I guess. I mean, I wasn't going to marry her, but I didn't expect her to kick me to the curb."

He was upset because he hadn't been the one to initiate the breakup. It was funny how people responded negatively to what they wanted when it was given to them. Clearly, the way they received their wish made a considerable difference in the perception of how it was fulfilled.

"Now you're ready to meet the right woman," Sarah said. "She's out there somewhere."

Mike grimaced before taking a sip of water. He probably found it hard to believe, and truth be told, Sarah had no idea if he'd ever meet the right woman, but she knew being available and unattached helped.

As they stood there pondering her prediction, Walter walked in and meowed.

"He wants a snack," Mike said. He headed to the

cupboard and pulled out the cat's bag of treats.

Walter usually hid when company was over but always came around for Mike. Her brother was good with animals, and even though he didn't want children, he was good with kids. He had a great job too. Plus, he was funny and smart. He was a great catch—he just needed to find an equally great catch for himself.

"I'd better head home and make some food," Mike said. Before Sarah could tell him that Caleb was bringing dinner and he was welcome to stay, he added, "I took some meat out and have to cook it tonight." On his way out the door, he called, "Let's go to a movie one day soon."

"Sounds good," Sarah called back.

As she watched her brother drive down the street, she realized Donna was part of the past, her name added to the list of contenders who hadn't made it to the finish line of Mike's life. She had been the best of the bunch but couldn't get him to commit. Sarah hoped Mike would find the woman he was looking for. Unfortunately, he wasn't into modern dating apps, so he'd have to meet her in the real world, and luck would have to be on his side. One of them deserved good luck. She'd been down on hers lately and hoped by next year it would improve.

Heather and Caleb arrived shortly after Mike left. Caleb said hello and dropped off a meal he had cooked but couldn't stay to eat because he had to run to class. Jeff came home soon after, and the three of them ate the roasted chicken with brightly colored steamed veggies, which was healthy but flavorful and way better tasting than any chicken Sarah had ever made.

With a forkful of broccoli, Heather turned to Sarah and said, "Grandpa invited me to go condo shopping this weekend. Do you want to come?"

Sarah had just seen Norman a few days ago, and they'd be going to her next chemo session together. She wanted to let him into her life but didn't want him around all the time. "I think I'll pass." Then, worried that may have sounded rude, she added, "I tire easily, and I don't want to slow you guys down."

Heather seemed to understand. And it wasn't like Sarah was lying entirely. It was nice that they were bonding, and she hoped they would have fun. It was a shame that Sarah and her father hadn't done those kinds of things when she was a kid. She understood he was busy working, but your daughter is only a child once, and you can't go back in time and relive those days.

It then occurred to Sarah that Norman hadn't invited her to go house hunting. Heather had. Maybe he didn't ask her because he knew she'd be tired from treatment. He was probably being thoughtful, but for some reason, Sarah was miffed.

She gave the matter more thought as she loaded the dishwasher but couldn't figure out why it would bother her. Finally, she shrugged it off and waved goodbye to Heather, who was meeting some friends from school after dinner, then joined Jeff in the living room.

Sarah and Jeff watched a heartwarming romance while holding hands. They hadn't been intimate since AC chemo started, and it felt good to have a date night, even if it didn't include sex. Sarah looked forward to sleeping with Jeff after the fourth and final treatment. It wasn't that they couldn't do it now, but avoiding contact with all bodily fluids would make it complicated and strange. In addition to that, the end of AC meant Sarah would be able to cry on Jeff's shoulder without causing him harm, she wouldn't have to wipe down the toilet after each bathroom visit, and hopefully, the mouth sores would lessen, and the bone pain and constipation would end.

"What are you thinking?" Jeff asked. It was usually Sarah who asked Jeff that question. He had never done it to her before now.

"I was thinking about how things may improve when I finish AC. Of course, I still have twelve weeks of the weekly chemo afterward, but Dr. Zimmerman says it's not as harsh."

Jeff squeezed her hand. "I hope she's right." He shifted positions so he was facing Sarah. "I don't know how you can have such a positive attitude while going through all this."

Sarah's emotions rose and fell so much that she worried she was driving Jeff insane. It was a relief to hear he thought she had a good attitude. "I figure it's better than dwelling on all the bad stuff."

Jeff smiled, but there were tears in his eyes. He reached for her and took her in his arms. "That's good," he said, sniffling. "It's good to stay positive when things are tough."

As Jeff held her, she felt his tears moisten the side of her neck. He wasn't sobbing, just releasing pent-up grief.

Sarah rubbed his back the way he rubbed hers when he tried to comfort her. It always helped when he did it, so she hoped it would help him too.

Sarah handed Jeff the box of tissues she always had nearby, and he blew his nose. She wished she could do something to cheer him up. As she considered ideas, a good one came to mind.

"Are you in the mood for chocolate chip cookies?"

Jeff wiped his eyes. "I'd love cookies, but what about you?"

Sarah hadn't eaten dessert since she'd had the PET scan. "I'm sure one cookie won't hurt." She rose from the sofa. "Let me make sure I have everything I need before making promises I can't keep."

After rummaging through the pantry and refrigerator, Sarah found all the items needed to make a batch of cookies for Jeff. First, she preheated the oven, then mixed the ingredients in a large bowl. Next, she rolled the dough into small round balls before putting them onto a nonstick pan. The experience relaxed her, taking her back to a simpler time when life was less complicated, and everyone in her family was in good health.

The scent of chocolate chip cookies filled the house as Sarah ensured there was adequate milk. She poured a small glass for herself and a large one for Jeff. When the cookies cooled, she put several on a paper plate. Jeff appeared without being called, and they sat at the kitchen table.

Jeff ate his first cookie as Sarah savored the first bite of hers. It was decadent. A thousand times better than green juice. Of course, she would never say that to Heather, but it was true. Eating only one would be nearly impossible.

Jeff took a swig of milk. "These are amazing," he said, grabbing cookie number two.

They were no different than the last batch Sarah made, but she figured Jeff thought these were better because he hadn't eaten them in a long time. She chewed her next bite slowly, letting the chocolate melt in her mouth, wondering why vegetables couldn't taste as good as cookies. She never overate spinach or green beans and had to force herself to stop.

But she did stop at one cookie, even as Jeff began eating his third. He finished his milk, let out a satisfied sigh when he was done, then kissed Sarah on the cheek before throwing his paper plate in the trash. Sarah put the remaining cookies in a clear container and left them on the counter. Between Jeff and Heather, they'd be gone soon.

Afterward, she and Jeff went to bed and watched a stand-up comedy special. Sarah hadn't heard of the man, but he made Jeff laugh harder than any other comic had before. She watched his smiling face in the dim bedroom light, clinging to hope that there would be many more evenings like this in the years to come. She'd do her best to get well so they could grow old together as planned. If luck were on her side, they'd have a chance.

The following day, with Heather off on a condo hunt with Norman and Jeff running errands, Sarah decided to have a "Me Day." She washed her face and applied a hydrating mask. After removing it, she put on makeup as she had worn it before. The smoky eye, which had looked sexy with her long blonde hair, didn't go well with the chemo scarf. She looked like she should be gazing into a crystal ball and telling someone their fortune instead of exuding sex appeal.

Sarah pulled the scarf off her head and stared at herself in the mirror, feeling discouraged. She washed her face again and started her makeup over from scratch. This time, she only put on tinted moisturizer, lip gloss, and mascara. She donned her chemo scarf and turned from side to side, satisfied with the more natural look. It wasn't sexy by any means, but she appeared healthier. A little less bedraggled overall.

The remaining chocolate chip cookies beckoned, their siren song calling to Sarah from the other room. She blocked the treats from her mind and made a veggie omelet instead. Just in case luck wasn't entirely on her side, she figured returning to a healthy diet would increase her odds of growing old with Jeff, seeing her daughter graduate college and get married, and maybe even becoming a grandmother someday.

Chapter 14

As she gazed out the train window, Sarah thought of her first chemo session. It was hard to believe it was only six weeks ago. So much had changed since then; it felt like a decade had passed. Sarah actually felt a decade older. Her reflection in the window showed that she looked it, too. She glanced at her father sitting opposite her with his eyes closed. His once full head of hair had thinned and turned gray. Age spots dotted his skin, and his body seemed frail. To her knowledge, he was in good health, but he was getting up there in age. Who knew how long he'd be around?

Norman opened his eyes and found Sarah staring at him. "Sorry. I didn't sleep well last night."

"Bad dream?" Sarah asked.

"Heartburn. I didn't think my dinner was spicy, but I guess it was."

Now that he was awake, Sarah figured they might as well chat. "How was condo shopping? Did you find a place you like?"

"We saw a few. One was too small, one was too far away, and one was too expensive."

Too far away. It was weird to hear her father prioritize being close to family. Having him say a property was too expensive was also surprising as Norman had always liked the best and had great taste.

"So, the search continues next weekend," Norman said. "The realtor is going to show us a few more places she thinks I'll like."

Sarah assumed "us" meant him and Heather. Although her daughter was busy with school, she'd make time for her grandfather, especially since they had just reconnected after so many years. "Finding the right house can be a daunting task. I'm glad Heather can help."

"She's been wonderful," Norman remarked. "She points out the positives and negatives of each condo. Little details I miss. A woman's opinion is invaluable in this situation."

The last time Sarah had looked, she was a woman.

She wasn't well enough to search for homes, but she still wanted to be asked, so she could politely decline because of poor health.

"When I view a place," Norman continued, "I see four walls, windows, appliances. If the price is right and it's in the correct location, I'm interested. I don't pay attention to which direction the home faces for nice sunsets or the feng shui of the room, whatever that means."

Sarah chuckled. Heather must've mentioned those points.

The train came to a stop, and three people stood to get off.

"Linda picked out our last house," Norman said. "She knew what looked good and how to decorate well." Norman looked lost after mentioning Linda. Sarah considered reaching out to put a hand on his shoulder to comfort him, but the distance to his train seat was longer than the length of her arm, and after thinking of it for too long, the moment had passed.

"Have you talked to her lately?" Sarah asked.

"I talked to her last week. She had a question about the water heater. She also asked about you."

At least they were civilized and could have a conversation without screaming at each other. And even though Linda didn't want to be married to Norman anymore, she'd been kind enough to inquire about her.

Sarah studied Norman. It was sad to think that her father had worked hard all his life to be successful, only to lose so much in the end. Since then, all he'd gained was a sick daughter, a funny son-in-law, and a granddaughter he seemed to cherish. She could see why he liked having Heather around. With her help, he'd find a home that suited his needs and had great sunsets. Its feng shui would be correct, which could help him enjoy life more.

As Norman started looking out the train window, Sarah's thoughts turned to Linda. She wondered if the age gap was really the issue or if they had problems and drifted apart. As Sarah thought more about it, she realized the details didn't matter. They were divorced, and her father had to figure out what to do with the rest of his life.

The conductor announced that the next stop was theirs. The ride had gone by quickly as they chatted, and now they were getting ready to disembark. The pair remained quiet on the cab ride to the hospital, each in their own world. Norman had his life to think of, and Sarah had hers. She had a few questions for Dr. Zimmerman and mentally reviewed them so she wouldn't forget. Considering her memory wasn't what it used to be, she probably should've written the questions down.

Dr. Zimmerman entered the examination room and smiled warmly. "How have you been?" she asked as she started the breast exam.

Sarah told her about the reconstruction decision as the doctor felt the lymph nodes under her arm.

"You're moving forward," her doctor said. "That's good." She didn't give an opinion on the option Sarah chose. She probably wanted to remain neutral.

Dr. Zimmerman asked her to take a deep breath and listened to her lungs. As Sarah exhaled, she remembered the question she wanted to ask. "I heard about special gloves for the upcoming weekly chemo. Can you tell me where to get them?"

"You can buy the cold gloves online. They have booties too. I'll have the nurse give you the details." She pressed on Sarah's abdomen and said, "I suggest getting both to protect your hands and feet from neuropathy. It doesn't happen to everyone, but it's best to wear the gloves and booties to play it safe."

When Dr. Zimmerman finished the exam, Sarah dressed and met with the nurse, who gave her a printout listing two brands of cold gloves and booties the hospital recommended. "Get these before the first session," the nurse said. "Many patients are four and four, but you're four and twelve, so you'll need them."

Sarah's brow furrowed in confusion.

The nurse clarified. "Some breast cancer patients get four AC chemo treatments followed by four Taxol. Since you're triple-negative, you're getting twelve Taxol, so your chances of developing neuropathy are higher."

Wonderful. This keeps getting better.

Sarah thanked the nurse for warning her and put the printout in her purse, planning to order a set of gloves and booties immediately. She had seen women with coolers in the patient waiting area. Now it made sense why they were carrying those things around. She didn't know if she and Jeff owned a cooler and would check with him when she got home.

Sarah followed the nurse into the treatment area. Her shoulders slumped when she didn't see Nancy in their usual spot. After the nurse started her on fluids, Sarah glanced at the woman in the chair next to her. Her eyes were tired, and her pupils dilated as she stared into space. It reminded her of the way Mike looked when he was stoned. Cold gloves and booties covered her hands and feet, which made Sarah wonder if the weekly chemo would make her feel high. She considered asking the woman about it, but it didn't look like her fellow cancer patient was in the best frame of mind to chat. So instead, Sarah closed her eyes.

Someone tapped her on the shoulder. She opened her eyes and saw Nancy. The nurse was taking her to the chair the stoned cancer patient had previously occupied. Sarah lifted her chin to acknowledge Nancy as she sat down. Then the nurse started talking to Nancy, and Sarah heard her friend say she was in pain.

Sarah pretended to be busy with her phone. She didn't want Nancy to think she was listening to their conversation.

After Nancy's nurse left, she asked Sarah how it was going.

"Today's my last AC treatment, so I'm pretty psyched."

Nancy nodded. "Amen to that." Nancy hid her pain well, even when it was unnecessary to do. She could be herself here, of all places, but maybe she'd gotten into the habit of pretending she was okay.

The nurse returned with Sarah's chemo. She glanced at the red bag of fluid, feeling thankful and fearing it in equal measure. Then, after it was set up and dripping into her line, she turned back to Nancy. "They gave me info about cold gloves and booties. Did you use those?"

"I did. Unfortunately, I still ended up with some numbness in my fingers and toes. But who knows how bad it could've been if I hadn't worn them?"

Sarah sighed. She didn't like hearing that the gloves weren't foolproof. All she could do was buy them and hope for the best. "The person in the chair before you wore them. She looked high."

Nancy laughed. "It's the Benadryl. They give it to you before Taxol, so you don't have an allergic reaction. Unfortunately, a few patients have gone into anaphylactic shock. Benadryl prevents that."

Sarah's eyes bulged. "That's not scary."

"Not at all. Nothing scary is happening here."

Sarah and Nancy shared a look of camaraderie before her friend added, "There's a pill form of Benadryl for allergies, which can make you drowsy. The Benadryl we get goes into the bloodstream via the port, so it's much stronger. Just wait. You're going to feel like you're floating in your chair."

Sarah imagined being wasted while sitting in a chair with cold gloves and booties on her hands and feet. She didn't care for the idea, but how she felt about the prospect didn't matter. The experience was coming down the pipeline, whether she liked it or not.

A series of loud beeps rang out, and a group of nurses rushed to one of the private treatment rooms. All the patients in the group treatment area watched them go.

"Do you think it's an allergic reaction?" Sarah asked Nancy.

"Maybe. Hopefully, it's not worse."

Sarah's muscles tensed. She knew cancer was deadly but hadn't expected a fellow patient to die while receiving treatment. Growing more anxious with each passing moment, she craned her neck to see what was happening in that room, but she couldn't see far enough down the hall from where she was seated. None of the other patients spoke as the commotion took place. Instead, each seemed to be waiting with bated breath to learn what was happening. Eventually, the door to the waiting area opened, and a nurse led an older man down the hall and into the private room. Nurses had never brought anyone from the waiting area into the treatment area since Sarah became a patient. She turned to Nancy, hoping she knew what that meant.

"That's not good," Nancy said, frowning and shaking her head. She was the only person who had uttered a single word since the drama began. After that, time seemed to stand still until a nurse emerged from down the hall to check on Sarah.

The young woman fiddled with buttons on her machine. "How are you doing?" she asked. "Would you like something to drink?"

"I'm fine," Sarah said. "But I'm wondering, what just happened?"

"Medical emergency," the nurse replied.

There was something in her tone that reeked of formality. She checked on Nancy next. When she had moved on to another patient and was out of earshot, Nancy whispered, "Medical emergency is code for none of your business."

Sarah smirked. "Yeah, I got that. Makes sense with privacy laws, but I just wanted to know if the person is okay."

No one learned what happened to the woman. Several patients asked, but the nurses stayed mum.

Sarah's machine beeped, signaling the end of her session. A nurse flushed her port, unhooked the line, then attached the Neulasta on-body injector to the back of Sarah's arm before leaving.

"I'll be back in two weeks. Will you be here?" Sarah asked Nancy.

"I will." She reached for her phone. "Why don't I give you my number, though, just in case."

Sarah and Nancy exchanged phone numbers. Nancy told Sarah to call or text whenever she felt like it. Sarah told Nancy to do the same.

Somehow, the act of exchanging numbers made their friendship official. In the midst of one of the saddest rooms in the hospital, Sarah stared into space and smiled.

Chapter 15

On the train ride home, Sarah started feeling nauseous. The nurse gave her medicine during treatment that controlled nausea well, but the queasy feeling in her stomach surged with every bump and turn. She'd never felt this lousy right after chemo and wondered if she would make it home before getting sick. She rose, eager to find the train car with the bathroom.

"Are you okay?" Norman asked.

Sarah shook her head and kept her mouth closed. She rushed to the end of the car, opened the door, and entered the next. No bathroom. She continued racing to the next car, trying to ignore the watery sensation in her mouth. She hit paydirt with the third car, and thankfully, no one was in the lavatory.

Sarah locked herself in, crouched down, and vomited. Shaking and sweating, Sarah tried to calm down. Unfortunately, she heaved a second time. Most of the contents of her stomach made it into the toilet, but some managed to get on the toilet seat and floor. Once her stomach settled down, Sarah grabbed a wad of toilet paper and wiped her mouth. She took another and used it to clean up the toilet seat and floor before reaching into her purse and trying to figure out how to clean the area so it wouldn't be dangerous to the person who used the restroom next. A bottle of hand sanitizer was all Sarah had. She squeezed some onto a fresh wad of toilet paper, wiped the toilet seat and surrounding areas to the best of her ability, and then flushed.

Dizziness struck when Sarah stood. Between nausea and the train's movement, it was all she could do to stand without tipping over. Once she got her bearings, she washed her hands and took a deep breath. She'd have to go out and face everyone now. With any luck, no one would have heard anything, and she could quietly return to her seat.

The train conductor she and her father had met on a previous trip was there when she opened the door.

"Are you okay?" he asked, glancing inside.

Heat rose in Sarah's cheeks. "I'm fine. Just a little nauseous from chemo, but I'll be alright."

As Sarah stepped out of the restroom, she wobbled, and the train conductor caught her before she fell. "Here," he said, steadying her. "Let me help you back to your seat."

Everyone stared at the unlikely pair as they traversed the train. Sarah guessed it wasn't every day that you saw a man in uniform with a cancer patient hanging on his arm. She wished she'd worn her bucket hat so she could pull it down and cover her face. But there was no way to hide from this embarrassing situation, so she held her scarf-covered head as high as possible and avoided eye contact with the other riders as they passed.

The conductor lowered her into the seat next to

Norman, who turned and spoke with the conductor in hushed tones about what had happened. Sarah closed her eyes and rested her head on her father's shoulder, listening to them talk. Within a few minutes, she couldn't stay awake any longer and fell asleep.

Norman shook Sarah's shoulder gently. "Our stop is next."

Groggy, Sarah opened her eyes. She yawned and realized her breath must be horrific but didn't dare put a mint in her mouth. Instead, she grabbed her purse and stood. Norman stood, too, and put his arm around her like the train conductor. Sarah could walk on her own now but let her father help. Other riders politely allowed them to pass before exiting the train themselves. There was a time not so long ago when she wouldn't have let them wait on her. Today, she pursed her lips into a grin, grateful for the break.

"I'll stay with you until Heather or Jeff gets home," Norman offered after walking Sarah to her front door.

Sarah pulled her house keys from her purse. "You don't have to do that."

"I know. But I want to," Norman said.

Sarah smiled at her father, who looked tired and concerned. "I'll be fine," she assured him. "Thanks for all your help."

After unlocking the door, Sarah turned back to her dad. She hugged him, thinking he was more of the father she had always wanted him to be today. Norman held her in his arms for quite a bit longer than expected, then rubbed her back before letting go.

"Call me if you need anything," he said as he walked away.

"I will," Sarah said before going inside.

Exhausted, Sarah removed her shoes and climbed into bed, fully clothed. The sound of Walter's paws on the blankets came soon after, and she used the last bit of her energy reserves to pet him. The cat, who usually slept by her feet, burrowed as close as possible to her face. He seemed to know that his mommy needed his special brand of feline medicine more than ever today.

It was past dinnertime when Sarah woke. She padded to the family room and found Jeff and Heather watching TV.

"Mom!" Heather practically shouted upon seeing her. "How are you feeling?"

"Not great," Sarah answered honestly, for once.

Jeff got up and helped her to the sofa. "Norman told us what happened. Is there anything I can do?"

Heather chimed in before Sarah could answer. "Yeah. Is there anything we can do?"

Sarah sat down. She couldn't think of anything, but just being with them helped.

Jeff put his arm around her. "How about some crackers? Do you think you could eat some of those?"

"Maybe," Sarah said, afraid to try.

Everyone got up and headed to the kitchen. Sarah sat down at the table as Jeff pulled her favorite crackers from the pantry. He put several on a plate and brought them to her. Heather trailed her father, a tall glass of water in hand. They both sat down and waited for Sarah to eat.

"Here goes nothing," Sarah joked. She bit into the first cracker, reminding herself it only tasted bland because of chemo, not because the recipe had changed. She took a sip of water afterward. Just enough to wash it down. When her stomach didn't reject the first cracker, she ate a second and third. She took a few more sips of water, and then the three of them waited in silence.

"So far, so good," Sarah finally said.

Jeff exhaled a sigh of relief. Heather, whose face was a study of apprehension, relaxed.

"I guess it was only a matter of time until I barfed."

Neither Jeff nor Heather laughed.

Since humor was ineffective, Sarah said, "Remember that chemo is cumulative, and AC is super strong, so it makes sense I'd feel worse after the final treatment." As Sarah said the words aloud, she suddenly realized she might be in for a tough two weeks. She'd been so excited to finish AC that she forgot the cumulative part.

Heather snapped her fingers. "I'll tell Caleb to cook bland dinners going forward."

"Good idea," Jeff said, pointing at his daughter for emphasis. "And I'll buy some ginger ale."

Sarah was glad that the suggested solutions seemed to lift her family's spirits. She had no doubt that if she implemented them and took her nausea medication, things would be fine. If they weren't, she would only have to endure two more weeks of struggling before things improved. She'd come this far. Surely, she could do that. All she had to do was remind herself that she was getting closer to the end each day. Plus, she could reach out to

Nancy if things got too crazy.

The next morning, Sarah logged into Facebook and stared at the ads dashboard. She scanned its rows of metrics and drew a blank. Usually, she'd see data and compare it to the day before, then make necessary changes to the campaigns. Now she wasn't sure what the data meant. And the harder she tried to figure it out, the more confused she became. She'd already accidentally turned off an ad and feared she could do worse if she attempted to work today. The mental fogginess improved toward the end of each treatment. She'd ignore the ads and hope nothing went wrong until then.

Walter sat by his toy basket and meowed at Sarah. She walked toward him, pulled one of the many plush mice from the basket, and threw it across the room. Walter tore across the carpet and pounced, doing a backflip after catching the mouse. He batted it around for a bit and returned to the basket. This time, he didn't have to meow at Sarah. She knew the drill and sat down, throwing mouse after mouse until the basket was empty and Walter had run out of steam.

The short play session wore Sarah out. She returned to bed and napped, waking when her arm beeped. The doorbell rang as she rubbed the sleep from her eyes. She rose to answer it and smiled when she saw Beverly.

"Perfect timing! My medicine just finished dispensing."

Beverly came into the house and set her purse down. She regarded Sarah with concern. "How are you doing?"

"Better. Not as nauseous." Heather must've told her

about the incident on the train. Her mother was probably upset that she wasn't there when it happened.

"Good," Beverly said. "Now, let's get this thing off your arm."

They went to the bathroom, and Beverly loosened the tape holding the device. "I'll bet you're glad this is the last time we have to do this."

"I am," Sarah said, facing the shower curtain as her mom stood behind her and pulled it off.

Beverly washed her hands after throwing it away. Then her cell phone buzzed, and she picked it up and began texting. Sarah thought that was odd because her mother preferred talking on the phone.

"Who is that?" Sarah asked, curiosity trumping manners.

Beverly ignored her daughter and kept typing. When she finished her message, she looked up. "Your father."

"You're talking to Dad?"

"We're not talking; we're texting."

Sarah was stunned. Surely, this was a strange dream as there was no way her parents could be talking to each other, let alone texting. Sarah blinked a few times. She was definitely awake. And there Beverly was, standing in her bathroom, texting Norman.

Beverly put her phone on the bathroom counter. "He wanted to know how you're doing today."

"Why doesn't he just call me and ask?"

"He didn't want to disturb you, in case you were working or sleeping."

Beverly had gotten a new cell phone number last year.

Sarah doubted Norman had it. Before she could ask how they were texting each other, her mother said, "Heather called me last night and told me you got sick on the train. I wanted to check on you, but it was too late to call." Beverly frowned. "That's when I realized there would be times bad things would happen, and I wouldn't be there. I'm only with you half the time. The other half, Norman is in charge."

Sarah didn't think either of her parents was in charge when they took her to treatment, but she could understand why her mom might have that point of view. Heather was an adult, but Sarah still felt protective of her. If she and Jeff were taking their daughter to doctor appointments, they might think they oversaw her care.

Beverly continued, bringing Sarah back to the conversation. "So, I asked Heather for Norman's phone number. I called him this morning and suggested that we keep in touch while you're beating cancer. That way, we both know what's happening. He thought it was a good idea and asked me to let him know how you're doing today."

Sarah nodded. If she were in Beverly's position, she'd do the same. "And Richard doesn't mind?"

"Richard understands. That said, I don't want your father to call and chat for extended lengths of time, so I'm texting. Of course, if there's an emergency, he's welcome to call, but I think a simple text to keep each other in the loop should suffice."

Sarah stood in awe. Norman and Beverly were on the same team. They weren't best buddies, but they didn't hate each other and were back on speaking terms because she was sick, and Norman had finally decided to be a dad. Heather had gained a grandfather, and Jeff gained a father-in-law he seemed eager to get to know.

What about Mike?

Why hadn't Norman tried to reconnect with his son?

Chapter 16

Mike showed up at Sarah's place on Saturday afternoon with an armful of DVDs. They had planned on going to the movies, but Sarah wasn't feeling well enough to leave the house, so Mike brought the entertainment to her.

"I got these from the library." Her brother sat on the sofa and spread the DVD's out on the coffee table so Sarah could see each cover. "There's a comedy, a horror flick, and some sappy shit I figured you might like."

Sarah eyed the movie Mike thought would interest her. Its cover had a couple holding hands as they walked on the beach with a dog by their side. Her brother never watched those kinds of movies, and Sarah didn't want to subject him to one now. Scary films were his favorite. Sarah tolerated them but found most to be too gory for her taste.

"Let's watch the comedy," Sarah suggested, figuring it would appeal to them both. She could certainly use a laugh.

With that decided, Sarah went to the kitchen and put a bag of popcorn into the microwave. She brought napkins and two glasses of water the family room while it cooked, then returned and put the popcorn into a large bowl before setting it on the coffee table and offering some to her brother.

Mike grabbed a handful. "I heard about what happened on the train. Man, that totally sucks."

Sarah reached for her glass of water. "Yeah, and of all the places it could happen!" She shook her head, embarrassed by the memory.

"But you're doing better now?"

"I haven't thrown up again, but I still feel like crap."

Mike's face fell. Sarah knew it was hard for her brother to hear his kid sister was suffering. Instead of asking about her symptoms, he glanced around and asked, "Where is everyone today?"

"Jeff had to finish a project at work, and Heather is with Dad, looking at condos."

Mike chuckled.

Sarah smiled at her brother. "What's so funny?"

"Norman. He's made up this shopping for a condo BS so he can spend time with Heather."

Norman no longer had a home and claimed he wanted to buy one near his family. Shopping for a condo with the help of a relative seemed reasonable to Sarah. "He's staying at a hotel, so it could be legit," she suggested.

Mike reached for another handful of popcorn. Before putting it into his mouth, he said, "Mark my words, they'll be looking at condos weekend after weekend, and he won't buy one."

Sarah considered his comment. This was their second weekend looking. Norman hadn't liked any of the properties the realtor had shown him the first time, but that was normal. Doing a thorough search before spending that kind of money was to be expected.

Sarah moved on. "Did you hear that Mom and Dad are talking again?"

Mike was about to grab a third handful of popcorn but stopped. "You're kidding."

"Completely serious."

Mike eyed his sister with suspicion. "Let me guess. He lost Linda, and now he's trying to get Mom back."

That hadn't occurred to Sarah. It was possible, but she doubted that was her father's intention. "No," she said. "They're keeping in touch because they both take me to doctor appointments."

"Oh. That makes sense. Sucks that Mom is stuck talking to him, but it may be hard not to in this case."

"They're not talking. They're texting," Sarah mentioned, parroting Beverly's words.

"Talking. Texting. It's all the same." He rolled some popcorn around in his hand as though it helped him think. "I still don't trust him. He wouldn't think twice about making a move on Mom."

Sarah chuckled.

Mike's brow furrowed. "What's so funny?"

"I'm visualizing that happening. Mom would probably roll her eyes and walk away."

"And if Richard got wind of it, he'd beat Dad's ass."

Sarah burst into laughter at the image of the two older men duking it out. Mike must've envisioned the same scene because he put his glass on the coaster and laughed. Her brother went on to describe the imaginary altercation in detail, with Richard landing specific punches before putting their father in a headlock and making him beg for release. There was no need to watch a funny movie as this was the most fun she'd had since she had gotten sick.

Once she caught her breath, Sarah reflected on the time they had shared since Norman arrived. "It's weird having Dad around," she said. "I mean, I appreciate him taking me to treatment because it takes some of the burden off Mom, but sometimes I still feel angry that he thinks this will somehow make up for abandoning us as kids."

Mike nodded. She had expected him to launch into a long list of things for them to be angry about, but this time, he stayed quiet.

"He's been great with Heather. Whether he's going to stay here and buy a place, I don't know. But he's been a better grandfather to her than he was a father to us." Sarah paused, deciding whether to ask her brother something that could offend him or, worse, hurt his feelings. That was the last thing she wanted to do.

Mike leaned forward to study her. "What's on your mind?"

Her brother had always been good at reading her. Hiding things from him was tough. Sarah figured it was best to share. "I've been wondering why Dad hasn't contacted you since he's been back."

"Because he's a strategist."

Sarah shook her head and gave a couple of rapid blinks. She'd expected Mike to express anger over the continued neglect—not an actual theory. "How so?" she asked, pulling her legs onto the sofa to get more comfortable.

"He reached out to you first, hoping you would give him another chance because he's old and you're sick."

Sarah nodded. So far, this made sense.

"Then he focused on Heather. She's young and sweet and doesn't really know him, so she's an easier target. Mom's a tougher nut to crack because she wants nothing to do with him. But he's part of the team now, and she has to talk to him if she wants to stay in the loop on the days he takes you to chemo."

Sarah supposed that could be considered a strategy. But she didn't think Norman had preplanned all their interactions and that each was part of some diabolical scheme. Perhaps since she and her father had been spending more time together, she had begun to think of him less as a monster and more as a normal person with flaws.

"So, how do you fit in?" she asked.

"I'm supposed to fall in line after he's got everyone else on his side. But, since we always fight, he's leaving me for last, hoping I don't cause any problems." Mike smirked, indicating he had no intention of cooperating with Norman.

"You might be right," Sarah said.

"Oh, I'm right. One hundred fucking percent."

Mike got up to use the restroom. While he was gone, Sarah refilled their glasses of water and threw away the used napkins. It would be nice if Mike were there the next time Norman came to dinner, but she didn't expect him to fall in line just because she had decided to give her father a second chance.

When her brother returned, Sarah said, "I changed my mind. Let's watch the horror flick."

Mike smiled brightly, then grabbed the DVD and put it in the player before sitting down and starting the film. Sarah watched as teenager after teenager entered a house where a madman was hiding and got murdered one by one. When the first kid met a gruesome demise, her brother said, "Oh, snap!" When the second one followed in his footsteps and died in a different but equally horrific manner, Mike cringed and shouted, "Hell, no!"

The plot was thin, and the characters were basically the same. The most amusing aspect of the movie was her brother's commentary. It made watching it together worthwhile. Sarah nodded off for a few minutes here and there but woke and could still follow along. When it ended, Mike informed her that the series had four more movies.

"You enjoy those on your own," Sarah joked.

Mike grinned. "I will." He gathered the DVDs and stood. "I should probably get going so you can rest."

Sarah stood too. "Thanks for coming. I had a good time, but you're right; I'm tired."

She and her brother hugged before he left, then she went to her room and took a nap.

When she woke and trudged downstairs, Heather was at the kitchen sink rinsing veggies for the juicer, and Jeff was pulling food from a takeout bag sporting a logo of a popular healthy chain.

"Hey, honey." Jeff smiled and reached out a hand to rub her back. "I got soup and sandwiches on the way home from work. I hope that's okay?"

"That's great," Sarah said, appreciating their help.

As they ate, Jeff talked about the project his team had been working tirelessly to finish on time, and she was glad it was done so that he didn't have to worry about it anymore. It was bad enough that her reaction to the chemo added extra work to his busy schedule. Sarah missed cooking and performing some of the more basic household tasks she had previously done with ease. Before, she could lift the large cast iron pot from the cupboard and vacuum the house. Now the pot was too heavy, and pushing the vacuum for extended lengths of time was hard. Sarah knew treatment would be difficult but didn't expect to feel useless all the time.

"How about your day?" he asked.

"What's that?" Sarah asked, coming out of yet-another chemo fog. "Oh yeah, my day. Mike stopped by and brought along one of those awful horror movies."

"The kind where all the teenage kids get murdered?" he asked.

Sarah's jaw dropped. "How did you know?"

Their banter was interrupted when Heather said, "Grandpa mentioned Uncle Mike today."

"Really?" Sarah asked, her interest piqued. "What did he say?"

"He said he plans to reach out to him soon. That he's just waiting for the right time."

That sounded like a strategy. If it weren't, Norman

would've already contacted Mike.

"He also talked about Grandma a lot," Heather added. "He told me how they met and described all the fun places they used to go on dates."

Sarah blew on her spoonful of soup, thinking this sounded familiar. Suspiciously so. "How'd house hunting turn out?"

"It was a bust. One place had a foundation problem, and Grandpa said he wouldn't consider it. The other had been renovated, but the workmanship was shoddy." Heather lifted her sandwich. "So the search continues."

Sarah was about to take a bite of hers when her stomach flipped over. What if Norman didn't return to help Sarah beat this disease? Linda had divorced him, and he was alone. What if he was trying to regain what he lost all those years ago?

Chapter 17

The following week, the mental fog lifted just enough for Sarah to finally understand what was happening with her clients' ad accounts. She made the necessary changes to each campaign and answered emails. Unfortunately, she had been too slow to reply to one person, and he had sent a second email asking for data. Sarah responded, apologizing for the delay, and attached the updated spreadsheet for him to review.

Just a few hours of computer work had already worn her out. She doubted she'd be able to hold down a job at the ad agency as she battled cancer and was glad she had started her own business. There were no paid vacations or guarantees she'd consistently make money, but she did all right. And she had signed up on Jeff's work health insurance plan after starting the business, which helped. They had chosen the high deductible PPO because before Sarah got sick, neither took medication, and they only went to the doctor once a year for a free physical exam. They learned the hard way that life was unpredictable, and although they had saved money on low premiums, they had to pay the five thousand dollar out of pocket before the insurance covered everything at one hundred percent. Sarah had hoped to use that money for travel.

But instead, it was gone after receiving the bill for the PET scan.

Sarah logged into the health insurance website to make sure all the claims were being paid and that none were being rejected. There were so many claims it was overwhelming. Two pages of them so far. Sarah spotted one for a recent chemotherapy visit. Her eyes widened when she saw that it cost thirteen thousand dollars. That was one costly bag of red fluid. She couldn't believe the insurance company had to pay that every two weeks and was grateful she had signed up on Jeff's plan.

Sarah breathed a sigh of relief after learning all claims were either paid or in the process of being paid. The total dollar amount for her care this year was staggering; she knew it would only go higher as time passed.

Sarah went to the living room, turned on the TV, and channel-surfed. She selected one of those sappy stories her brother knew she liked, and then Walter joined her. As Sarah petted him, she realized he was a leisure expert. And he didn't seem to feel bad about doing nothing. Instead, he reveled in its glory as only a feline could.

Shortly after the movie ended, Sarah's phone buzzed. She was happy to see a text message from Nancy. "*How are you doing?*"

Sarah replied. "*I've had lots of fatigue and brain fog, but it's getting better. How are you?*"

Bubbles appeared on the screen as Nancy typed. "*I'm alive and talking to a friend, so I consider myself blessed!*"

Nancy put a smiley face emoji after her text. She had never mentioned what stage her cancer was when it returned, and Sarah didn't want to pry. Unsure what to talk about, Sarah switched the subject and recommended the feel-good movie she had just watched. Nancy told her that she would check it out, then said she'd see her at chemo before saying goodbye.

The conversation had been short but sweet. Just what Sarah needed to brighten her day. Afterward, Sarah ventured out to check the mail and found a box on the porch. She brought it into the house and opened it. Inside were the pink gloves and booties for her new chemo sessions. She tried them on. The gloves resembled oven mitts. The booties had a Velcro belt that wrapped across the foot to keep them snug. Jeff had a lunch cooler that he thought might work, so Sarah found it and checked it for size to make sure that the container would hold both the gloves and booties, plus several ice packs.

Sarah wished she had the energy to clean the house but wasn't feeling that good yet. Instead, she went to her bedroom and pulled the breast cancer treatment handbook she'd gotten from the hospital off the bottom shelf of her nightstand. She'd read the chemotherapy and surgical options chapters but thought there was one on breast cancer and sexuality. Since she and Jeff were headed in that direction soon, she figured she would read it now.

Halfway through the chapter, Sarah grew concerned. She learned that many menopausal women who received chemotherapy experienced painful intercourse. Worse still, women polled in multiple studies reported that the condition increased with time. Sarah assumed the issue would improve after finishing treatment.

Sarah turned the page, eager to find the solution. The author recommended over-the-counter vaginal moisturizer. It didn't work immediately, but it supposedly repaired what chemo and Mother Nature collectively broke.

The author said gynecologists often prescribe estrogen cream to fix the problem if the vaginal moisturizer doesn't work. However, in the same paragraph, she mentioned that most breast cancer patients couldn't use estrogen creams.

Wonderful, Sarah thought. *Just wonderful.*

The chapter ended with the check with your doctor because each case is different disclaimer. It also mentioned that new technologies were on the horizon to fix the issue.

"Technology!" Sarah scoffed. How pathetic was it when you had to turn to technology to have relations with your spouse?

In all, the handbook told Sarah that she didn't have much time. She rushed to her laptop and placed an order for the product the author mentioned. When she received the email confirmation of her purchase, she inwardly groaned. Sarah used a pricey moisturizer for her face. She never thought she'd have to buy one for her private parts.

Sarah closed her laptop. She'd learned more than enough for one day and was ready to take a nap.

After falling asleep, Sarah had a nightmare that she was trapped in a clear plastic bubble, watching Jeff and another woman on a dinner date. The lady looked a lot like her before she had gotten sick—vibrant and full of life. She and Jeff flirted with each other throughout the meal. The scene instantly switched from the restaurant to a hotel room. Jeff and the woman were kissing, and then they began groping each other. Sarah pounded against the bubble wall, but it kept her captive, powerless, and alone.

She woke with a start. Walter was sitting on the bed, staring at her. She breathed deeply when she realized it was just a dream, then reached out to pet Walter. The cat came closer before curling up next to her and starting to purr. It didn't take a psychologist to figure out what the nightmare meant. Sarah feared losing her husband to another woman because of her illness. She also feared losing her femininity because of the medication used to treat the disease.

On Saturday, Heather went downtown with Caleb. Now that Sarah had finished AC, this was her opportunity to be alone with Jeff.

Thankfully, the moisturizer Sarah had ordered arrived the previous day. She went to the restroom, applied more moisturizer, then donned a favorite black nightie and put on pink lip gloss. When she looked in the mirror, she saw a cancer patient in lingerie. Not quite as sexy as the women in those catalogs, with their long flowing hair and tan legs. Sarah retrieved her chemo scarf from the dresser drawer and tried it on. Although it covered her bald head, it added zero sex appeal, so she put it away in favor of wearing nothing.

Sarah peeked out the bathroom door and noticed Jeff had dimmed the bedroom lights. He had taken off his shirt and was lying in bed. Suddenly, Sarah wasn't sure if this was a good idea. She hadn't been this nervous when they'd first slept together. Now her fear was off the charts. She worried she might look so terrible that he wouldn't be able to get an erection. She worried she might have the issue mentioned in the breast cancer handbook and have yet another problem to overcome.

Only one way to find out, she thought, taking a deep breath. She entered the bedroom, and Jeff turned to look at her. He smiled as she approached, as he had done many times before.

"Are you well enough to do this?" he asked. His eyes shone the same soft green they'd been a few months after Heather was born. He had been equally worried twenty-three years ago to resume their sex life as he was now.

"I'm fine," Sarah lied. She hadn't felt well since she'd started chemotherapy and doubted she'd feel well for many months, but she didn't want to put this off any longer. She had to know what would happen when they had sex.

Jeff studied her. He knew her better than anyone and had to know she wasn't telling the truth.

"If it doesn't work out, we can stop," he assured her.

Sarah nodded, determined not to let this encounter crash and burn. She'd been repeatedly poked with needles and had endured painful mammograms. Sex was a good thing. It brought pleasure into people's lives. She and Jeff deserved some joy after all they had been through these last few months.

Once Sarah came closer, their lips met. Jeff's kisses

were gentle at first, but then they grew more passionate, reminding Sarah that he'd gone without her for a long time as she fought this disease.

As kisses trailed down her neck, there was an awkward moment when Jeff's lips neared the chemotherapy port. She braced herself. Surely, nothing was as much of a turn-off as a chemotherapy port. But he simply whispered an apology and moved to the other side of her neck.

Jeff caressed the healthy breast. As he began to shower it with affection, Sarah's heart seized at the thought that she would lose the other one in a few months. She tried to shake it away—to stay in the moment with her spouse.

"Is it safe to touch the other one?" Jeff asked, his hand extended in midair.

Sarah nodded, too overcome with emotion to speak.

Jeff cupped her cancerous breast lightly. He kissed it softly until Sarah could no longer hold back her tears. She wiped them away with the back of her hand and sniffed.

Jeff looked up. "Am I hurting you?"

Sarah shook her head.

As Jeff continued, Sarah let her hands wander over his body. They began making love, and to Sarah's surprise, there was discomfort even though she had used the moisturizer. It felt like the inside of her vagina was being ripped to shreds even though it wasn't dry.

Sarah stayed silent. She wanted to please her husband and knew he'd stop if she told him there was a problem. The moisturizer took time to work, she reasoned, so this issue would probably get better soon. But instead of enjoying the experience with the man she loved, she was frustrated beyond belief.

Today was one of those days when she was exasperated that she was stuck fighting this horrible disease.

Chapter 18

Sarah and Beverly arrived at the hospital early for Sarah's appointment. With time to kill, they chose to grab a coffee and relax. After Sarah took a sip of her decaf latte, she opened the cooler Jeff had given her and checked inside. The ice packs had softened, but the gloves and booties were still cold. She had been worried that they wouldn't stay chilled on their journey downtown, but so far, all was well.

Fifteen minutes before Sarah's visit with Dr. Zimmerman, she checked in with the woman at the front desk, and then a nurse showed her to the exam room while her mom stayed in the waiting area reading a book. The nurse took her vitals, and Sarah changed into the medical smock after she left.

Dr. Zimmerman walked in with a big smile. "I've got good news."

Sarah had no idea how there could be good news at this point.

Dr. Zimmerman sat down before continuing. "An immunotherapy drug has been approved for triple negative, and you meet the required criteria, so I can give it to you if you're interested."

Sarah didn't know what to say. She hated taking yet

another medication but wanted to use every tool available to beat breast cancer.

"The immunotherapy drug helps your body fight cancer," her doctor explained. She described how it worked alongside chemo before ending with, "Studies show it prevents recurrence and helps patients live longer without one."

Sarah immediately thought of Nancy. Maybe she wouldn't be back here if this immunotherapy drug had been available a decade before.

"What are the side effects?" Sarah asked.

"Some patients get diarrhea. Since you've struggled with constipation during chemo, this may help." Dr. Zimmerman paused, then added, "One of the major side effects is thyroid dysfunction. But we'll monitor your numbers every visit, so we'll know if that occurs. If it does, we can refer you to an endocrinologist."

Sarah didn't know much about the thyroid gland. All she knew was that hers worked, and she wanted it to keep working. After all she'd been through up to this point, she was reluctant to become a guinea pig, let alone experience long-term effects that may not have been discovered yet.

"Do you need time to think about it?" her doctor asked.

Sarah thought about taking some time to talk about it with Jeff, Heather, Beverly, Mike—even Norman. No. She shook her head. No matter what input she received, she knew that she didn't want to miss out. "I'll give it a try."

Dr. Zimmerman nodded, then proceeded with the breast exam. She felt the cancerous lymph nodes under Sarah's arm and mentioned that they seemed to be shrinking. Sarah had noticed they appeared smaller the last time she looked at them in the mirror. So maybe the situation was finally improving.

Sarah changed back into her clothes after the doctor left, and then a nurse returned and offered to put her gloves and booties in the freezer so they'd be cold before the Taxol infusion. The young woman wrote her name on a large plastic bag and stuffed the gloves and booties inside before taking her to the treatment area.

Sarah's jaw dropped when they arrived. Half of the patients had needles sticking out of their faces and hands. "What on earth?" she asked aloud.

"It's acupuncture," the nurse said. "You can receive a complimentary session today."

Sarah spotted Nancy in a reclined chair. Her eyes were closed, and her body was covered with needles. Sarah didn't know why anyone would want to be poked with more needles than necessary and didn't plan on partaking in the insanity.

The nurse put her in the seat next to Nancy. Sarah kept quiet until the acupuncturist approached and offered to turn her into a pin cushion.

"I'm good," Sarah whispered to the woman.

The acupuncturist came closer and asked, "Are you sure? It helps to lower stress."

"You should try it," Nancy mumbled from under the needles.

Sarah winced. Why wouldn't this woman lay off? Couldn't she see that her friend had been sleeping? "I'm not a big fan of needles," she explained.

"These needles don't hurt," the acupuncturist replied.

"They don't," Nancy agreed.

Sarah found it hard to believe that being repeatedly stabbed with a slew of needles didn't hurt, but how could she say no now?

"Fine," Sarah begrudgingly acquiesced, driven by the desire to alleviate the tension headache that had recently started. She closed her eyes and braced for impact.

"All done," the acupuncturist said a minute later.

Sarah opened her eyes, surprised to see long needles sticking out of her face. She had been waiting for the woman to start and was shocked to learn she had already finished. Sarah thanked her, and then her nurse arrived and started her on fluids. Sarah reclined her chair after she left to have the same experience as Nancy.

"You were right," Sarah said to Nancy. "It doesn't hurt."

"I told you."

"But I don't feel anything happening. They're just...there."

"That's because you're still talking," Nancy murmured. "Sit back and enjoy."

The women were silent as they let the acupuncture needles go to work. Sarah focused on her breath, making sure it was deep and even, then tried to relax her shoulders, which had been tense since Dr. Zimmerman mentioned adding more medication to her treatment plan.

Ten minutes later, light snores filled the air. Sarah opened her eyes and saw a fellow patient asleep on the other side of the room. She wore lavender gloves and booties, a purple paisley headscarf, and had acupuncture needles on her face. Sarah laughed inwardly. It was an interesting sight, to say the least.

A nurse came to check on Nancy. The movement seemed to bring Nancy to enough of a state of consciousness that she began talking again. "What do you do for a living?" she asked Sarah.

"I have my own business," Sarah replied, finally becoming relaxed. "Online marketing."

Nancy nodded. "Cool."

"What do you do?" Sarah asked.

"I used to work for the newspaper, back when people bought newspapers. Now I write blog posts. It keeps me busy, but not too busy if I don't feel well."

Sarah was happy to hear that Nancy could work in a similar field and, more importantly, that she could work when she chose to and not have to answer to demanding bosses.

Nancy continued. "Thankfully, my mom left me some money when she passed, and I was able to pay off my condo and set some money aside to pay for my son's college. He still has loans, but they're not that big, so he won't be saddled with debt forever."

"That's wonderful," Sarah said, knowing that must be a weight off Nancy's mind.

The acupuncturist returned and started removing needles from the patients who had them put in before

Sarah arrived. She pulled them out of Nancy shortly after Sarah's nurse started her on Benadryl and other premeds.

"This may make you sleepy," Sarah's nurse warned.

Within a few minutes, Sarah felt even more relaxed than she had with the acupuncture. After ten minutes, she was wasted. It was a more powerful high than she'd gotten with Mike a few times when they were younger, minus the coughing associated with smoking a joint.

"How are you feeling?" Nancy asked.

Sarah turned to her. "Like I'm floating in my chair. You weren't kidding. This is some potent stuff."

Nancy chuckled. "It's nice while you're here because it makes you chill. But it lasts a while, so plan on being groggy throughout the day. Don't drive until it wears off."

"I won't," Sarah promised. It would be an easy promise to keep since she hadn't been driving since treatment began. She supposed she could drive now that she had finished AC and her mind wasn't as foggy, but she wouldn't drive after taking Benadryl, which Sarah decided to dub sleepy juice.

Nancy and Sarah watched as nurses gathered around a patient who had finished chemo. They led her to the area to ring the bell, and after she did, cheers erupted, followed by thunderous clapping. Everyone was all smiles, especially the woman who was about to leave the treatment area for the final time.

Don't come back, Sarah thought as she watched the woman leave.

Sarah couldn't bear to look at Nancy. She didn't want

to see the smile she had managed to find even though she had been unlucky enough to return.

Shortly afterward, a nurse arrived with Sarah's gloves and booties. She handed the ice-cold bag to Sarah and said, "Time to put these on."

Sarah put the gloves on first, then bent over to put on the booties, which was impossible with the gloves on. She started over—booties, then gloves. "That's cold!" Sarah said.

Her nurse gave her an empathetic smile. "You can take them off if it's too cold. But remember to put them back on again."

As Sarah nodded, Nancy's nurse removed the line from her port. Nancy was getting ready to leave before Sarah's nurse started her on the new chemo medication.

Sarah eyed her friend. "I wish my brother could see me now."

Nancy pulled her phone from her purse and snapped a photo of Sarah. "Now he can," she said, smiling as she sent the ridiculous-looking picture.

Once the women said their goodbyes and the acupuncturist removed Sarah's needles, her nurse turned on the meds and said, "I'm going to stay with you for the first ten minutes to make sure you're okay."

Sarah waited patiently to feel any changes.

Her nurse studied her. "Any shortness of breath? Fever? Chills?"

Sarah shook her head.

Ten minutes passed, and the nurse said she'd stay five minutes longer just to be sure. When nothing unusual happened, she pointed out the call button to Sarah before leaving.

The gloves were cold, but Sarah didn't dare take them off. She'd follow the instructions and hope her hands made it through the process unscathed. Nancy's hadn't, but Sarah was determined to be an exception as having chemotherapy-induced neuropathy didn't sound fun.

Sarah closed her eyes, finally succumbing to the Benadryl. She woke when her nurse returned to start the Carboplatin. The nurse said the second chemotherapy drug didn't require gloves and booties, so she removed them and set them aside before falling back asleep.

At the end of Sarah's session, a younger woman was in the chair Nancy had previously occupied. She was talking on her cellphone while receiving chemo, clearly work-related. Customer service, from what Sarah could tell. The woman had her laptop out and frantically typed after she hung up the phone. Sarah felt so bad that she had to work while fighting cancer that she didn't interrupt her while gathering her things and heading to the waiting room to meet her mom.

"How did it go?" Beverly asked after she closed her book.

"I made it through the first of twelve sessions," Sarah said with a wan smile.

Beverly offered to carry the cooler, and an exhausted Sarah let her. Then, they took the cab to the train station and boarded their train five minutes before it left. Sarah was thankful they had made it in time because she couldn't wait to get home and climb into bed.

On the way there, Sarah told Beverly about the immunotherapy drug. Beverly agreed it was worth trying. Sarah pulled her phone from her purse. "My friend took a picture of me." She showed the photo to her mom. "Check it out. It's funny as heck."

Sarah texted the photo to her mom and Mike. Beverly studied the picture and laughed so loudly that the other passengers glanced her way.

As Beverly began a little text-fest with Richard, Sarah laid her head back and started to drift off.

"Norman loves the photo," Beverly murmured. "He's glad you made it through today's session and that you're going home."

Sarah's eyes opened dully. Beverly had been texting her father? She knew her parents had agreed to communicate with each other during this time, but for some reason, it irked her that they were getting along. Beverly's behavior was beyond reproach. Norman, on the other hand, was the one Sarah had to watch.

Chapter 19

Jeff studied the picture of Sarah. He didn't even crack a smile. Having anticipated inevitable laughter, Sarah felt her grin go slack when she saw sadness in her husband's eyes.

"We were just having fun," Sarah said, trying to lighten the mood.

"Fun," Jeff repeated, handing the phone back to her. "That's good."

Her husband suddenly seemed to be in a daze.

Sarah continued. "I thought it was nice that they gave us free acupuncture." She set her phone aside and made eye contact with Jeff. "It didn't hurt. Actually, it was incredibly relaxing."

Jeff nodded. The silence loomed between them before he finally said, "I wish I could go down there with you. I can't believe I used all of my vacation days." Sarah was about to tell him that it was okay when he added. "Seeing that picture made it more real. It's like, I know you go down there for treatment, but I've never seen you do it. Now I have." His voice cracked on the last word.

Sarah reached for his hand. "Getting chemotherapy isn't painful. Only its side effects stink." This wasn't how Sarah had thought it would go. She felt terrible seeing Jeff on the verge of tears.

He sniffed and cleared his throat. "Who took the picture?"

"My friend Nancy."

Jeff's expression brightened. "You have a friend at the cancer center?"

"I do," Sarah said. "I see her every time I'm there, and we talk through the whole chemo session."

After hearing that Sarah had a buddy, Jeff smiled. "That's nice."

Sarah wanted to move on from the image of her getting chemo and focus on Nancy.

"She has the same kind of breast cancer I have." Sarah didn't mention that Nancy's was a recurrence. Her goal was to turn this conversation into a positive one, not upset Jeff more. "She's a single mom with a kid in college, studying to be a doctor. And she writes blog posts for a living now that she left the newspaper industry."

"She sounds interesting," Jeff said. "Seems like you two have a lot in common."

"We do." The main difference was that their cancer journeys had started a decade apart. Although Sarah didn't want Jeff to know that it was Nancy's second time doing battle with the disease, she decided to share something she hadn't told him yet. "Have you heard of cancer ghosting?"

Jeff tilted his head. "No. What's that?"

Sarah explained the phenomenon and then told him it happened to Nancy.

"Man!" Jeff said. "That's one of the strangest things

I've ever heard."

Sarah went on to tell him about the research she did online. She relayed the stories of women not inviting their cancer patient friend out to dinner and told him of the relative who had shunned a woman after they heard she was ill. Jeff didn't ask Sarah how her friends treated her because he knew she'd lost touch with them after starting her own business.

Sarah wondered if she should tell him about the story that shook her to the core. Unsure but taking a chance, she said, "There was another post about a man leaving his wife when he learned she had cancer."

Sarah met Jeff's gaze and said no more. The unspoken question hung in the air, waiting to be answered.

Jeff leaned forward and said, "I'll be here no matter what happens. You don't have to worry about losing me."

A weight Sarah didn't know she had been carrying was lifted from her heart after hearing his words. Happy tears spilled down her cheeks as she wrapped her arms around the man she loved. Jeff squeezed her tightly before kissing her forehead, each cheek, and finally, ever so gently, her lips.

Earlier, Sarah had been flying high on Benadryl. Now, she was floating on a cloud of bliss. They continued kissing. It didn't progress into anything passionate but stayed sweet, like a fuzzy blanket keeping Sarah safe and warm.

When their lips parted, Sarah snuggled up next to Jeff. For some reason, she thought of the woman who rang the bell at the end of treatment. She wasn't sure if she had told him about that.

"Have I ever told you about ringing the bell?" Sarah asked.

"No," Jeff replied.

Sarah turned toward Jeff and explained what happens on the last day of chemotherapy.

"I don't care if I'm out of vacation days," he said. "I'm calling in sick so I can see you ring that bell!"

Sarah smiled. It wasn't necessary, but it would make the occasion more memorable if he were there.

Jeff continued. "Heather will want to go if I go, and I'm sure your mom will want to be there."

"Which means Norman would want to go, too. And Mike won't want to miss it if everyone else is going."

Jeff's smile turned into a grimace. "Talk about awkward." He put his hand on hers. "But we'll deal with it when the time comes. Together."

Chapter 20

The week passed quickly, and before Sarah knew it, she was back at chemo again. Nancy sent a text, letting her know she wouldn't be there this time because her white blood cell count was too low. Sarah tried to sound upbeat when she replied, sending her well wishes and telling her that she hoped to see her soon.

Sarah's white blood count was low but not low enough to miss treatment. She had been lucky in that respect. Today the team was adding the immunotherapy drug to her regimen. Sarah chose to focus on its benefits and not think of the possible side effects that could occur.

When her nurse finished accessing her port, Sarah asked, "Can my family come to my final session to see me ring the bell?"

Her nurse hesitated. "We don't like having too many non-patients in the treatment area, but I'm sure we can make an exception for a few minutes."

Sarah thanked her and then grew drowsy as the drugs kicked in. She watched a woman across from her read a book. Each time she turned a page, Sarah's eyelids grew heavier until she finally nodded off.

"Sarah," her nurse said softly, waking her. "You're done for the day."

The nurse flushed her port, and then Sarah removed her gloves and booties and put them in her cooler before meeting her dad in the waiting room. He was chatting with the person in the chair beside him but wrapped up his conversation when he saw her coming.

Norman took the cooler from her. "Did you get acupuncture today?"

"Not today." They left the waiting room and headed toward the elevator. "But I did start the new immunotherapy drug."

The elevator dinged, and then the door opened. "How did that go? Did you have any negative reactions to it?"

Norman was asking more questions than he usually did, the kind of questions Beverly would ask. He must've seen Sarah's eyes narrow in suspicion because he added, "Your mother wants to know."

He pulled out his phone and began typing on the cab ride to the train station. Sarah knew he was texting her mother, giving her the answers to the questions she had undoubtedly told him to ask. Sarah briefly considered telling him about the bell-ringing ceremony but changed her mind. She would run the idea by her mother next. Although Norman would be included, he would learn of it after everyone else, as there was a hierarchy of importance in how family data spread. Since her mother had always been there, she had secured the number two spot after Jeff.

Once they boarded the train, Sarah saw the conductor who had helped her when she was ill. He greeted Sarah and Norman before checking their tickets. He didn't linger because the train was packed, which was okay with Sarah because she was too tired to chat with someone she barely knew, even though he was nice.

As they entered the suburbs, Sarah noticed a few trees with yellow and orange leaves. She had been so wrapped up in the details of her life that she hadn't seen the season change until today. It was mid-September already. Her favorite time of year. She and Mike used to play outside together after school when they were kids, enjoying the warm weather and blue skies. As Mike got older, he raked leaves for neighbors to make extra money. Sarah preferred taking long walks by herself and collecting the prettiest leaves, which she glued to cardboard paper, creating a fall collage that her mother hung on the wall.

Norman's voice brought her back to the present. "Remember that pumpkin patch we went to?"

Sarah scanned her memories and came up blank.

"The place with the hayride and the hot apple cider."

Sarah remembered it now. She had been very young when they went, and for some reason, she didn't remember Norman being there, just Beverly and Mike. "We did the hayride and picked out a big pumpkin to take home and carve, right?"

Norman smiled. "Right."

An image of a glowing pumpkin on the front porch came to mind. Sarah didn't know if Norman or Beverly had carved it but assumed it must've been her father since he was talking about it now. Apparently, they had done some fun things as a family. Sarah wished she could recall more of those times instead of remembering the instances of him not being there and letting her down.

"Too bad we're not there now," Sarah said.

Norman let out a heavy sigh. "We could go next year."

They could, Sarah thought.

She, Norman, Jeff, and Heather could go to that fair and take a hayride if she got better. They could pick out a pumpkin and carve it the way they had all those years ago. Sarah had been a planner before, knowing what she wanted to do in five years, ten years, and beyond. Now she realized they were just plans, that none of us were guaranteed our next breath. But if they were all alive and doing well next fall, they could go. They *should* go, she decided.

Norman pulled his phone out again and started typing.

"Is that Mom?" Sarah asked.

Her father didn't reply until he finished writing whatever he was writing. When he was done, he looked up. "That was Linda."

"Linda?" Sarah asked, surprised to hear that they were talking again.

"Yeah. She called me out of the blue the other day, asking about you. I told her that Beverly and I take turns taking you to treatment. I let her know things are going well here. Well enough, considering the circumstances. And that Heather is helping me find a house. Then she told me to text her with updates about you." Norman smiled. "I thought that was nice."

Sarah didn't know what to think. On the surface, Linda's concern seemed decent, but she hadn't sent a get-well card or tried to contact Sarah since the diagnosis.

Why was she so interested in her well-being now?

Sarah gazed out the train window. What if Linda was jealous because Norman and Beverly were talking again? Her father had been sulking after the divorce, but now he had moved on. His life was busy and full. Perhaps hearing things were going well here made Linda question her decision to break it off. Or maybe learning that he was involved with Beverly brought out a competitive streak, and that's why she wanted him to text her the same info Norman gave her mom. But then, people could be thoughtful without having an ulterior motive.

Chapter 21

Sarah and Beverly boarded the train. It seemed like Sarah had just gotten off it with her dad, and now she was back. She wasn't having fun, but time was definitely flying. Nancy had texted, saying her white blood count was most likely high enough to return to treatment this week. Sarah was glad because she looked forward to getting her opinion about something.

Once Sarah and her mom were seated, Beverly said, "I counted the number of treatments you have left and realized the last one is on the same week as your birthday."

Her mother had been in planning mode ever since Sarah mentioned Jeff's suggestion to turn the bell-ringing ceremony into a celebration. And since Sarah's birthday was the same week, it made even more sense to do something fun.

Beverly continued. "Heather and I were trying to figure out if it was better to get reservations at a restaurant downtown or order food and a cake at home."

"A party at a restaurant near the hospital sounds great, but I don't know how well I'll feel, so it might not be the best idea."

"I keep forgetting that." Her mother shook her head,

obviously embarrassed. "I'm so focused on celebrating the end of chemo that I didn't remember you'll still be feeling its effects."

Sarah appreciated her mother's efforts and didn't want her to be discouraged. She put a hand over hers and said, "I'm sure whatever you plan will be just right."

Beverly squeezed Sarah's hand and went on to describe the benefit of ordering food from one restaurant over the other. She rattled off a list of menu items from each establishment, impressing Sarah with her memory skills, and eventually decided to run it by Heather before making the final choice.

"I invited your father," Beverly mentioned.

"Sounds good." Sarah realized that Norman would have to be included going forward. "Poor Richard. Tell him I'm sorry."

Beverly dismissed her comment with a wave of her hand. "He understands. Norman doesn't bother him."

Richard managed to stay calm and collected during this family drama. Sarah hoped he would remain that way as time passed and that Norman wouldn't get on his last nerve.

Her mother hadn't mentioned whether Mike would be coming. Sarah would love for her brother to be at the bell-ringing ceremony and the party, but she didn't want him to have to put up with Norman just because of her.

"I do have one request for the party," Sarah said. "I'd like chocolate cake with chocolate frosting."

"No problem," Beverly replied.

Sarah had been doing a good job of avoiding desserts

while receiving treatment. Although she planned to continue eating healthy going forward, she wanted to indulge in something decadent to celebrate the day she was born.

They arrived at the hospital fifteen minutes before Sarah saw Dr. Zimmerman. Sarah headed to her appointment while her mom grabbed a coffee at the hospital coffee shop. The doctor's visit went smoothly, with no new symptoms to report. Afterward, a nurse took Sarah to the treatment area, where Nancy was seated, taking a sip of water.

The women nodded to acknowledge one another, preferring not to talk until Sarah and her nurse had finished doing their thing.

After the nurse accessed Sarah's port and started her on fluids, Sarah told Nancy, "Glad to have you back. I mean, not that I'm glad you're getting chemo, but that you're back, finishing your treatment. And so I can see you."

Nancy smiled. "I know what you mean."

Then, Sarah realized Nancy had been here when she first started. "How many more treatments do you have left?"

"Five. Then I have surgery six weeks later."

Nancy would finish before Sarah. She was happy for her friend but sad because she would miss hanging out with her.

"Have you made a decision on reconstruction?" Sarah asked.

Nancy took a deep breath and let out a heavy sigh. "I

liked the natural look of flap reconstruction, but since I can't do it again, my options are getting an implant or no reconstruction." She paused, then said, "I'm going with no reconstruction."

"That's what I was going to do, but now I'm having second thoughts."

Nancy gave her an empathetic look. "It's a big decision. You have the right to change your mind as often as you like." Nancy paused. "I'm doing what's best for me at this stage of my life. Having a breast was more important to me before. Now I want to enjoy whatever time I have left and not spend it in the hospital."

Sarah and Nancy held each other's gaze.

"Any particular reason you're not sure anymore?" Nancy asked.

Sarah was still thinking of what Nancy had just inferred. "I don't know. It's just a feeling, a worry, really, that I'm messing up." Sarah tried to think of a way to answer the question better. She racked her mind and added, "Recently, my husband and I had a heart-to-heart conversation. He told me that no matter what happened, he would always be there for me."

"That sounds like something a good man would say." Nancy smiled warmly at Sarah, and Sarah didn't dare mention that the conversation occurred because she told Jeff that Nancy's sister had ghosted her because of cancer. "So, why would that make you worry about your surgical choice?"

"I guess it's because I don't want my husband to live with less. I mean, he's saying he'll love me no matter what, and that's wonderful to hear, but why should he have to live with less if I can get the implant? Maybe I should do the additional surgeries so I can look the same."

Nancy nodded but didn't speak. Sarah wondered if she was going to say anything.

"Do you want to know what I think?" Nancy finally asked.

"Yes."

"I think this isn't about your husband."

Sarah's brow furrowed.

"You told your husband you chose no reconstruction. He said he supported your decision and then told you what every cancer patient wants to hear, that he's with you no matter what happens. He truly loves you, Sarah. But the question is, do you love yourself?"

Sarah sat in her chair, dumbfounded. She didn't understand how loving herself had anything to do with her concerns about looking good for Jeff.

"What I'm saying is," Nancy continued, "take how your husband may or may not feel out of it and ask if you love yourself. If the answer is yes, you're on the right track."

Sarah's nurse arrived and started the Benadryl. As the drug relaxed her from head to toe, she continued thinking of Nancy's comment. Sarah guessed she loved herself. She ate right and made sure to brush her teeth twice per day. She wanted to live a long life, which was why she was here doing all of this. But deep down, Sarah knew that wasn't what Nancy meant. She had been referring to loving oneself at a core level. Not because someone else loves you. These were the kinds of concepts that reminded Sarah of famous philosophical statements that sounded great on paper but were difficult to apply in real life.

Sarah knew what it felt like to be loved by her husband, mother, daughter, and sibling. Each love was different and could be described if necessary. Self-love was harder to put into words. Sarah tried remembering a time when she looked in the mirror and had a positive thought. Often, she'd inwardly groan about one imperfection or another, chastising herself for not having a smaller waist, better posture, and fuller lips. If she couldn't be satisfied with how she looked as a human being with all her body parts, how would she feel when she was missing a breast?

The nurse returned with Sarah's gloves and booties. Sarah put them on and closed her eyes, realizing she didn't love herself as she was supposed to. She wanted to. She really did. But she didn't know how to do it.

Nancy was gone when Sarah woke, but she'd sent a text.

"Whatever decision you make is the right one."

Sarah appreciated her friend's vote of confidence and planned to reflect on their discussion more when she got home.

Once they were on the train, Beverly asked, "How did the session go?"

"Okay," Sarah said, still groggy. "Made it through another one, so that's good, right?"

Beverly smiled sadly. "Right."

Her mother pulled her phone from her purse and began typing. Sarah didn't have to ask who she was texting. She already knew her mom was telling her dad that she was okay.

Sarah closed her eyes, picturing her dad texting Linda that information after he'd finished talking to her mom. It was strange to have people communicating with each other about you every week. She understood why, but it still felt odd.

After working on her clients' ads the next day, she typed Nancy's first and last name into her computer's search bar, hoping to find one of her blog posts. Sarah's eyes widened when she saw plenty of links. Nancy had not only written blog posts, but she'd written published articles as well. Most were about religion. How it helped in good times and bad. She mentioned God's love several times, reminding Sarah of one of Nancy's texts, where she'd said she was blessed. Reading her friend's articles painted a fuller picture of who Nancy was. It made sense that she said the kind of things she said. Uplifting comments. Why she asked questions that made Sarah think.

Nancy's name was listed as a choir member at her local congregation of the African Methodist Episcopal Church. Sarah could picture her standing next to fellow parishioners, smiling and singing songs that filled her heart with joy. She was glad that Nancy was part of a supportive community since her mother was gone and she and her sister no longer talked.

Sarah contemplated the subject of religion. She liked the idea of God, of a father figure watching over her, and that she would go somewhere amazing after she died. It all sounded terrific. Unfortunately, there was no proof. Sarah used to believe in the Easter Bunny and the Tooth Fairy, but she had learned that they were fictional characters created by grownups to make childhood fun. Maybe grownups had created God to make being an adult less terrifying. Sarah didn't know but thought it couldn't hurt to believe if, like Nancy, it brought positivity into your life.

If there was a God, Sarah wondered what it would feel like to be loved by him.

Just then, Walter approached. He jumped up onto the chair and sat on Sarah's lap. Usually, he curled into a ball, and Sarah petted him until he fell asleep. Today, he sat facing her. He looked into her eyes for a long time without blinking. Sarah gazed back at the cat, transfixed.

In the stillness, Sarah could feel something pass between them. Something comforting and powerful. A connection that could only be described as love.

Walter finally blinked, then turned and curled into a ball. Sarah automatically began petting him, her mind now furiously at work.

If she could feel this way about her cat, why couldn't she feel this way about herself?

Chapter 22

Mike stopped by that weekend to say hi. Her brother chatted with Jeff for a little bit before Jeff excused himself to run errands. Things he and Sarah used to do on Saturdays when she was well.

"Jeff looks tired," Mike mentioned as he and Sarah entered the living room.

Sarah sat on the sofa. "I noticed that, too." Poor Jeff had so much to do at work and home. Caleb's dinners were incredibly helpful, but her husband was still overwhelmed. Sarah assumed part of it was emotional exhaustion. That everything was becoming too much. "But thankfully, this will be coming to an end soon."

Mike sat in the chair opposite Sarah. "Mom told me about the bell-ringing thing. That's cool."

"Will you be able to make it?" Sarah asked.

"Of course, I'll be there. I wouldn't miss it for the world."

Sarah smiled, pleasantly surprised. "Even if Dad's going to be there?"

Mike leaned back and clasped his hands behind his head. "I'm not going to let that prick ruin things for me."

Sarah knew her brother would behave, considering the

circumstances. She remembered Linda contacting Norman, asking about her and wanting to be updated weekly. She told Mike about it and asked, "What do you make of that?"

"I think she's crazy."

Mike was a master of human behavior. He explained how and why people did things, so lumping Linda's actions into the crazy basket wasn't a good enough answer for Sarah.

"How so?" she asked.

Mike released his hands from behind his head and set them on his lap before leaning forward. "Think about it. She's with Dad all those years, then is smart enough to jet. What kind of person wants to reconnect with him?" He paused before answering his own question. "A crazy person. That's who."

Linda had always seemed mentally stable when Sarah interacted with her. She had been pleasant and acted more like a friend than a stepmom, which made sense as there wasn't much of an age difference between them. Linda must be genuinely concerned about Sarah's health. That was all there was to it.

"Let's forget about Dad's love life," Sarah readily transitioned. "How's yours? Have you met anyone?"

"There's a new saleslady at the dealership that's pretty and smart. Word is she's recently divorced, so I asked her to lunch, but she shot me down. She says she's not ready to date yet."

"Hmm," Sarah replied. "Maybe she'll change her mind as she gets to know you more. Try to become friends first and keep being nice. She may let her guard down as time passes."

Mike nodded. Heather and Norman were looking at condos together, but since her brother didn't mention it, Sarah stayed mum.

"You look different," Mike said.

Sarah did a mental catalog of herself. He'd seen the scarf before, and she hadn't lost any more weight. "Well, I'm losing my eyebrows and eyelashes." Sarah jutted her chin forward so her brother could take a closer look at her face.

Mike studied her. "You're right. Just a few eyebrow hairs left." He sat back in his chair. "The good news is they will grow back."

"All my hair will grow back eventually. But it doesn't make it any easier to handle now."

Mike's eyes widened. Sarah hadn't meant to sound rude, but getting used to being bald had taken time. Losing her eyebrows and eyelashes was another hurdle. Each section of hair was like a treasure she had lost.

"Even my nose hairs have fallen out," she continued, trying to smooth over her earlier reply. "You probably don't think much about the function of nose hairs—neither did I—but apparently, they're necessary, and without them, I've been getting bloody noses."

Sarah had seldom if ever, seen Mike at a loss. Finally, he stammered, "It'll all work out. You'll see. I mean, it has to."

Sarah managed a smile and said, "I know."

But she didn't know, and there was no way he could

assure her that the outcome would be positive. So it was just a nice thing to say.

Seeming to sense there was nowhere to go but in circles on the subject, Mike began telling Sarah about a buddy he ran into from high school. They spent the next hour reminiscing about the fun times he and Mike had, and Sarah was glad to hear that her brother's old friend was doing well. He'd gone to college and became an accountant. He was married with kids and had a grandkid on the way.

After Mike left, Sarah was home alone. His story made her think of her old work colleagues. Suddenly, she had the urge to call one of them but chose not to, sticking with her original decision not to contact them because too much time had passed, and it would feel weird.

Sarah had a few good friends in high school. One had moved out of state, the other had gone to college elsewhere, and they had also drifted apart. However, many people stayed connected to old classmates on social media. Although Sarah used those platforms to run client ads, she rarely used her personal account. She preferred to use social media for business, targeting people via interests and behaviors. To her, it was a place to make a living. Now she wondered why she hadn't been more active on it herself.

As she pondered the reasons, Jeff pulled into the garage with a car full of groceries. Once he made it into the kitchen, his arms were overflowing with bags from several different stores. He set them down and pulled a square white box out of one. "Check out tonight's dessert," he said as he presented it to Sarah. "No added sugar pumpkin pie."

Sarah felt her face brighten. "Thanks!"

She kissed him on the cheek and playfully slapped his behind as he turned around to unpack the other bags. They flirted with each other the way they had before she got sick. And for a few minutes, Sarah forgot that she was bald and had no eyebrows or eyelashes. She was her old self, relaxed and carefree. If only she could figure out how to be that way all the time. For now, she'd take what she could get.

If things worked out as her brother predicted, she would make sure to enjoy every moment of the rest of her life. Maybe she would even become active on social media and reconnect with childhood friends. She could also get in touch with old coworkers and see how they were doing now.

Sarah gathered all the plastic shopping bags so Jeff could drop them off at the grocery store the next time he went. She was hungry for a change and looked forward to eating dinner with Heather and Caleb. Since treatment started, she was never hungry and only ate because she had to. But the no-sugar-added pumpkin pie sitting on the counter had kick-started her appetite. She loved all pumpkin spice offerings at this time of year.

Caleb and Heather set covered platters on the dining table when they arrived.

"I made a mini-Thanksgiving dinner," Caleb said in greeting, "so I could try out some new recipes before the real Thanksgiving."

"Smells great," Sarah replied. She felt bad he went through so much trouble cooking it, but Heather had assured her it was no problem, saying Caleb wanted to experiment on them.

Once the table was set, everyone sat down to enjoy the small turkey, green beans, and potatoes. And the green beans weren't the gravy-laden casserole Sarah usually made, but the kind of green beans found in a fancy restaurant.

"These potatoes look good," Jeff commented after removing the tray's lid.

"It's a French version of scalloped potatoes," Caleb explained. "I used Yukon Gold potatoes, rosemary, and gruyere cheese."

Sarah hadn't been this excited about a meal in a long time. She couldn't believe their good fortune that Heather was dating a prospective celebrity chef. Everyone filled their plates, then dug in.

"Mmmm," Jeff said after taking a bite of the potatoes. "These are the bomb."

Caleb and Heather shared a blank look.

Since Sarah was pretty sure that people hadn't used that phrase since her daughter was in diapers, she took a bite of the potatoes and interpreted, "Jeff's right. These are the best."

The group chatted about their meal as they ate. Caleb seemed happy to describe the ingredients used in each dish and how it was cooked. His whole face lit up when he talked about food. It was rare to be that passionate about one's work. Sarah met Heather's gaze as he spoke, and the two women shared a small smile, acknowledging how much fun they were having without intruding on Caleb's time to shine.

When Jeff helped himself to seconds, Sarah surprised herself by doing the same.

"Look at you, Mom." Heather's head bobbed with approval.

Sarah smiled. She knew her family didn't want her to lose too much weight. She now wore the jeans she had kept in her closet for over a decade, thinking she might fit into them again someday. She had almost put them in the donate pile last year, but hoping she'd return to her old size kept her from doing it. Thankfully, she hadn't because they came in handy at this time.

Heather and Jeff discussed how this college semester was going as they ate. Sarah listened, proud that her daughter had managed to keep up her grades. Afterward, Sarah and Heather cleared the table as Jeff cut the pie. He brought everyone a piece as Sarah offered coffee or milk to drink.

Although it was no added sugar, the pumpkin pie tasted sweet, probably because she had limited her intake of the substance and could notice small traces of it now. She stared into space in culinary bliss and mused, "I could eat the whole pie."

Everyone's laughter brought her back into the moment, and Sarah laughed too. Although she appreciated the fresh green juice Heather made for her every day, she enjoyed comfort food more. She especially enjoyed having them all together as a group. These meals had become one of the few bright spots in her life.

When the plates were empty, Sarah asked Heather how the house hunting was going.

"Grandpa bought a place," Heather said, her eyes bright. "I can't believe I forgot to tell you."

Sarah couldn't believe it either. Norman had actually bought something. He would be living in town, probably for the rest of his life. While a part of her felt glad, there was also a surge of concern.

Heather pulled her phone from her pocket and began tapping the screen. "Here's a link to the property." She handed the phone to Sarah and added, "There are a bunch of photos."

Sarah took the phone from her daughter and scrolled through the images. It was a large condo with one bedroom and an open concept. The appliances looked new, and the colors were neutral throughout.

"It's only five years old," Heather said. "So many of the older condos needed a lot of work. Grandpa said he doesn't have the time or energy to deal with that."

Sarah clicked the map listing and noticed it was nearby. About ten miles away.

Jeff had scooted over so he could look at the photos with Sarah. "That's pretty close to us," he commented. "That will be nice. Won't it, honey?"

"Yeah," Sarah answered. "That will be nice."

As the others continued talking about how much Norman had paid for the property, Sarah zoned out, trying to figure out how she felt about the news.

It should be nice to have your father close by.

Who would want their parents to be far away?

Sarah and Norman had shared some good times since he'd returned. Fleeting moments of positivity that bubbled to the surface past the ever-present quiet rage. Maybe there would be more of those in the future. Maybe they would become the father and daughter they were supposed to be all along.

As soon as she had the thought, Sarah quickly dismissed it. Allowing herself to hope for unlikely outcomes was a habit she had outgrown years ago. Instead, she pushed the idea out of her mind and rejoined the conversation, asking Caleb if he would give her the recipe for the French scalloped potatoes.

Chapter 23

Sarah checked the time. It wasn't like her father to be late to pick her up for a chemo session. She put on a light jacket and made sure the lid on the cooler was snapped shut. Then, tapping her foot, she glanced at the clock on the wall. They had to leave within the next ten minutes if they wanted to make it to the train station on time.

When Sarah finally called her dad, it went straight to voicemail, which was odd. What was she supposed to do now? She pictured Norman lying on the floor of his hotel room, suffering from a heart attack. But then, he could just as well have slept in, and if she missed her appointment, she'd be in trouble. Not showing up to treatment was a no-no; if it happened more than once, a patient could be dropped from the program.

Sarah grabbed her car keys and hurried to the garage. She pulled out of the driveway and zipped to the train station. Luck was on her side since she didn't get a ticket. Now if that same luck could extend to her appointment, it would be a good day indeed.

Sarah jumped out of the car, slung her purse over her shoulder, and lugged her cooler, which had somehow gotten heavier because she was in a rush. She managed to cross the train tracks and get to the side of the platform she needed to be on to board the train a minute before it arrived.

Sweating and out of breath, Sarah dropped the cooler and collapsed into a seat. It took a few minutes for her heart to stop hammering in her chest. She used to be able to run for a decent distance without being winded, but that wasn't the case anymore. Once she calmed down, she adjusted her chemo scarf, which had slipped from its original position during the commotion, then she opened her cooler and pulled out a bottle of water. It was a small one that she had managed to tuck between the booties and gloves.

After she took a sip, a conductor she didn't know asked for tickets, and she showed him the one she had bought on her phone. As soon as he continued, she checked to see if her father had called, but he hadn't, which sent her heart beating faster for a different reason. Scanning the train entrance to make sure she wasn't in a quiet car where no one was supposed to talk, Sarah called him again. This time, she left a message. "Hey, Dad, it's Sarah. I waited for you but had to go to the train. You've got me worried now. Give me a call when you can."

As the train headed to the city, Sarah considered calling Jeff to let him know what was going on. But she hated to bother him at work and decided it was better to tell him about it when she got home.

Ogilvie Transportation Center seemed bigger to Sarah today. When she came to Chicago with someone else, they usually chatted as they made their way to the cabs.

Being alone in the large crowd made her feel nervous and small.

As Sarah walked with the herd to the escalators, several people bumped into her without any apology. They just continued on their way, oblivious to her plight. Sarah worked to assume the best—that they were most likely lost in thought of their own impending appointments and meetings.

Sarah exited the building and hopped into a cab. It felt weird to be locked in the car with a total stranger, but it was what people did.

Once the cab driver dropped her off at the hospital entrance, she gave him a generous tip and climbed out, happy to have made it on time. She took the elevator to the fourth floor, checked in, and glanced around for the familiar faces she had come to know. Many patients were here each time Sarah was here, and so were the people who came with them. Occasionally, one group would replace another, and the cancer treatment cycle would begin again. It broke her heart that so many women were in the same position as her.

A few minutes after being transitioned into the exam room, Sarah was surprised when an Asian male oncologist stepped in to greet her. He introduced himself, shook her hand, and explained that he was filling in for Dr. Zimmerman, who was on vacation and would return next week. Sarah tried to forget he was a man as he did the breast exam. As he palpated her breast and felt her underarm, she pictured her doctor holding a well-deserved tropical drink by the beach.

After the exam ended, a nurse took Sarah to the treatment area. Nancy waved as Sarah arrived, brightening the room with her smile. That was when Sarah noticed that Nancy had a full head of hair, a wavy bob that she didn't have before. Sarah could usually spot wigs because the texture was too shiny and perfect, but this one looked amazing.

The nurse put Sarah next to Nancy. After she attached the line to Sarah's port, Sarah turned to Nancy and said, "I love your wig."

Nancy beamed. "Thanks."

"It's great to see you so happy."

"Well, this smile is part wig and part desperation." Nancy leaned in and lowered her voice. "I made sure to use the restroom before they hooked me up, but my bladder is ready to burst."

Sarah winced, knowing that being connected to the chemo drip made it almost impossible for women to just get up and go. "So, where did you get the wig?"

"Online. It's made of real hair. Pretty pricey, but I'm meeting my son's girlfriend for the first time this weekend, so I decided to treat myself to a new look."

Sarah nodded. "Great idea—and how exciting that you get to spend time with your son!" Sarah's excitement centered more on the idea that Nancy wouldn't spend another weekend alone.

"My son says they're getting serious. I hope I like her."

"I'm sure you will," Sarah said.

The nurse returned to start Sarah on fluids. During that time, Nancy's bladder had finally reached its limit.

After the nurse unplugged Nancy's machine, Nancy wrapped the cord around one of its hooks and pulled the rolling rack draped with bags of medicine down the hall to the bathroom, making sure not to let it slide too far away because the line from the port in her chest was connected to the medicine bag on the rack. Sarah made sure not to drink too much water before treatment as having to use the restroom became a production. She had done it on several occasions, and after fumbling a couple of times, she now knew how to balance all the moving parts for a successful bathroom break.

Sarah checked her phone. Still no message from her dad. She didn't want to sound the alarm and start making calls before getting chemo. Heather was at school, and Jeff was at work. She would wait a bit longer and see if her father called.

Sarah's nurse arrived mid-conversation and started the Benadryl. Soon, the floating in her chair sensation came over her, and it felt like her hair was growing even though she didn't have any, like the roots on her scalp buzzed with an energy of their own. Sarah usually fell asleep after chemo started, but now that Nancy had returned, she forced herself to stay awake so they could chat. Sarah mentioned that she had read some of Nancy's articles, and they discussed philosophical ideas until Nancy's treatment session ended.

After Nancy left, Sarah rechecked her phone. No missed calls. Sarah closed her eyes to focus on ways to deal with her father's disappearance.

It seemed like she had just fallen asleep when her

nurse woke her, saying she was done. She watched through groggy eyes as the nurse flushed her port and disconnected her, and then Sarah packed her gloves and booties into the cooler and used the restroom before getting ready to go.

Thankfully, a cab was right outside the hospital, and she didn't have to roam the streets of Chicago searching for one. Sarah lugged her cooler through the train station. It was so heavy. And she was so tired. She felt as if she were sleepwalking.

Sarah reminded herself that she would be sitting down soon as she checked the information board for her train's track. She headed in that direction and boarded the train. Although the seats weren't comfortable, she found respite in the faux leather bench and set her purse and cooler next to her so they were close to the window, and her body shielded them from view.

The train filled up quickly since it was close to the workday's end. Sarah averted her gaze from the other passengers, not in the mood to deal with anyone's lingering stares or questioning eyes. Soon, the train departed, and the constant rumbling sound lulled Sarah to sleep.

"Tickets!" the conductor shouted.

Sarah's head snapped up. She rubbed her eyes, quickly ensured her purse and cooler were beside her, and pulled her phone from her bag. She opened the app and held the ticket up so the conductor could see it.

His brows knitted together as he examined the ticket. "You're on the wrong train."

"What?" Sarah asked, disoriented.

"You're on the wrong train," the conductor repeated. "You want the Union Pacific Northwest line. You're on the Union Pacific North line, heading toward Kenosha."

Sarah gasped. "Where are we now?" she asked, panicking.

"Next stop is Glencoe."

That was an hour from Sarah's house. She couldn't believe she had made such a stupid mistake. She apologized to the conductor and gathered her things, grateful that she hadn't gone all the way to Wisconsin. Things could always be worse.

As Sarah got off the train in Glencoe, raindrops began to fall. She scanned the station for a covered waiting area and walked toward it, thinking of her umbrella, which was in the backseat of her car. Somehow, she never had it when she needed it.

Sarah shuddered as a gust of wind whipped past. It always seemed colder by the lake, and the weather changed hourly this time of year. She made it to the covered waiting area and sat down. She was the only passenger there. Everyone else had gone home, and it was getting dark.

Mentally and physically exhausted, Sarah pulled her phone from her purse and saw a text from her brother, checking in.

She called him. He picked up on the second ring.

"Mike. I need help."

"What do you mean you need help? What's wrong?"

"I'm in Glencoe. Somehow, I boarded the wrong train."

"How's that possible? Didn't Dad double-check before you guys left?"

"He's not here," Sarah said.

"What do you mean he's not there?"

"He didn't show up to take me to chemo, so I went by myself."

"Son of a bitch!" Mike continued cursing. He spat a string of expletives so long that Sarah lost track of all the words used. When he returned to the conversation, he said, "Sit tight. I'll be there as soon as I can."

Sarah disconnected and put her phone in her pocket. She knew she should call Jeff and Heather but was too embarrassed about her predicament and too tired to explain it again. The temperature dropped as the sun set, and Sarah rubbed the upper arms of her damp jacket, trying to get warm. Something terrible must have happened to her father. Once she got home and explained everything to Jeff and Heather, they would find out what happened and see if he needed help. He was getting older and could have fallen. He could be lying on the floor in his hotel room, unconscious, or worse.

Thunder rumbled overhead, and shortly afterward, it began to pour. Sarah berated herself for today's debacle as she shivered, her teeth clattering like castanets as she shook. She prayed Mike would be careful on the way over. She would never forgive herself if he got into an accident because of her.

Time passed slowly as Sarah sat in the covered waiting

area. Her bladder, which she had emptied before leaving the hospital, felt full again—probably from the pre-treatment fluids she had received. Tapping her foot, she tried to push the need to urinate from her mind. She also made a mental note to dress in layers from now on and to buy a travel umbrella that would fit in her purse so she would never be without one again.

Sarah looked up when she saw Mike's car pull into the train station. He parked as close as he could to where she was sitting, then hopped out and quickly closed the distance between them. Mike grabbed her cooler and ushered her to his car. He opened the passenger side door and helped her in before pulling something out of the trunk.

Mike returned to the car, started it, and turned on the heat. He had pulled a blanket he kept for emergencies from the trunk and wrapped it around Sarah's shoulders. Then, he looked her up and down. She waited for the impending, "I told you so. I told you he wouldn't change his stripes." But it never came.

Instead, through clenched teeth, he said, "I'm gonna fucking kill him."

Chapter 24

Jeff opened the front door as she and Mike walked toward it. As Sarah stepped inside, Jeff pulled her into a tight embrace and didn't let go for a long time.

"My car," Sarah said, remembering it was still at the train station.

"Heather and I already got it," he murmured into her ear.

Heather entered the room and rushed toward her mother. Her eyes seemed to glow a lighter blue when she was anxious, and they were certainly glowing now. "Are you okay?"

"I'm fine," Sarah assured her. "Just a little tired." She removed her jacket and handed it to her daughter. "Has anyone heard from Norman?" she asked, glancing from Heather to Jeff.

"I called and got voicemail," Jeff said.

"Should we go over there and see if he's okay?" Sarah asked.

"Don't worry about Dad," Mike replied. "He's fine."

There was no way her brother could know that, but the tone of his voice meant they wouldn't be discussing the matter further. Sarah could hear Jeff and Mike talking as Heather took her to the bedroom, where a pair of dry pajamas and fuzzy socks with foot grips were lying on the bed. Sarah changed and climbed under the blankets, then Heather took her damp clothes away, turned off the light, and left without asking questions.

As she turned on her side, her foot made contact with a furry form, and a moment later, Walter crawled toward her and snuggled up to her chest. Sarah wrapped her arm around him and quickly nodded off.

When she woke the next day, Sarah could vaguely remember Jeff sitting beside her in the dark, gently stroking her head. She felt well-rested and a bit hungry, so she rose and headed to the kitchen.

Sensing an opportunity to score a meal, Walter trailed Sarah and repeatedly rubbed her legs until he achieved the desired result. Jeff had left a veggie egg bake for Sarah in the cast iron pan. She reheated it on low, put a slice of bread in the toaster, and then made a cup of coffee.

As she ate her food, Sarah wondered why she had called Mike instead of Jeff when she was stranded. Had Jeff been hurt by that? She would mention it when he got home.

When Sarah finished eating, Jeff called.

"Hey, honey. How are you feeling?" Jeff asked.

"I'm okay. I just ate breakfast." Sarah wanted to tackle the other topic since he was on the phone. "You know, I had Mike come and get me yesterday because he sent a text asking how I was doing. For some reason, I called him right after reading it. I should've called you instead."

"That's no problem. The important thing is that you made it home safely." Jeff paused before asking, "Have you heard from your father?"

"Not yet. I really think we should go over there and check on him."

"Me too. Let me see if I can get off work early. I haven't had much success with these kinds of requests, but I'll try."

Jeff's longtime boss had recently retired, and his new boss wasn't as friendly. The man was all business and didn't show much concern for workers' personal plights. Jeff made great money at the company and had terrific benefits, so he had learned to keep his mouth shut and his head down, especially since the health insurance coverage was crucial now.

Sarah went to the restroom after she hung up. When she returned to the kitchen and picked up her phone, she noticed a new voicemail from Norman. She listened to the message.

"Hey, honey. It's Dad. Sorry I missed your appointment. I got the days mixed up and didn't realize it was my week. I went to visit Linda and will be back tomorrow. Let's reconnect then."

Sarah breathed a sigh of relief. She was glad that Norman wasn't sprawled out in his hotel room, unconscious, or that he hadn't been in a car wreck. She quickly texted Jeff and told him that Norman was okay, so he didn't leave work early, then headed to her desk.

Before sitting in her chair, she stopped and thought about what her father had said. She listened to the message again and found his nonchalant attitude about the situation irritating. He didn't seem concerned about what may or may not have happened to her when he made such a careless mistake.

Don't worry about Dad, Mike had said. *He's fine.*

Sarah shook her head as she realized she had wasted time worrying about him. She felt like such a fool. "I can't believe I fell for this crap. Again!" She stormed the house, shouting at the walls. "Why do I keep making the same mistake over and over? Isn't that the definition of insanity? Doing the same thing and expecting different results?"

Walter crouched in the corner of the room, watching Sarah with a fearful look in his eyes.

Sarah turned to her cat. "Mommy's an idiot. Did you know that? Yeah, Mommy's a total chump!"

The phone rang again. This time, it was Mike.

"How are you feeling?" he asked.

"Not good," she admitted.

"Why? What's going on?"

Sarah told her brother that Norman called. She told him exactly what he said in the voicemail message.

"'Let's reconnect then'?" Mike mocked. "Who says that kind of shit to their kid?"

Sarah only used that phrase with business partners. She would never say something like that to Heather. Neither would Jeff.

"Give me that asshole's address," Mike said. "I'm gonna be there when he gets back tomorrow. He's not getting away with this."

"I'll go with you," she suggested, hoping to diffuse the situation before it got out of control.

They agreed on a time, and Sarah hung up. Although she was angry, she would have to be the calm one tomorrow to prevent her brother from doing something he'd later regret. Now that Linda was calling, and Norman had gone back to see her, he'd withdraw his offer on the Illinois condo and move back to North Carolina, and they could be the family they were before he had come back into their lives.

At dinner that night, Jeff and Heather listened to Sarah explain why her father hadn't shown up to take her to the chemotherapy appointment.

"It's possible that he forgot," Jeff said as he cut into his steak. "But to be on the safe side, I'd like Beverly to take you to your remaining treatments. She and I discussed it and agreed that would be best."

That explained why Beverly hadn't called Sarah yet. She thought her mother didn't know, that Mike had spared her the story so she wouldn't get upset. Not only did Beverly know, but she had already stepped in to complete the job she had set out to do on her own. Norman was a blip on her radar, a short-term storm that briefly caught her attention but one she had already forgotten.

Sarah nodded in agreement before digging into her steak. She could understand why he wouldn't trust Norman with her care going forward.

Sarah dried the dishes as Heather washed them. Her daughter was quiet while she worked, most likely contemplating things and forming an opinion of her own.

When Jeff left the room, she said, "Dad and I were

worried about Grandpa, but Uncle Mike talked to us last night and told us we had nothing to worry about." Heather put a clean bowl into the rack and frowned. "I guess he was right."

Sarah began drying the bowl. She had a pretty good idea what Mike had told them after she fell asleep. Her brother was enraged and needed to vent, and they were upset and wanted to hear what he had to say. Mike didn't sugarcoat unpleasant events the way Sarah did. Instead, he presented them in all their ugly wonder, letting others marvel at the stark reality of how they occurred.

Sarah put the bowl in the cupboard and turned back to her daughter. "Grandpa does things like this. That's why we grew apart."

Heather removed her dish gloves. "But I thought he was trying to make it up to you. Why would he do the same thing he did before and think that it's okay?" As Sarah considered how best to reply, her daughter put her hands on her hips and huffed. "Unbelievable," she said before stalking out of the kitchen and heading to her room.

Sarah wiped down the counter, knowing it was easily believable. The only good thing was that Norman had done this to her and not Heather. She was glad her daughter could see how Norman operated and learn from her mistake.

Jeff was sitting on the sofa reading a non-fiction book he got from the library. He closed it when he saw Sarah approach. "I hope you don't mind that Beverly and I discussed your remaining treatments. She called last night after Mike left, and we got to talking."

"I don't mind," Sarah said, easing into a chair.

Jeff's expression grew serious. "Norman knew when the chemo appointment was and didn't show. I counted on him to take care of you, and he let me down. I don't appreciate him doing that to me."

Sarah didn't bother saying that was how Norman was because Jeff already knew. He'd patiently listened to the stories after asking why her dad wasn't around. In the past, he'd been empathetic, telling her he was sorry to hear it and that maybe things would change down the road. Then her father returned, and he was filled with unwarranted optimism. Now he was getting his own dose of Norman and didn't like the taste.

Jeff removed his reading glasses and leaned toward Sarah. "Mike said you two are going to see him tomorrow."

"We are," Sarah said. "He wants to hold Norman accountable for his actions, and I'm going along to make sure Mike's fists don't connect with my dad's face."

Jeff's eyebrows rose.

"Mike has never gotten physical with Norman," Sarah added, "but you never know."

Their previous fights had been loud arguments that ended with slamming doors. Since Norman currently resided at a hotel, Sarah hoped to keep noise to a minimum. She didn't want another guest to get upset and call the police.

"Don't worry about tomorrow," Sarah reassured him. "I know how to handle Mike."

Jeff's shoulders seemed to relax. He turned on the TV, and they began watching an episode of a mystery series they enjoyed. Heather joined them after it started, still looking miffed but gradually relaxing as the show played. Then Walter arrived. He jumped onto the sofa and curled up next to Jeff, oblivious to the family drama in his house.

Sarah texted her father the following day about her plan to visit. She left out the part about Mike coming along.

As she showered, she became less and less in the mood to visit Norman. She was supposed to be resting, but she couldn't exactly let Mike rip into their father without someone level-headed to diffuse the situation.

Sarah donned fleece-lined leggings and a tunic sweatshirt since the temperature had dropped. She pulled the curtain aside and looked out the bedroom window up to the dreary sky—a perfect backdrop for today's event. A wave of melancholy overcame her as she pictured the scene between her father and Mike. It was a shame that it had to be this way, but as usual, Norman had brought it on himself.

When Mike texted that he was almost there, Sarah put on her jacket, grabbed her purse, and donned her bucket hat. She left the house when she saw him pull into the driveway.

"Are you sure you want to do this?" Sarah asked after she got into the car.

"Of course, I'm sure. I want him to know it was a bullshit move to put you in harm's way."

Mike put the car in reverse after Sarah buckled her seatbelt. He drove the speed limit to Norman's place, probably for Sarah's benefit. "The Girl from Ipanema" played on the radio. Its jazzy vibe seemed more appropriate for lounging by the pool with a daiquiri than heading to a fight. Mike knew the lyrics and sang along, which made it even more bizarre. He was unusually calm.

They pulled into the hotel parking lot and got out of the car. Sarah turned to her brother. "Let's be mindful of the noise level."

Mike raised his hands in protest. "I'll be quiet as a mouse."

They nodded at each other and headed to Norman's room. Once there, Mike knocked. Sarah inwardly cringed.

Norman opened the door. His face fell when he saw them standing side by side.

Smiling, Mike asked, "Is now a good time to 'reconnect'?"

Chapter 25

"Sure. Please, come in," Norman stammered as he stepped aside.

Norman led Mike and Sarah toward the small kitchen table. He sat in one of the chairs, but Sarah chose to stand. Mike decided to stand, too.

"So, here's the deal," Mike launched right in. "You were supposed to take Sarah to chemo. It was your day. Your responsibility." Mike let that sink in before adding, "But you didn't show. And since Sarah couldn't miss a treatment, she drove herself to the train station. She made it to her session on time but boarded the wrong train on the way home because she was heavily sedated and confused. I picked her up in Glencoe. In the rain."

Norman glanced at Sarah and shifted his weight from one hip to the other. Instead of empathy, she saw fear in his eyes. He seemed to be looking for a way out of this confrontation and trying to form a response that would satisfy them both.

"I'm so sorry," he told Sarah. "I mixed up the dates when Linda called. She broke up with her boyfriend and wanted to talk, so I flew to North Carolina thinking it was your mom's week. I would never have gone if I had known it was my week. I would have asked Linda to come here."

It sounded like an honest mistake. If it were anyone but Norman, Sarah would believe it.

Mike shook his head. "Why don't you cut the crap? You're a retired businessman who knows how to use a calendar. You knew it was your week to take her to chemo, but you chose to blow it off and focus on yourself."

Mike's words rang true for Sarah. They connected with an old pain she ignored, peeling the scab off a wound she thought had healed. Emotion bubbled in her gut as Norman replied to Mike.

"I didn't blow it off. I made a mistake."

Mike took a step closer to Norman. "Your mistake is being self-centered. Always has been. Always will be. Everything is always about you."

"You don't think I have a right to work things out with my ex-wife?" Norman asked.

Mike smirked. "You have the right to do whatever you want. Nobody cares about your love life. In fact, you *should* get back with Linda because she's the only woman interested in you."

Norman jumped from his chair. "You have a smart mouth."

"I know," Mike replied. "It's one of my many charms."

Father and son were face to face as the bickering continued. It was no longer about Norman not taking Sarah to chemo. Instead, it was about everything that had happened through the years.

"What about that time you were supposed to come to Sarah's parent/teacher conference?"

"I got a flat tire," Norman said.

"And her fourth-grade talent show?"

Norman folded his arms in front of his chest. "I missed my connecting flight."

"You got a flat tire. You missed your flight," Mike quipped. "You've got an answer for everything, don't you? A never-ending supply of excuses."

"They're not excuses!" Norman exclaimed.

Sarah's body tensed, and her eyesight blurred with welling tears until the fight started sounding like white noise. It hummed in her ear, growing louder each minute. She desperately wanted it to stop.

"Be quiet," Sarah said, speaking for the first time since they arrived.

They kept on, oblivious to her soft-spoken voice under their incessant shouting.

"Shut up!" She shouted over them, an adrenaline surge rushing through her. "Shut the fuck up!"

Silence. Mike and Norman turned to her, eyes wide, mouths agape.

"I have cancer. I don't need additional stress." She looked at her dad and said, "I don't want to do this anymore."

Norman reached out to her, but Sarah pulled away. "Don't," she said, tears finally spilling down her cheeks. "Just leave me alone."

Norman's mouth opened as if he was going to say

something, but Sarah dealt the final blow. "You're never going to be the father I wanted you to be. So stop trying to pretend you care when you don't."

With that said, Sarah ran out of the hotel room. An older woman in the unit next to theirs had her door cracked open to see what was going on, and Sarah eyed her as she flew past, unashamed of what had occurred.

The sound of her brother's footsteps echoed behind her. Then, finally, he caught up to her in the parking lot.

"That was epic!" he said, high-fiving Sarah. "Way to fucking slay!"

Sarah and Mike shared a commiserative look as their palms smacked together, then they hopped into the car and laughed. They continued laughing all the way home, Sarah's tears now coming from joy instead of grief.

Mike pulled into Sarah's driveway. Her brother beamed with pride as he waved goodbye. Sarah lifted her chin as she waved back, feeling oddly exhilarated as she entered her empty house. Jeff and Heather had gone out to dinner because Sarah said she'd grab food with Mike, but food was the last thing Sarah wanted right now. She took off her shoes and climbed into bed, relieved that this small but turbulent chapter of her life had finally come to an end.

Chapter 26

A few days passed with no word from Norman, which was just fine by Sarah. She'd caught up on some reading and created a few new campaigns for her clients before it was time to get chemo again.

Beverly arrived at the appointed time to take her to the train. She had a small paper bag in her hand.

"What's in the bag?" Sarah asked as they got into the car.

"Protein cookies. They're made with hardly any sugar. I thought it might be fun to try."

Beverly hadn't called to discuss what happened with Norman. Mike had undoubtedly filled her in, and she was moving on to bigger and better things, like cookies that wouldn't negatively affect Sarah's bloodwork.

After Beverly handed her the bag, Sarah pulled out a peanut butter cookie, unwrapped it, and took a bite. Her eyes widened as the cookie melted in her mouth. "These are delicious," she said when she'd finished eating. "No kidding. They taste like the real deal."

Beverly's broad smile was the only reply Sarah got.

Shortly after they boarded the train, Sarah heard her mom's phone vibrate. Beverly pulled it from her purse and frowned before pushing the phone to the bottom of the bag and zipping it closed. It could only have been Norman, but no matter. Today was her day to beat cancer. It wasn't about her dad.

Beverly told Sarah about a new show she and Richard had started watching as they headed downtown. Time passed quickly as they chatted, and before they knew it, they were already at the hospital.

Dr. Zimmerman was in good spirits as she examined Sarah. She looked different, though. Sarah couldn't figure out why and then realized it was her hair. It used to be to her shoulders. Now it was chin-length.

"I like your hairstyle," Sarah said as they finished.

Her doctor smiled. "Thanks. There have been lots of changes in my life, so I figured it was time for a new look."

Dr. Zimmerman had never mentioned anything personal before, but Sarah understood the desire to reinvent oneself. Sarah couldn't wait to try a new style once her own hair grew back.

When her doctor left, Sarah dressed, and a nurse took her to the treatment room. Nancy was there and had already started her session.

"How's it going?" Nancy asked after Sarah got situated. "Tell me about your week."

Sarah hesitated, then figured what the heck. "I got into a fight with my dad. So we're not speaking to each other anymore."

"Oh, no!" Nancy said.

Sarah tried to explain so Nancy would understand.

"It's okay," Sarah added. "We never got along well anyway."

She gave Nancy an abbreviated backstory of their relationship from childhood until he showed up at her front door wanting to help. Nancy listened to their history without comment, the conversation pausing when nurses came to check on either of them, then resuming when they left.

Sarah told Nancy about Norman taking her to treatment. That he and her mom alternated weeks until her father blew her off, and she mistakenly boarded the wrong train and had to be picked up by her brother. She explained that Mike wanted to hold Norman accountable, then told her the details of the big fight.

Nancy whistled under her breath. "That's a lot of drama for a cancer patient." Nancy took a sip of water, then turned to Sarah. "Do you want my opinion?"

Sarah nodded. She valued Nancy's opinion very much.

"There's no room in your life for toxic relationships. Especially now." She paused, making sure Sarah digested that advice before adding, "But there's one thing you have to do."

Sarah leaned closer and asked, "What?"

"You have to forgive your father," Nancy said. "Do it for your health."

Chapter 27

Sarah reflected on Nancy's advice throughout the week. It made sense to forgive people and stop holding a grudge because letting anger and resentment fester could make a person sick. And wasn't she sick enough?

As Sarah washed the breakfast dishes, she thought about Nancy's sister. She had wronged her horribly and didn't deserve mercy, but Sarah presumed she'd given it to her.

"Do it for your health," Nancy had said. Words spoken by a person willing to do whatever it takes to beat this disease.

Sarah drank green juice, avoided sweets, and went to treatment. She was using all the tools in her arsenal to get well. But this forgiveness thing was complicated. It seemed harder than chemo. Plus, she had no idea where to start.

When Beverly came for lunch later that day, Sarah told her what Nancy had suggested.

"That's excellent advice," her mom said. "You don't have to see your father if you don't want to, but you should forgive him for not being the person you want him to be."

The mention of Norman's shortcomings reminded

Sarah of the vow she made when she learned she was pregnant. She promised to put Heather's needs first. To always be there for her daughter so she would feel loved and supported and hopefully become a well-balanced adult. She had given Heather everything because her dad had given her so little.

"I don't know how to forgive him," Sarah admitted.

Beverly leaned back in her chair and regarded her daughter. "It's something you decide. That's it. You don't have to call or text and say I forgive you. You just choose to forgive and move on with your life."

Sarah gave her mom a small smile. "It sounds easy when you say it like that."

"It's easier said than done, that's for sure."

The women dug into their chicken salad sandwiches and left the subject behind. Beverly didn't say if Norman had texted her that day on the train, and Sarah didn't ask. She'd told her father to leave her alone, and he still hadn't contacted her. For once, he was doing what she wanted him to do. Yet, for some reason, she felt oddly sad about how things ended.

The following day, Nancy texted that she would be in costume at their next treatment since it fell on Halloween. Sarah hadn't dressed up for the holiday in many years but felt it could be a nice distraction from the grueling treatment.

Heather drove Sarah to the Halloween store, which was huge and bustling with customers. A fairy princess costume caught Sarah's eye after she walked in, but unfortunately, it was only available for kids.

She and Heather headed to the adult section. They had sexy fairy costumes—the kind she'd worn when she and Jeff went to Halloween parties when they were young. Sarah pulled a skeleton costume from the rack. She was thin and bald and figured the style might work well. Heather found two contenders: a female superhero and a sexy witch.

They scanned the store for other choices before going to the fitting room. The attendant suggested they share a room since the store was packed, which was okay with Sarah. She wanted to see her daughter in the outfits anyway and get her opinion of the one she chose.

Heather changed clothes faster than Sarah. She donned the Wonder Woman costume, turning from side to side, checking it out in the mirror as Sarah undressed.

"I love it!" Sarah exclaimed. "I was a big fan of that show when I was young."

"It's cute," Heather said, her tone somewhat skeptical.

Heather zipped the dress of the sexy witch costume as Sarah donned the skeleton one. She removed her chemo scarf and stared in the mirror.

"It's perfect!" Heather said, gazing at Sarah's reflection.

"It is, isn't it?" Sarah agreed, thinking she looked pretty cool.

Halloween music played in the background, and the song switched to "Monster Mash." Sarah lifted her arms and began swimming midair as she sang the lyrics, then she paused and started doing the twist. Heather copied her mother, laughing as she danced. Both women shimmied around the dressing room, acting silly and free. For those few minutes, Sarah forgot she had cancer.

When the song ended, Sarah smiled at her daughter. "This was fun. Let me buy both costumes."

"You don't have to do that," Heather said. "I can buy my own."

"I know. But I want to."

The women changed and took their costumes to the register. Sarah paid the young man, whose everyday look paralleled Halloween, and they were on their way home. Heather had plans with Caleb that evening and left to meet him shortly after they returned, so Sarah and Jeff had the house to themselves.

Jeff eyed the shopping bag sitting on the bed. "You found a costume?"

Sarah lifted the bag and smiled. "Yes, I did."

"Why don't you try it on?" Jeff suggested.

Sarah took the bag to the restroom and changed into the skeleton costume, removing her chemo scarf to complete the look.

"It's not the kind of costume I used to wear," Sarah said as she emerged from the bathroom. "It's more scary than sexy."

"It's scary cute," Jeff said, pulling her close.

He pressed his lips against hers, gently at first, but when she didn't say she was too sick or too tired, he became more passionate. Sarah didn't know how her outfit could arouse him, but if it worked for him, she wouldn't complain. She had been using the vaginal moisturizer as directed and hoped it would hurt less this time. Thankfully, it did, but it wasn't how it was before chemo, so she wouldn't rule out technology down the road.

Sarah had to make it to the end of the road before she could worry about that. Sex was important, but she had to be alive to partake. As Jeff lay beside her, snoring lightly, she considered how far she'd come since she'd been diagnosed. She was almost done with treatment, and then she'd have surgery—and most likely radiation afterward.

The thought of losing her breast brought Sarah down. Every day that passed, she got closer to looking like the women in the mastectomy pictures online. Sometimes she visualized herself that way to prepare, but she knew there was no way to prepare for what was coming. Knowing a thing would happen and experiencing it were two different things. Luckily, the hospital had counselors who could help. She didn't know if she would talk to one, but knowing they were there if she needed them was comforting. It made her slightly less afraid.

Heather must've told Beverly about Sarah's costume because her mother was dressed as a ghost when she picked her up on Halloween.

"I love your costume!" Sarah said as she stepped outside.

"I love yours too!" Beverly replied before hugging her.

Sarah rubbed her head. "It's the first time I've gone out without my hat or scarf. I kind of have to if I want to rock this look."

"Agreed," Beverly said as they headed to the car.

When they got to the train station, other passengers glanced at them and smiled. Most stared at Sarah much longer, then nodded approvingly as they realized what was going on.

A little boy pointed at her. "Look, Mommy! A skeleton."

Sarah waved at the child, happy to have made his day.

People didn't have fear in their eyes when they saw Sarah today. Instead, they seemed to like what they saw. Ironic, considering she was dressed as a skeleton instead of a cancer patient. Maybe it was because she felt confident in her costume. Since she wasn't embarrassed by the way she looked, people treated her differently.

Some of the admissions staff and medical assistants wore costumes at the hospital. Sarah hadn't expected Dr. Zimmerman to participate in the holiday, but she walked into the exam room wearing black sequin cat ears. It dressed up her white lab coat and hinted that her oncologist might be a lot of fun outside of work.

After discussing how Sarah was doing this week, Dr. Zimmerman said, "It looks like the immunotherapy drug is causing trouble for your thyroid gland. The good news is if it breaks your thyroid, you have a better chance of beating cancer. The bad news is that your thyroid breaks in the process."

Sarah closed her eyes and shook her head. She didn't want the immunotherapy drug to cause a new health problem.

Dr. Zimmerman continued. "The numbers indicate hyperthyroidism, which causes weight loss. So that would explain why you're losing weight even though you're eating three meals per day."

Sarah nodded. It made sense.

"That tends to happen with this drug," her doctor added. "It causes hyperthyroidism first, then the numbers swing in the other direction, and patients get hypothyroidism."

"Then I'll gain a bunch of weight?" Sarah asked, alarmed.

"You could gain some, but we'll send you to the endocrinologist, and you'll get medicine to balance everything. Don't worry about your thyroid. It can be managed with medication."

Sarah's festive mood soured upon hearing this news. She hadn't given her thyroid gland much thought before, but it seemed essential, like something to be cherished, not broken. She didn't want to take medication to balance it, but it seemed she had no choice.

When Dr. Zimmerman left, she removed her gown and donned her costume, trying to think positively. If the drug broke her thyroid, she had a better chance. She wished the medical community knew how to cure diseases without creating new ones.

Sarah went to the treatment room and spotted Nancy in an orange velour pumpkin costume and matching hat with a green carrot top attached.

"So cute!" Sarah said as she approached.

"Yours too! It's genius," Nancy complimented.

Sarah asked the nurse to take a picture of her and Nancy before starting the chemo session. Sarah pulled her phone from her bag and leaned toward Nancy, who was seated, and they both grinned as the nurse took a few snaps.

Afterward, Sarah sat down and got started on fluids. When the nurse left, she asked Nancy, "How was your week?"

"Interesting."

Sarah raised an eyebrow. "Interesting, how?"

"My sister called."

"Wow!" Sarah said, stunned. "What did she say?"

"She left a voicemail saying she wants to see me and asked if she could stop by this weekend."

Sarah couldn't believe it. "What are you going to do?"

Nancy took her time replying. "I was thinking I could ignore her and go to my grave proving a point, or I could see what she has to say."

Sarah waited for her friend to tell her which choice she'd made.

"I'm going to call her," Nancy said.

Chapter 28

No one in the family asked about Norman after Sarah had told him to leave her alone. They were united in helping Sarah decompress and forget. She couldn't forget her father entirely because he was her dad. But with him gone, she didn't have to deal with the frequent drama his presence brought.

Work also kept Sarah busier than usual because she'd landed a new client. A referral, no less. Although she wasn't looking for more work, she was grateful a current client had sent a new one her way. Creating campaigns for their business took her mind off the blisters in her mouth, chronic constipation, and nausea. Thankfully, she had only thrown up that one time on the train. But there had been many times she was on the verge but managed it with anti-nausea medication.

The week went by quickly. Sarah spent a lot of it researching the thyroid gland online. She hadn't realized how important it was. And now that she knew, she couldn't understand how Dr. Zimmerman could act like breaking it was no big deal. But since she'd played the whole thing down and said the endocrinologist would handle it, Sarah didn't bother telling Jeff. If it became a bigger problem, she'd bring it up. For now, she'd keep it to herself.

Mike called on Saturday to ask how Sarah was doing. "I hope you're taking it easy," he said.

"I am," Sarah assured him. And even though he didn't ask, she said, "I haven't heard from Dad."

"He's long gone by now," Mike said.

Sarah stood by the window watching rain drops fall. "Unfortunately, I'm still thinking about him."

"What the fuck for?"

Sarah sighed, then went to the sofa and sat down. "I'm trying to forgive him."

"Why do you want to do that?"

Sarah tried to think of the best way to explain. "It's supposed to help me heal. I don't have to see him again, but I have to forgive him to get well."

"I thought chemotherapy and green juice did that."

"They do," Sarah said. "But this is just another tool."

"Sounds like BS, but if you wanna try it, give it a shot. Marijuana is a tool, too. Just saying."

Sarah laughed. Her older brother was in good health and prayed to the weed gods daily. In return, they took great care of him.

"Have you made any progress with the new saleslady?" Sarah asked.

"She quit a few days ago."

"How come?"

"She went on a test drive with a guy who drove like a maniac. He almost crashed."

Sarah didn't think she could let strangers drive her around every day. "Did you at least get her number before she left?"

"Nah. She's history. Wasn't meant to be."

They dropped the subject and discussed the bell-ringing ceremony. Mike wanted Sarah to remind him which day to take off work because he hadn't put in his request yet. They chatted about other things before hanging up, and afterward, Sarah was in a better mood. She did light household chores as Jeff ran a few errands, checking her phone intermittently to see if Nancy had sent a text.

Jeff noticed Sarah peeking at her phone on Sunday night. "Any word from your friend?"

Sarah set the phone on her nightstand. "Not yet. I'm guessing she's busy and will tell me about it the next time I see her."

Jeff nodded. Oddly enough, he seemed as interested as Sarah in learning what had occurred.

On Tuesday, autumn abruptly turned to winter, so Sarah wore a wool hat downtown and stashed her chemo scarf in her purse to wear when she got to the hospital. Beverly didn't interact with her phone on the train ride.

Nancy sat in the treatment room, staring into space. She looked up when Sarah arrived. That's when Sarah noticed that her sunny smile was missing.

"How's it going?" Sarah asked after sitting down.

Nancy's eyes were dull, and her lips formed a thin line. "My pain meds aren't working. They're trying to find a solution."

Sarah gave Nancy an empathetic look. "I hope they can give you something that helps."

Just then, Nancy's nurse appeared, so Sarah adjusted her chair to give them privacy. Thankfully, Sarah's bone pain went away after she stopped using Neulasta. She still had plenty of frustrating side effects, but pain wasn't one of them anymore. Knowing that Nancy was suffering broke Sarah's heart.

When they could talk again, Nancy said, "They're going to give me something new."

"That's good," Sarah replied.

They sat in companionable silence until Nancy asked, "Did I tell you my sister called me?"

Sarah nodded. "You mentioned it last week."

Nancy shook her head, seeming embarrassed. "With all the pain meds, sometimes I forget what we discuss."

"No worries. I've been forgetful, myself."

"Well, I saw her." Nancy paused as if taking time to gather her thoughts. "She apologized for not being there when I needed her."

Sarah thought that was a good start.

"It ends up she had a lot of problems she hadn't told me about. She said she couldn't handle all of them at once, that when she learned of the cancer recurrence, she snapped."

Sarah had something to say about prioritization but held her tongue.

Nancy let out a heavy sigh. "Her marriage was in trouble, her hours had been cut at work, and she was forced to find a second job to make ends meet, and then her son became addicted to drugs."

That was a lot of problems. But still, Sarah thought,

she didn't have to abandon her sister.

Nancy's eyes got glassy. "My nephew left home. He's on the streets with bad people. No one has heard from him. And my sister got a divorce. She did her best to save the marriage, but God had other plans."

Sarah's opinion about the situation evolved as her friend spoke. What Nancy's sister did to her wasn't right, but the woman had valid reasons for being overwhelmed. People dealt with problems in different ways. Maybe when confronted with another one, all her sister could do was pretend it didn't exist.

"I'm sorry that all those things happened to her," Sarah said.

Nancy lifted her chin, managing not to let tears fall. "Me too. She's a good person. She didn't deserve any of that."

Sarah thought Nancy was a good person who didn't deserve what had happened to her, either. The conversation paused when Sarah's nurse arrived with her medication. She verified her name and date of birth before they gave it to her, and when the nurse left, Sarah turned to Nancy, hoping to hear more.

"Then time passed, and one day, she said it was like she woke up from a fog and realized ignoring me while I was sick was a huge mistake." Nancy swiped a tear from her cheek with the back of her hand. "I'm thankful my sister is back. I missed her so much."

If their chairs weren't so far apart, Sarah would've reached over and given Nancy's hand a little squeeze. "I'm glad you two were able to reconnect."

Nancy reached for a tissue and blew her nose. She took a few steadying breaths to regain composure and, to Sarah's surprise, had more to say.

"My sister got a new job. Full-time with good benefits. Even though it pays well, her rent is pricey, and since the lease is up soon, I suggested she come and live with me."

The level of Nancy's kindness knew no limits. It astounded Sarah.

"And what did she say?" Sarah asked.

"She said yes." Nancy smiled brightly. "She cried at first, saying she didn't deserve that after how she'd treated me, but I told her to forget the past and move in. I told her we could help each other."

"That's a great idea! I'm sure you could use help. Plus, it would be nice having your sister around."

Sarah didn't say what she was genuinely thinking, that it would be nice to have her sister around for as long as she had left. There was no point saying the words aloud. Not when Nancy was sitting next to her, fighting for her life.

She could beat this disease. She'd done it before, and she could do it again. But Nancy would have a better chance with her sister by her side, giving her another reason to live.

Chapter 29

Sarah stared at her computer screen, frustrated that the CPC on her new client's ad had risen over the last few days. The graphic was on trend and the copy snappy, but it wasn't getting as many clicks as she'd hoped, so she spent the afternoon creating several new ad graphics and rewriting the copy to see if people would respond to the second version more.

When she finished, she sat on the floor with Walter. First, she brushed his hair with the grooming glove. Then he wanted to play with his toys. Sarah held the wand with feathers attached to a string overhead as he rolled back and forth, batting it. Once he was amped up, she threw his toy mouse across the room, and he raced toward it and pounced. They repeated the process many times until Walter grew tired. He still had a lot of energy for a six-year-old cat. Not as much as when he was a kitten, but he still played hard.

Heather offered to make dinner—an easy chicken recipe Caleb had given her. Sarah wanted to help, but Heather wouldn't let her. So Sarah hung around anyway, claiming she wanted to see how the meal was made when she just wanted to spend time with her kid.

Sarah heard the garage door open, her signal to set the table and pour glasses of water for the family. After greeting her husband, they sat down to eat.

Jeff took a bite. "This tastes good," he told Heather. "Light and flavorful."

Sarah turned to her daughter. "Everything I eat still tastes bland, so I'll have to take his word for it."

Heather frowned. "I'll make it again when chemo ends," she promised.

That was something to look forward to. Being able to taste one's meal and decide if it was good or bad. Oddly enough, Sarah could taste the chocolate chip cookie she'd eaten recently and remembered liking the pumpkin pie. It was a bit of a paradox. Probably having something to do with the sugar content of the food.

Heather's phone rang. She usually silenced it at dinnertime. Her eyes grew wide as she glanced at it, then picked it up and said, "Hi, Grandpa."

Jeff and Sarah looked her way.

"I'm fine," Heather said. "How are you?"

Silence ensued before Heather added, "Sure. Caleb and I can help with that." There was a pause, and then Heather said, "Okay. We'll see you then."

Heather disconnected and set the phone down. "That was Grandpa. He wanted to know if Caleb and I could help him move into the new condo next weekend."

"He's still buying the condo?" Sarah asked.

Heather shrugged. "I guess so."

Jeff cleared his throat. "That comes as a surprise." He made eye contact with Sarah.

Sarah couldn't believe her father had decided to stay. Suddenly, she needed to move. "I'm going for a walk," she said, rising from her chair.

Jeff's mouth opened halfway, but he said nothing as she marched to the hallway closet, donned her winter gear, then slipped out the front door.

Sarah strode down the sidewalk, breathing in the chill autumn air. Why would Norman stay in Illinois? She'd told him to leave her alone, which meant their relationship was over. So why would he buy the condo if they weren't going to spend time together?

Sarah stopped to look at the full moon. That's when it hit her. Norman hadn't called her; he'd called Heather. He wanted to stay in the area and have a relationship with his granddaughter.

It was a stupid move because Norman would be Norman, and Heather would eventually grow tired of his behavior like Sarah and Mike. Then, once she stopped talking to him, he'd live in a condo surrounded by a family he never saw.

That wasn't Sarah's problem. If he wanted to make a major mistake, it was his choice.

It would make her situation more complicated, though. She planned to forgive her father for his failings but hadn't planned to see him again. That could be tough if he was still in the area and visiting Heather.

Why did Norman always have to be so difficult?

Sarah let out a heavy sigh as she went home. She opened the door and stepped inside, and there stood Heather, looking distraught.

"You're not mad at me, are you?" Heather asked.

Sarah rushed to her daughter and said, "No, honey. I'm not mad at you. I'm just surprised that Norman is staying after our fight. But that has nothing to do with you. If you want to spend time with your grandfather, you should."

Heather didn't look convinced.

"Your relationship with him is separate from mine. You don't have to ignore him out of loyalty to me."

"Are you sure?"

Sarah smiled at her daughter. "I'm sure."

Heather's shoulders relaxed, and the two women hugged. Then, Heather headed to the kitchen to do the dishes while Sarah walked down the hall to the bedroom, where she found Jeff sitting in bed.

"Are you okay?" he asked as she drew near.

"I don't know," Sarah answered honestly.

She climbed into bed, and Jeff said, "You should do what's best for you. If that means creating boundaries, so be it. You don't have to be involved with your father just because Heather is."

"Great minds think alike," Sarah said as she reached for Jeff's hand.

"The main thing is that you not let it cause stress," Jeff added.

No stress, Sarah thought. *Right.*

Jeff turned on the TV after it was obvious that Sarah had no more to say. Instead of the news, he chose an episode of their favorite comedy sitcom, and soon after, he laughed at one of the actor's snarky jokes. The skit was funny; under normal circumstances, Sarah would have enjoyed it.

She lay next to Jeff, wishing it wasn't too late to call her brother. Unfortunately, Mike went to bed early because he started work early, so this particular piece of gossip would have to wait until the next day. Sadly, she was awake past midnight, thinking about her predicament as Jeff lay beside her, sound asleep. Not stressing about it wasn't an option. She was still trying to forgive her father. Now she had to construct a plan to create boundaries.

The next day, Sarah called Mike on his lunch break.

"That's not funny," Mike said when she told him Norman was staying.

"I'm not joking. He called Heather and asked her and Caleb to help him move."

There was a long pause before Mike said, "He has nothing to gain by staying here. He must have oldtimers."

Sarah didn't want to correct her brother and tell him the disease was called Alzheimer's. "He could have a slight case of it. He forgot to pick me up for chemo. Maybe he was telling the truth and mixed up the days?"

"I doubt it, but it's possible. Remember, assholes grow old too."

Sarah chuckled before agreeing, and then Mike had to return to work. After they hung up, Sarah considered the possibility that her father could be suffering from mental decline. She had been so focused on all his shortcomings that she hadn't even entertained the thought. Her heart opened ever so slightly before reminding herself there was no proof he had any cognitive dysfunction and that she wanted nothing to do with him either way.

Sarah focused on her new client instead. She tinkered with his campaign, then stared at her laptop in disbelief.

"What's wrong?" Jeff asked as he entered the room.

Sarah looked up. "Every time I roll out a new ad, the CPC climbs a few days later."

"Is it happening across the board?"

"No. This is the only campaign that's possessed."

Jeff smiled warmly. "I'm sure you'll figure it out. You always do."

Jeff had a dental cleaning appointment, so Sarah wished him luck before returning to her desk. She spent the afternoon creating new audiences to test. If that didn't work, she'd create all new ad copy and go in a different direction with graphic design.

The hours passed quickly as she worked, and for once, she didn't feel as bad as she usually did. There were brief glimpses of wellness from time to time, with fatigue eventually taking her down. She finally succumbed to it later in the afternoon, knowing if she didn't, she'd end up doing more harm in the ads dashboard than good.

The sound of voices woke Sarah. She checked the nightstand clock and realized it was time to eat dinner, then climbed out of bed and headed to the kitchen. Walter nibbled on wet food as Jeff opened a pizza box.

When he saw Sarah, he said, "I know we're trying to eat healthier, but I was in the mood for pizza. I got a sausage for me and Heather and veggie for you."

Sarah appreciated her husband adding vegetables to hers. "That sounds good," she said, grabbing paper plates from the cupboard so there would be less to clean afterward.

Heather put a few small slices on her plate. "I ate lunch not long ago but can't say no to pizza."

"More for me," Jeff said with a grin.

After they sat down, Sarah asked Heather, "What did you have for lunch?"

"Tacos."

Heather usually elaborated on what kind of taco she'd eaten and how it compared to tacos she'd eaten before. Her one-word answer seemed odd to Sarah.

"I went to lunch with Grandpa," Heather added.

Sarah tried to hide her surprise. Instead, she nodded approvingly and said, "That's nice."

"He wanted help picking out a sofa," Heather continued.

Sarah's mouth was full. After she swallowed her food, she asked, "Did you guys find one?"

Heather got up to get another piece of pizza. "Eventually, but it took forever because so many good ones were out of stock." She sat back down. "Plus, we got a late start. We were supposed to have lunch first, then shop, but for some reason, Grandpa went to the furniture store instead of the restaurant, so we didn't eat until after we found the couch."

"Didn't you tell Norman where to meet you?" Jeff asked.

"I told him the name of the restaurant, but I texted him the name of the furniture store. He must have got confused."

Sarah took another bite of pizza. This time, there was no ulterior motive for making such a mistake. Perhaps her dad was suffering from mental decline. "What kind of sofa did he buy?" Sarah asked, trying to be polite.

Heather wiped her mouth with a napkin. "A light gray sectional. One of those big ones, so there's room for everyone to sit."

Everyone, Sarah thought.

Who the heck was that?

But it was none of Sarah's business, so she didn't ask.

Chapter 30

Nancy was all smiles on her last day of treatment. Sarah sat next to her, anxious to hear how things went last week while being somewhat sad that she wouldn't see her friend from now on. The nurse attached the line to Sarah's port and offered her a warm blanket. Sarah accepted it since the room had grown colder as the temperature dropped outside.

"Last day," Sarah mentioned once they were free to chat. "You must be thrilled."

"I am. The only thing I'll miss about this place is seeing you."

Sarah smiled. "Let's get together one day when we're both feeling better. Something easy, like meeting for lunch."

"I'd like that," Nancy said.

Dr. Zimmerman walked through the treatment room. She rarely did because she was so busy with patients, most of whom looked up at her as she passed.

When their doctor was gone, Sarah turned back to Nancy and asked, "How was your week?"

"Busy. I did some cleaning and reorganizing to make room for my sister. She came by twice with boxes, and I helped her unpack." Nancy paused. "I helped as much as I could, that is."

Sarah gave her a knowing look. "I hear you."

"She's going to make Thanksgiving dinner for me, my son, and his girlfriend."

"That will be nice," Sarah replied.

Thanksgiving was right around the corner, which meant Sarah, Jeff, Heather, and Caleb would go to Beverly and Richard's house for an epic feast that Beverly and Caleb would cook. Sarah realized for the first time that Norman would spend the holiday alone. She pictured him sitting on a large gray sectional sofa in his new condo and felt sad. But he had chosen to move there even though it was a bad idea. It wasn't Sarah's fault.

"How was your week?" Nancy asked Sarah. "Have you made any progress on forgiving your dad?"

Sarah sighed. "I took one step forward and two steps back."

Nancy gave Sarah an empathetic look and waited for her to explain.

Sarah continued. "I planned to forgive him for the past but discontinue our relationship in the future. Then, out of nowhere, my daughter told me he called and asked her to help him move to the new condo. I had no idea he was still buying it. I assumed he would've gone home."

Nancy stayed quiet.

"Last weekend, he and my daughter went furniture shopping. He bought a large sectional sofa, so there was room for everyone to sit."

"It sounds like your father isn't giving up on you."

"What do you mean?" Sarah asked.

"Even though you got into a fight and told him to leave you alone, he stayed. So he's hoping you'll change your mind down the road."

Sarah let out an exasperated sigh. "That's my fear."

"Why is that so scary?" Nancy asked.

Sarah drew a deep breath and stared into the distance as she let it out. She turned to Nancy and said, "Because I don't want to be forced into a dysfunctional relationship. Time is short, as we've both learned, and I want to spend my time with loving, supportive people. I don't have the energy for drama."

Nancy nodded in agreement before asking, "What if you could eliminate drama?"

"I did by cutting ties with my dad."

"That's one way to do it, but there's another way."

"I'm all ears," Sarah said, eager for her friend to dispense this arcane truth.

Nancy wrinkled her forehead. "I have to warn you that it's not easy to do."

Sarah had figured as much.

"The key is to let go of expectations and accept people for who they are." She paused to let Sarah absorb that before continuing. "For instance, if your father is unreliable and self-absorbed, you can acknowledge those traits without wanting to change them. He's a senior citizen, so he's unlikely to change whether you want him to or not."

Sarah listened without comment as Nancy went on to say, "If you can accept him as he is and not let his character flaws aggravate you, there's a chance you could actually enjoy each other's company."

Sarah gave Nancy a sideways glance.

"Remember, I said it wasn't easy," she reiterated.

Sarah stared out the hospital window and began rapidly tapping her fingers on the chair as she gave the concept some thought. It sounded good in theory, like eating right and exercising or saving ten percent of one's income. Everyone knew they should do those things, but it was tough.

"It's something to think about," Nancy said. "No one is saying it's what you have to do."

Sarah bobbed her head. She sat there, considering her family's negative traits. Heather didn't keep her room as tidy as Sarah would've liked, preferring a more lived-in look, and Jeff had that annoying habit of not rinsing the sink after brushing his teeth. Mike swore too much, and Beverly repeated things a little more these days, but none of their habits were deal-breakers. They could be overlooked, just as her bad habits were overlooked by the ones she loved.

Why was it so different when it came to Norman?

Sarah realized it was because his bad habits were ten times worse than everyone else's. They were toxic. And disregarding them would require the patience of a saint. Sarah appreciated Nancy's good advice but felt it would be impossible to take this time.

Just then, Nancy's nurse came to check on her, followed by Sarah's nurse, who had Sarah's cold gloves and booties ready for her to don before starting the chemotherapy which could cause neuropathy in her hands and toes.

"Are you going to ring the bell today?" Sarah asked Nancy when they'd left.

"No. It's not the same the second time."

The two women were quiet for the rest of the session. Nancy's ended before Sarah's, and when she rose from her chair and gathered her things, Sarah felt the true meaning of "bittersweet."

"Good luck with your surgery," Sarah told her.

"Thanks." Nancy slung her purse over her shoulder and smiled. "I'm looking forward to that lunch date. In the meantime, don't be a stranger. Feel free to call or text."

"I will," Sarah promised.

Sarah watched Nancy leave the treatment room, wondering if she'd ever see her again. Both wanted to meet in the future, but it would only happen if the fates allowed.

Closing her eyes, Sarah circled back to their earlier talk. Nancy had proposed an elegant solution to her problem, one she had used with her sister. Instead of preaching benevolent words, she spoke from experience, which made her advice carry considerable weight. The only thing Sarah couldn't figure out was how Nancy had accomplished such a feat.

Chapter 31

Saturday was moving day for Norman. Heather showered and poured herself a bowl of cereal for breakfast, rushing to finish before Caleb arrived.

Sarah sat at the kitchen table with a cup of coffee in her hands. "I feel funny that Caleb knows about the argument Norman and I had. I'm worried he will think less of me."

Heather lifted a spoonful of cereal to her mouth. "He understands. His family has had their fair share of fights."

Sarah knew all families had problems. She just didn't want Caleb to get the wrong impression. To an outsider, Norman may look like a sweet older man who only wanted to help and was being mistreated by his children.

"Don't worry," Heather said.

Her daughter tipped the cereal bowl so she could drink the remaining milk, then took her dish to the sink before disappearing to her room. When she reemerged, she had a large, wrapped box in hand.

"What's that?" Sarah asked.

"A Keurig coffee machine. Grandpa had an old-school coffee pot, but it broke."

Sarah took a sip of her coffee and said, "That's thoughtful."

Heather was such a good person. She could probably do everything Nancy had suggested with ease. *A byproduct of youth*, Sarah thought, realizing she had become jaded with time.

"I won't be home for dinner," Heather said as she set the gift down so she could put on her coat. "Caleb and I are going to the airport with Grandpa."

Sarah was confused. "Why are you going to the airport?"

"To pick up Linda."

Sarah's eyes grew wide. "Linda's coming to visit?"

"No, she's moving here." Heather grabbed the gift, adding, "I guess she wanted to make up with Grandpa, and he said he would try again, but only if it was in Illinois."

Genius, Sarah thought. *Leave the younger man she had cheated on him with behind and make a fresh start while simultaneously building a relationship with his granddaughter.*

That wasn't the plan of a man suffering cognitive decline. On the contrary, Norman's mind seemed to be working just fine.

Chapter 32

The next two chemo sessions were boring without Nancy around. Sure, there were other patients Sarah could've talked to, but she was almost done with treatment, so it didn't make sense to get friendly with someone new. Plus, it wouldn't be the same. Sarah and Nancy had thought-provoking conversations that stayed with Sarah long after she left the hospital. And they had the same type of breast cancer. They were meant to meet each other and connect. Sarah was sure all the other women at the cancer center were wonderful, but she had no desire to befriend any of them at this time. Soon, she'd be out of this place and, hopefully, never return.

After Sarah's nurse came to check on her, a text arrived from Nancy: "*Only one more session left!*"

The two women texted back and forth about restaurants they wanted to try, preferring to make plans than discuss the disease. Nancy mentioned a Thai place she'd read about, and Sarah suggested a family-owned Italian chain that Caleb loved. They sent each other menus to peruse, and by the time they finished chatting, Sarah's session ended.

Nancy was having surgery a week after Sarah's birthday, only two weeks away. Of course, that meant Sarah's surgery was fast approaching. She still wrestled with her decision to have no reconstruction but reminded herself that she could get breast reconstruction later. The breast surgeon said chemo was the hardest, and surgery wasn't as bad. Sarah had never had surgery but figured if they gave her good drugs afterward, she would survive.

The next day, she was still thinking of her upcoming surgery after she finished working on her new client's ad, which, thankfully, had started to behave and now had low CPC. She was on her way to the restroom when the doorbell rang. Since she wasn't expecting anyone, she ignored it. But then it rang again.

And again.

Annoyed, she padded to the front door, staying out of view as she approached. Then, peering out the side of the window, she saw who it was and gasped.

Sarah opened the door and came face to face with Linda. Her business casual wardrobe and short brown layered bob were the same.

"Hi," Linda said warily. "I hope I didn't wake you?"

"No, you didn't. I was just finishing work. Please, come in."

Sarah stepped aside and let Linda enter, wondering why she was coming by unannounced.

They went to the living room, and Sarah gestured for Linda to sit on the sofa. Silence ensued as the women sat opposite each other, and then finally, Linda spoke.

"I'm sorry to drop by without calling first, but I was

hoping we could talk." Linda shifted in her seat before saying, "First off, I'd like to say I'm sorry that this happened to you. It's so unfair."

"Thank you," Sarah said.

Linda paused, looking like she was trying to find the best way to say what she had to say. "As you know, your father and I had a rough patch, but we're trying to work it out."

Sarah nodded, thinking sleeping with her father's much younger business associate sounded like more than a rough patch. If she'd said it about anyone but Norman, Sarah might have pointed out the difference between adultery and a rough patch, but this time, she let it slide.

"Anyway," Linda continued. "Recently, I called your father and asked if we could talk. He came out to see me and somehow mixed up the dates he was supposed to take you to treatment." She looked down at her lap, obviously embarrassed. "Well, you know what happened after that."

Sarah wasn't comfortable with the direction this conversation was heading and willed Linda to get to the point.

Linda looked up and made eye contact with her. "Your father is just heartbroken over what happened. He's upset that you two aren't speaking and that he couldn't take you to the chemo treatments."

Sarah crossed her arms, wishing she hadn't answered the door.

"He mentioned the bell-ringing ceremony is next week. Last night, he was crying because he's going to miss it, and I felt awful because it's all my fault."

Sarah couldn't picture Norman crying over such a thing. And why would Linda blame herself?

"If I hadn't called and asked him to talk," she explained, "he wouldn't have come out to see me."

Sarah was about to mention that Norman was a grown man who knew how to use a calendar when Linda barreled ahead. "I feel so guilty that I not only ruined our marriage but that I ruined his new and improved relationship with you. I'm doing everything I can to fix our marriage, and now I'm here to see if there is any way you can forgive me for causing a problem between you and your dad."

"You didn't cause the problem," Sarah said. "It has nothing to do with you."

Linda frowned. "He keeps relating the two incidents. He hasn't said it's my fault, but I still feel I'm to blame."

Sarah sighed in frustration. It seemed that Linda wouldn't accept that this problem fell on Norman and Norman alone.

"Your father will never forgive me if he can't go to that bell-ringing ceremony. It will drive a wedge between us that I can't fix." She paused to take a deep breath. "Is there any chance you would allow him to come? For me?"

The desperation on Linda's face tugged at Sarah's heartstrings. Although this woman had done her father wrong, she had always been nice to her. Norman probably deserved the marital problems he experienced anyway. Most likely, it was karma coming home to roost.

But Linda, for whatever reason, wanted what they once had back. She was willing to do the work.

Linda wore a hopeful expression as she waited for Sarah's reply.

Sarah uncrossed her arms. "Can I think about it for a day?"

"Of course. Definitely." Linda pulled her phone from her purse. "Let me give you my number so you can call me tomorrow."

Sarah rose and grabbed her phone from the kitchen counter. They exchanged numbers, and then Linda headed to the door, perhaps anxious to leave before Sarah changed her mind.

Once she was gone, Sarah sank into the club chair, completely overwhelmed. Nancy's smiling face came to mind, along with her lofty advice. Sarah could forgive her father for not being the parent she had wanted him to be. Over the last few weeks, she managed to get to that point. But what Linda wanted was too much. If Sarah did it, she'd be giving in. She'd be saying it's okay to be a complete screw-up of a parent—that Norman didn't have to follow the rules her mother had followed but would still be included in the family either way.

No expectations, Nancy had said. *Accept the person as they are and don't require them to change.*

Sarah closed her eyes before taking a deep breath and letting it out. She wasn't sure she was capable of doing what Nancy had done. She wasn't even sure if she wanted to.

Stress kills, is how the saying went. And it was horrible

for cancer patients.

On the one hand, keeping her father out of her life seemed the right choice. She was going through treatment without drama. She could tell Linda no and stay on that path. Norman would still have Heather, and her daughter wouldn't push Sarah to try and reconnect.

As Sarah considered option number two, she couldn't figure out how it would benefit her. She wasn't a new age guru or religious, like Nancy, so having no expectations of people, especially of a parent, was out of the question. Norman wouldn't change. And she'd stopped thinking he would. If she allowed him back into her life, he'd annoy her again and again. That was a fact.

Linda had seemed desperate, though. The success of repairing her marriage hung on this event.

Sarah lay awake that night, weighing the options of each decision over and over. She knew Mike's opinion without asking and what Nancy would say. Heather wanted to stay neutral, and Jeff had made it clear that he was with Sarah no matter what she chose.

Now all Sarah had to do was make a decision.

She showered and ate breakfast in the afternoon, having slept late because she couldn't fall asleep until three am. She checked her clients' ads and made minor tweaks, then grabbed her phone and called Linda.

"Hello," Linda said after picking up on the second ring.

"Hey, Linda. It's Sarah. I wanted to let you know that you and my father are invited to the bell-ringing ceremony and birthday party."

"Wonderful!" Linda exclaimed.

Soon, Sarah would learn if it had been a wise choice or a terrible mistake.

Chapter 33

Dr. Zimmerman did a manual breast exam and felt under Sarah's underarms. She listened to her inhale and exhale and checked all the other little things she did every time they saw each other. When she finished, she stepped back and asked, "How are you feeling?"

Sarah was feeling a lot of things, but she knew her doctor wanted to know about her physical symptoms. "There's some numbness in the tips of my fingers and toes. I wore the cold gloves and booties for every session, so I'm not sure what happened."

"They prevent it for most people. But the more Taxol sessions you have, the greater the risk." Dr. Zimmerman saw Sarah frown and added, "The neuropathy could improve in time. Many patients have had it go away."

Sarah noticed her doctor had said it might improve. She wished she could tell her with certainty what would happen but realized there was no way she could know for sure. She was only a physician—one who was doing her very best.

"But today's the last day!" Dr. Zimmerman said with a wide smile. "I heard you've got quite a group gathered to see you ring the bell. That's not common, but we made an exception since you asked in advance. A nurse will come out and get your family when it's time."

Sarah smiled at her doctor, glad the hospital had been accommodating. After changing her clothes, she was taken to the treatment room and sat down before a nurse attached the line to her port. She started her on fluids and then began Benadryl. Sarah quickly became drowsy from the drug and closed her eyes, planning to rest so she could be awake for the party afterward.

Jeff, Sarah, Heather, Mike, Beverly, and Richard had taken the train downtown together as though they were having a fun family outing rather than a trip to chemotherapy treatment. Norman and Linda said they'd drive to the hospital instead, which made Mike happy. He wasn't thrilled that Sarah had caved to Linda's request, but like Jeff, he said he would respect her decision and promised to be on his best behavior. Her brother had even skipped his beloved weed today, saying he was already riding high because his sister was finishing chemo.

Toward the end of Sarah's session, her phone vibrated. Nancy had texted, "*You made it, girl. Congrats!*"

Sarah texted back, "*Thanks! I'll send you pictures from the party!*" She put her phone back in her purse and sighed deeply. She'd made it. Even though she didn't think she could. Sarah couldn't wait to hit that bell and get the heck out of this room.

A few minutes later, Sarah's machine beeped, signaling the end of her session. Her nurse arrived and flushed her port, and then she let Sarah use the restroom before taking her to the area where she was supposed to ring the bell.

"I'm going to get your family. I'll be right back," her nurse said before dashing off.

Sarah's relatives filed in one by one. Even Dr. Zimmerman appeared. Medical staff and relatives gathered around Sarah, surrounding her with love and hope. A brass bell protruded from the wall, its inner white rope beckoning to Sarah. She briefly made eye contact with each of her family members, then glanced at Dr. Zimmerman, who nodded at her, signaling it was time.

With one last look at her mom, Sarah grabbed the rope and swung it back and forth. The bell rang multiple times, followed by thunderous clapping and hoots. Although Sarah was tired from treatment, the experience gave her an adrenaline rush, making her feel awake and alive. Her brother high-fived her, and then Heather rushed in and gave her a big hug. Beverly hugged her next, followed by a quick hug from Richard, then Linda.

Norman wiped a tear from his eye and pulled Sarah into his arms. "I'm so proud of you," he said as he held her close.

Speechless, Sarah nodded after her father released her. Then she stepped forward and faced Jeff.

Her husband didn't say a word. Instead, he took her face in his hands and kissed her on the lips like in the movies. This caused another wave of clapping and hoots, making Sarah blush. She and Jeff pulled apart, and she turned to see everyone smiling at her.

As the medical staff returned to their duties, Sarah's family began to leave—everyone except Mike. Sarah saw him talking to Dr. Zimmerman. Her doctor handed him something, and then they smiled at each other before Mike arrived at Sarah's side.

"What's going on?" Sarah asked him on their way out.

Mike rubbed his hands together and grinned mischievously. "I just scored a date with your doctor."

"For real?" Sarah asked.

Mike nodded. "For real."

Everyone left the treatment room and went their separate ways, Norman and Linda heading to the parking lot and Sarah and the rest of the group heading to hail a cab to the train station.

On the cab ride over, Sarah was elated to be done with chemotherapy and stunned that her brother had asked Dr. Zimmerman on a date. He'd been looking for the right woman, and Dr. Zimmerman was everything he said he wanted. Sarah remembered her mentioning some changes in her life, changes that inspired a new hairdo. Perhaps, she'd gotten a divorce or survived a bad breakup. Sarah had no idea because she didn't know her that well. She briefly wondered if dating a patient's relative was allowed, then shrugged, not caring either way.

Jeff put his arm around Sarah after they got seated on the train. She snuggled up to him and watched Mike and Heather, sitting opposite her, chat animatedly. Mike was telling her one of his funny stories, complete with the colorful language he had become famous for, and Heather was laughing and slapping her knee. Her mom and stepdad were sitting nearby, silently holding hands, looking relieved that a big part of Sarah's cancer journey would soon be part of the past.

Sarah's eyelids grew heavy, and before she knew it, she was out. Jeff gently roused her before their stop, and she yawned, glad she'd had a chance to rest because the party would be starting soon, and she wanted to be awake enough to enjoy it.

Caleb greeted them when they got home. He'd been there all day, cooking up a feast. Jeff had offered to cater the event, but Caleb wouldn't hear of it, so Jeff offered to pay him instead. Caleb would only take enough to cover the groceries. He insisted that making the meal was his gift to Sarah.

Everyone hung their coats in the closet, and Sarah went to the restroom. As she washed her hands, she felt things were going well so far. She hoped things would continue to go well after Norman and Linda arrived. Eating and mingling for hours was a lot more difficult than clapping and cheering at the hospital. Not only did she and her brother just have a fight with her father, but Beverly would have to be friendly to her ex-husband and converse with Linda, a woman Beverly didn't even know.

As Sarah exited the bathroom, she saw Mike. She headed toward him and asked, "How did you score a date with Dr. Zimmerman? I mean, how did that conversation go?"

"I saw you look over at her, and the first thing I thought was, dang, she's fine. Then I realized she was your doctor, so I went over and introduced myself. Then

I asked if she was single."

"You went from hello, my name is Mike, to asking her marital status? Just like that?"

"Yep," Mike nodded. "Just like that."

Sarah was about to ask him what happened next but didn't have to because he continued. "When she said she was single, I took that as my cue to ask her if she'd like to get together sometime. She smiled, said she would, and then gave me her business card. She told me to call her and leave a message with my name and number and that she'd call me back to coordinate schedules."

"Wow," Sarah said, her mind blown. Things moved a lot more quickly these days, probably because everyone was so busy. If there was an opportunity to connect with someone, it had to be seized; otherwise, it could slip away as fast as it had occurred.

As Sarah contemplated the new world of dating, the doorbell rang. She looked up at Mike.

"Don't worry," he said. "Best behavior."

Norman and Linda walked in, a birthday present in Linda's hands. Heather took it from her and set it on the coffee table before hanging their coats in the closet and offering them something to drink. Mike and Sarah entered the room, and Caleb announced, "The food is ready. Feel free to grab a plate and get started." He gestured to the stack of plates next to the trays of warm food on the counter.

Heather started, followed by Norman and Linda. Beverly and Richard stood behind them, politely taking the serving spoon for each dish when they had finished putting a scoop of food on their plates. Jeff and Sarah were next, then came Mike and Caleb. Once everyone had their chicken marsala, mashed potatoes, and broccoli, they headed to the table. They sat in the same order, creating a buffer between Mike and Norman but putting Linda and Beverly at each other's side.

Jeff lifted his glass of beer and turned to Sarah. "To many more birthdays."

Sarah lifted her glass of water and clinked it against his glass. As she did, everyone said happy birthday at different times, creating a happy birthday echo. Sarah smiled and said thanks and then dug into her food.

"How are you liking the new condo?" Heather asked Linda.

"It's nice. I'm still learning my way around town."

Caleb put his fork down and told Norman, "There's a good butcher near your house. I'll give you his name."

"Thanks," Norman replied.

So far, Beverly hadn't spoken, perhaps because she didn't know what to say.

Linda turned to Beverly and said, "If there are any good nail salons nearby, let me know."

"There are a few," Beverly replied, appearing relieved to have something to add.

Sarah watched everyone chat, periodically glancing at Mike, who was immersed in his meal and seemed not to care that Norman was there. Jeff put his hand on the top of her thigh and gently patted it, sending a sign that all was going well and that she should relax.

Caleb and Richard talked about culinary school, and

Norman joined in, commenting on things here and there.

"Who wants cake?" Caleb said after Heather and Beverly cleared the table and put the plates in the dishwasher.

"I do!" Sarah exclaimed, eager for dessert after not having it in what felt like years.

Beverly put candles on the cake as Jeff dimmed the lights. Her mother brought it to Sarah's side of the table and set it down in front of her, and although they'd all said happy birthday earlier, they began singing the tune.

Sarah felt like a kid again, like when her friends came over to one of the many birthday parties her mom had thrown for her when she was young. She made eye contact with each family member as they sang, then inhaled and blew out the candles, wishing to grow old with Jeff.

Everyone clapped afterward, and Sarah smiled at her family, ready to eat. Caleb used a large knife to cut the cake, then began putting slices on plates. Heather ensured everyone had a serving and asked if they wanted milk or coffee to drink.

Sarah dug into the chocolate cake, making sure to get plenty of frosting on her fork. She put it into her mouth and sighed. It wasn't as good as it could be because of chemo, but it was the best-tasting thing she'd eaten since the cancer journey began.

The look on Sarah's face must've said everything because Heather grinned at her. "It's good, right?"

"So good," Sarah said.

After dessert, the group moved to the living room,

where Sarah opened her gifts. Jeff got her a cashmere sweater she had been wanting, and Heather and Caleb got her a Nutribullet, saying it was easier to use than the juicer, so she could continue making green drinks and smoothies with less clean-up time. Mike got her a book by her favorite author, and Beverly and Richard got her a gift card for several visits to the movie theater near her house.

Sarah reached for Linda and Norman's gift. She unwrapped it and discovered it was an empty photo album.

"For family photos," Linda said as Sarah opened the box.

Sarah looked at Linda and Norman and said, "Thanks."

She didn't print photos anymore, as most resided on her phone, but she decided to get into the habit so she could fill the album. It was a thoughtful gift.

Although Sarah was having fun, it had been a long day, and she was tired. She sat on the sofa as Beverly gathered the ripped wrapping paper and threw it in the trash, and Caleb and Heather washed the dessert dishes by hand. Linda went to the kitchen and offered to help as Jeff took a bathroom break.

Mike and Norman stood by themselves, looking like they had no idea what to do. Finally, Mike walked toward his dad, and they began talking. Sarah couldn't hear what they were saying because they were too far from where she sat, but she could tell from their body language that nothing was wrong.

Mike said he would never fall in line for Norman, but he had done it for her.

Sarah was grateful to have him as a big brother.

Chapter 34

Sarah stared at her laptop calendar, noting the mastectomy was only three days away. She'd been eyeing the date frequently in the last four weeks since chemo ended and sleeping twelve hours per day, trying to regain her strength. She'd been acting like the upcoming surgery didn't bother her because everyone thought she was strong when in truth, she was terrified and felt like an animal headed to the slaughterhouse, anxious to escape.

But unlike the animals who died for food, this surgery would save Sarah's life. She reminded herself of that whenever fear set in. She tried to think of the breast surgeon as a savior instead of a scary person with a scalpel. It helped a little, but mostly, the procedure frightened her.

Sarah's cell phone rang, grabbing her attention. She answered immediately after seeing it was Nancy, who'd had her mastectomy two weeks ago.

"How are you feeling?" Sarah asked.

"I'm all right." Nancy's voice sounded weaker than usual. Sarah waited for her to say more. "It's tough," Nancy added. "I had flap reconstruction before, so both breasts were there when I woke up." She paused. "It will take time to get used to this."

Nancy's usual sunny outlook was cloudy at best, which was to be expected after all she had been through. Sarah hoped that her friend would be given the time needed to accept her new look and thrive. Because if Nancy couldn't overcome this emotional hurdle, there was no chance Sarah could do it.

"My sister was a big help with the surgical drains," Nancy continued.

"My mom offered to do mine, which was great because the idea of emptying bodily fluids from a bulb and recording its levels made my husband and daughter queasy."

Nancy chuckled, and then they revisited their future lunch plans and chatted about that for a bit.

"Good luck with your surgery," Nancy said at the end of their conversation. "Look at the scar by yourself first," she suggested. "Then show it to your husband when you're ready."

"Okay," Sarah replied, appreciating the tip.

When Sarah hung up, she felt glum. Jeff entered the bedroom shortly afterward and sat down behind her. He gently massaged her shoulders and asked, "How is your friend doing?"

Jeff wasn't an eavesdropper, but he must've been able to glean who Sarah was talking to from what he'd heard her say. "She's all right. But she said it's tough."

Jeff focused on a knot in her left shoulder. "Good thing she can give you advice," he said softly. "I'm glad you two met."

Sarah was glad too. Many cancer patients made small

talk during treatment, but not everyone met a true friend.

The shoulder massage lifted Sarah's spirits. She started listening to a new audiobook afterward, pausing it when her brother stopped by to see her, which improved her mood more.

"How are things with Dr. Zimmerman?" Sarah asked after they sat on the sofa.

"We went on a second date, so I think she likes me." Mike threw his hands up and smiled. "Who knew that opposites attract?"

Sarah smiled, too, thinking everyone knew that adage. "Wouldn't it be funny if she was the one?"

"It wouldn't be funny. It would be awesome." Mike's expression grew more serious. "Maybe something good could come from all of this."

She and her brother held each other's gaze without speaking, and then he asked, "How's the old man? Is he bugging the shit out of you?"

"No," Sarah replied. "He's giving me space. Although, he and Linda will be in the waiting room with everyone else after the surgery."

Mike nodded. "Cool."

They discussed the upcoming mastectomy, and Mike told her he would pray for her. They hugged before he left, and Sarah took a bath afterward, needing time alone. As she soaked in the warm water, she thought about Christmas being right around the corner. Losing a breast wasn't on anyone's wish list, but beating cancer would be the best gift Sarah could receive.

It was all a matter of perception, she decided. And it

was better to think positively.

***

Heather was Sarah's shadow the last few days before the surgery, offering to make dinner, wash dishes, and empty the kitty litter. Her daughter took care of everything so Sarah could rest, all while studying for finals at school.

Jeff gave Sarah extra love and attention as well. He was always hugging her, rubbing her back, and being cuddly in general.

The night before the surgery, Jeff lit a candle before he and Sarah got into bed. He looked into her eyes as he unbuttoned her pajama top. It slid down her shoulders and landed on the mattress, and then he began gently kissing every inch of the breast she was going to lose.

Tears welled in Sarah's eyes as he said his unspoken goodbyes. She remembered the many wonderful nights they had shared throughout the years, noting this would be the last one like this. Tears spilled down Sarah's cheeks, and Jeff kissed them away. Then Sarah broke down. She began sobbing, and Jeff pulled her close.

"It's going to be all right," he whispered, rocking her back and forth.

Jeff handed her a box of tissues so she could blow her nose. While she did, he snuffed the candle before returning to bed. The rest of the night, he held Sarah in his arms. She was still in them when she woke the following day. It was as if he didn't want to let her go.

***

Sarah, Jeff, and Heather arrived at the hospital. Beverly, Richard, and Mike were there, along with Linda and Norman. Everyone had come together to wish Sarah good luck and said they'd be waiting for her when she woke up.

Jeff hugged and kissed Sarah one last time before she had to go. "I love you."

"Love you too," Sarah replied before walking through the double doors.

Because Sarah was having underarm lymph nodes removed, the surgeon said she'd need a procedure done before surgery. A procedure he preferred she was awake for even though she would get knocked out right afterward.

An ultrasound technician promised Sarah she wouldn't feel a thing. All they needed to do was mark the lymph nodes so the surgeon would know which ones to remove, and marking them meant sticking needles into Sarah's underarm.

"We're going to numb the area before we start," the female tech said. "You'll feel one needle prick. That's it."

Sarah took a deep breath and waited for the familiar sting. She closed her eyes as they went about their business, grateful she didn't feel the needles that followed the first.

"We're all done," the woman finally said, a warm smile on her face.

Sarah let out a deep breath and was taken to the

surgery area, where a team of people introduced themselves. Sarah's breast surgeon was among them. He smiled and assured Sarah that everything would be fine. However, she had to sign something before they started anesthesia. That's when she realized why they wanted her to be awake for the other procedure. It was because she had to be coherent enough to sign this form.

Soon, the anesthesia kicked in, and the next thing Sarah remembered was hearing someone repeatedly calling her name. She woke up in a room, feeling groggy and sore.

Jeff and Heather arrived a little later. Sarah couldn't talk much because she was tired, but she assured them she was doing okay.

The next time Sarah woke, her mom was at her bedside with a tray of food.

"I thought you might be hungry," Beverly said. "I ordered you something bland."

Instead of asking how Sarah was doing, Beverly went straight into mothering mode. Sarah ate a few bites of mashed potatoes and baked chicken. She hadn't eaten since the night before and was hungry but couldn't finish her meal because she was too tired.

A nurse woke her again to give her pain medicine. Beverly, along with the half-eaten tray of food, were gone. Sarah had to use the restroom, which meant getting out of bed, something she wasn't keen to do. Thankfully, her nurse was patient and kind. The young woman helped her out of bed and waited for her to finish before helping her back into bed again. The simple task exhausted Sarah. She closed her eyes and fell asleep right away.

The next day, a doctor came to check on her. He ensured all was well before saying it was okay for Sarah to go home. Jeff picked up her pain medication at the hospital pharmacy as a nurse told Beverly how to care for the surgical drains. Her mom had already watched videos on how to do them online. Still, she listened carefully as the woman explained the procedure, taking the written instructions and tucking them into her purse.

Jeff and Beverly went to get the car as the nurse helped Sarah into her mastectomy top, which snapped in the front and had inner pockets for the drains. Before the surgery, a nurse told Sarah she wouldn't be able to pull shirts over her head for a while. She recommended button-down blouses or the mastectomy top. Sarah had bought two mastectomy tops so she would have one to wear while the other was being washed. The breast cancer website she bought them from also had other helpful items: a pillow that provided protection from the car seatbelt and a shower lanyard that kept the drains secure. Sarah had purchased those as well, figuring anything that could make life easier during this experience was a must.

A nurse got her into a wheelchair and took her to meet her family at the hospital exit, and then Sarah climbed into the back seat of the car. Jeff carefully tucked the mastectomy pillow, which had armhole cutouts on both sides, under her arms. She could still feel the pressure of the seat belt on her chest, but it was mild. The pillow made her feel safe on the road.

Once they got home, Beverly helped Sarah get

comfortable in her bed, propping multiple pillows against her headboard so she could sleep on an angle, as lying flat on her back hurt her chest.

Jeff brought Sarah her pain medication and a glass of water. He set both on the nightstand, and then he and Beverly stood next to the bed, looking unsure of what to do next.

"Feels good to be home," Sarah said.

After she uttered those words, Walter jumped on the bed and walked toward her. Instinctively, she reached for her mastectomy pillow and put it over her chest, worried her cat may bump her wound.

Walter stopped in his tracks and curled into a ball near Sarah's hip.

"It's like he knows," Beverly said.

"He does," Jeff agreed. "The cat is super smart."

Sarah used her good arm to rub Walter's head. In return, he purred.

Beverly eyed Sarah. "We'll let you get some rest. We're here if you need anything. Just call out."

As Beverly left the room, Jeff bent down to kiss Sarah but stopped midway.

"It's okay," she told him.

He kissed her on the forehead. "I'm afraid of hurting you."

"Your lips are soft, so they won't hurt."

Jeff nodded. "True."

He left her with Walter and joined Beverly, who was spending the next two weeks at Sarah's house so she could take care of the drains and help her with whatever she needed while Jeff was at work. Heather had offered Beverly her bed, saying she could sleep on the couch. When Sarah heard them discussing it, she suggested Heather stay at Caleb's. That way, she could study in peace while her mom took care of Sarah. At first, Heather seemed like she wanted to argue back and forth about it, but thankfully, she didn't. Her daughter was able to see it was a win-win for all involved.

Sarah fell asleep again. When she woke, her mom sat next to her, reviewing the written instructions for the drains.

"We should do this," Beverly said, trying to sound enthusiastic but looking intimidated.

Although Sarah had given birth to a child, she couldn't bear to look as her mother completed the task. When Beverly finished logging the fluid output on the sheet the nurse had given her, she went to the bathroom to dispose of the drain bulb's contents and wash her hands. When she returned, she pulled her phone off the dresser and began typing.

"Are you recording the levels on your phone too?" Sarah asked.

"No, I'm updating Norman."

Her parents were communicating again. She guessed that if Mike managed to converse politely with her father at the party, her mother could resume her former role.

Heather and Caleb had stopped by to drop off dinner and see how Sarah was doing while she was sleeping. Sarah felt terrible that she had missed her daughter's visit but was grateful they had brought food so Beverly didn't have to cook.

Time passed fast. It was a blur of naps and pain meds, interspersed with drain duty and bites of food. Finally, the moment Sarah had been trying to avoid arrived. She had to shower, which meant taking off her clothes and seeing her scar.

Sarah grabbed her shower lanyard, a fresh towel, and a clean mastectomy top and headed to the bathroom. She removed her slippers, took off her sweatpants, and, after hesitating, began unsnapping her blouse.

Sarah stared at herself in the mirror as the top fell to the floor. The left side of her chest was covered with green and purple bruises. Her left breast had been replaced by a scar that ran from the center of her chest to her underarm. Sarah continued to gaze at herself in the mirror, feeling numb. She thought she'd be sad or angry, but for some reason, she felt strangely detached. The woman she saw was her, but it didn't feel that way. It was like looking at a person Sarah didn't know.

Chapter 35

Christmas was low-key since Sarah was still recovering. Her family ate dinner together and exchanged a few gifts, but that was all. Norman called to wish Sarah a Merry Christmas. He didn't invite her over or push for them to get together anytime soon, which allowed Sarah to relax. Perhaps, now that he and Linda were back together, they were busy trying to fix their marriage, or maybe Linda was advising Norman to give things time.

Whatever was happening behind the scenes, Sarah was just happy that there was no drama and that her father was a part of her life, if only in a small dose. Sarah was busy healing. Her mind was preoccupied with accepting her new body image and anxiously awaiting the pathology report. It was supposed to be ready soon. Then she'd know if she had beaten the disease or not.

Beverly told Sarah that the drain fluid levels were low enough to have them removed, so Sarah called the cancer center, and they managed to get her in with the breast surgeon's assistant the next day. She used her mastectomy pillow on the car ride to the train station but chose to leave it in her mom's car when they boarded the train. Sarah glanced back at it longingly. It had become somewhat of a security blanket she used to protect her chest. It wasn't easy to leave it behind.

Sarah held her arms in front of her chest as she boarded the train. It was the only thing she could do to make sure another passenger didn't accidentally bump into her. She also sat near the window so the people getting on and off at each stop wouldn't get too close.

"You must be excited to get those things out," Beverly said after the train started moving.

"I am, but Nancy told me it feels weird when they do it. And they don't knock you out or numb you. It happens while you're wide awake."

Beverly shook her head. "Of course!"

Although Sarah appreciated all the medical community had done for her, she felt that many things could be easier on patients if it weren't for health insurance policies. For example, a person could stay in the hospital a little longer after surgery and have a nurse care for them instead of sending them home with written instructions on how to do things they hadn't been trained to do. In addition, patients could be knocked out for procedures they didn't need to be awake for to experience less pain. But that wasn't protocol. Instead, things were done in a way that benefited insurance companies first and patients second. Sarah wasn't happy about it but had accepted that sad fact.

The cab ride to the hospital was another matter. Sarah usually wore a seatbelt in cabs, but without her pillow, she chose not to this time, desperate enough to forgo pressure on her scar to take a chance that the short trip to the cancer center would be safe.

Thankfully, it was. After Sarah checked in, she waited for them to call her name. When they finally did, her mom whispered, "Good luck."

Sarah went to the breast surgeon's office and sat down. Shortly afterward, the breast surgeon's assistant arrived. The man didn't look much older than her daughter.

After introducing himself, he sat in the chair opposite her and pulled out a manilla folder. "Your pathology report came in."

Sarah's breath caught in her throat. She held it, waiting for him to speak.

"It's good news," he said. "You got a pathologic complete response."

Sarah didn't understand.

"It means the cancer is gone."

"It's gone?" Sarah asked.

The surgeon's assistant smiled. "Yes."

Sarah tried to absorb the news, but after months of processing possibly terminal prognoses, it was hard to believe. "How do they know it's for sure gone?"

The assistant set the folder on the desk. "They test the tissue samples after they're removed."

The tissue samples. He meant her breast and underarm lymph nodes.

"Not everyone gets a pCR," he reiterated. "It's the best possible outcome."

Lightheaded, Sarah finally smiled. This was what every patient prayed to hear, and she was actually hearing it.

"Why don't we get started on removing those drains?"

The man reviewed the written log her mother had done and nodded. "The levels are definitely low enough for them to come out."

Sarah was still working through the good news he'd given her.

"This is going to feel strange," he warned. "But it will only take a minute, so sit still, and it will be over before you know it."

Sarah nodded. She took a deep breath and closed her eyes as he approached. She felt a tug near her ribcage, and then all at once, there was a sensation of something slithering out of the center of her chest, along with a wet, sloshing sound.

"You're all done," the assistant said. "I'm putting a bandage on it now."

Sarah blinked rapidly as she held the edge of the examination table. She breathed in and out several times, then sat up straight, thinking the experience was more than strange. It sounded like something she'd once seen in a science fiction flick.

The breast surgeon's assistant congratulated her again on her success. "Stay healthy!" he said on his way out the door.

Healthy.

One word. Two syllables.

It had seemed so out of reach, but Sarah had finally achieved the goal.

She met her mother in the waiting room. Once they were in the hospital hallway, Sarah turned to her and said,

"The pathology report came in. The cancer is gone."

Beverly's eyes widened, and then she gasped. She stepped forward to hug her daughter, and Sarah stepped back to avoid pressure against her chest—even the hugging kind. Both women laughed as they realized what had just happened.

"Let's tell everyone," Beverly suggested.

Sarah fished her phone out of her pocket and dialed Jeff. She never called him at work unless it was urgent, but today was the best kind of urgent.

"What's going on?" Jeff asked. "Are you okay?"

"Jeff," Sarah started but felt her throat close in on the words.

"Sarah?" His tone was increasingly anxious.

"Jeff," she repeated. "I'm cancer free."

"You're cancer…" Jeff paused. "Wait, you're cancer *free*?"

"Yep!" Sarah said, feeling the idea take root and grow into her reality.

"No more cancer?"

"Nope." She could feel herself grow giddy—the way she'd felt twenty-three years prior when she and Jeff had found out the baby would be a girl.

Sarah heard Jeff call out, "My wife is cancer free!" Cheers erupted in the background. He'd shouted the news to everyone in the office, which was unlike him.

"Looks like you're stuck with me," Sarah joked.

"And vice-versa," Jeff replied, playing along.

"Let's wait until Heather gets home to tell her."

"Sure thing," Jeff said before returning to work.

When Sarah finished her conversation with Jeff, her mother, who had stepped away to use her phone, returned to where she had previously stood. "I called Richard and let him know. I usually text Norman, but I think this time I'll call."

Sarah didn't want to call her brother at work because he could be with a customer, so she texted him, letting him know she'd beat the disease.

"*HELL YES!*" was his reply. "*WAY TO GO!*"

Sarah studied the city on the cab ride to the train station. She used to associate coming downtown with browsing fancy stores and eating at trendy restaurants. Now it reminded her of the cancer fight. She'd come back for follow-up visits, but that was it. She'd be thrilled if she never set foot in the area again.

On the train ride home, Sarah considered telling Nancy the good news but hesitated as Nancy hadn't shared the pathology results of her surgery with her. Sarah didn't want to say the wrong thing at the wrong time, so she decided to keep the news to herself unless asked.

Heather squealed with delight after hearing Sarah was cancer free. "I knew it!" she said. "Chemo plus green juice was the one-two punch!"

It was possible that drinking organic vegetables had helped. Sarah had no way of knowing for sure. "Thanks for making all those glasses of juice. I know it was a lot of work."

"You're worth it," Heather said, holding her gaze. "You're worth everything."

Sarah's eyes filled with tears. "Come here," she said. She used her right arm to lightly hug her daughter while using the left to protect her scar. "I love you so much," she told her.

"Love you too," Heather said as they pulled apart.

The next day, Sarah thought of all she'd been through so far. She had finished chemo, had the mastectomy, and had the drains removed. Along the way, an endocrinologist had prescribed medication that balanced her thyroid. She'd have to take that medication for the rest of her life, but the endocrinologist said it was a small price to pay in the grand scheme of things. The tips of her fingers and toes were still numb from chemotherapy, but Dr. Zimmerman said there was a chance that could improve in time. Next, Sarah had a consultation with a radiation oncologist at the nearby branch of her hospital. If she needed radiation, it would be daily for several weeks, so taking the train to the hospital downtown wouldn't work.

Beverly drove her to the appointment, which was only twenty minutes away. Sarah waited in the new doctor's office, hoping she didn't have to start another cancer treatment as she wanted to be done with all of this and move on.

The radiation oncologist entered the room and said hello. He made eye contact with Sarah and said, "I've reviewed your case and determined radiation isn't necessary."

Sarah was ecstatic. Things were finally looking up. They chatted for ten minutes more, the doctor answering the few questions she had before she met her mother in the waiting room.

Her mom raised an eyebrow after they stepped outside.

"I don't need radiation," Sarah announced.

Beverly looked skyward and put a hand on her chest. "Thank God. You deserve a break."

***

As the weeks passed, Sarah found it difficult to raise her arm. Whenever she tried, it felt like she was being stabbed in the underarm with an ice pick.

"Go to physical therapy," Nancy suggested. "I'm doing it, and it really helps. My PT says the sooner you do it, the better. That way, the shoulder won't heal in a hunched-forward fashion."

Sarah's posture wasn't the best since she spent a lot of time at her desk. So skipping physical therapy probably wasn't a good idea.

The next day, Sarah made an appointment with a physical therapist in her network. She set the phone down afterward, hoping they could help. It rang again. She lifted it back up and saw that it was her dad. Norman hadn't called her in a long time, opting to get information about Sarah from her mother or hear how she was doing when Heather visited him.

"How's it going?" he asked after she answered the phone.

"Okay, considering the circumstances."

Sarah told her father about going to physical therapy next.

"I'm available if you need someone to take you."

Sarah had planned to drive herself to the appointments. She had the mastectomy pillow and wanted to get back on the road as she had almost forgotten how to drive. But unlike the chemo treatments, which were downtown and required taking the train, physical therapy would be close to home. So if Norman said he would take her to an appointment and flaked, it wouldn't be a big deal. She could drive herself.

"The first visit is next week. I'll text you the date and time," Sarah replied.

Norman sounded upbeat now that Sarah had taken him up on his offer. Once again, she'd give him an opportunity to be her father.

Chapter 36

Norman rose from his seat as Sarah exited the physical therapy treatment room. He pulled her coat off the wall hook and helped her put it on, making sure the left arm went in first.

"Any progress?" he asked as they walked to the car.

"I'm at sixty percent range of motion." Sarah used her good arm to open the door. "She says that's not bad after ten visits."

Norman texted Beverly an update after starting the car. Even though sharing the information wasn't crucial, he'd been doing it since their first visit, and Beverly didn't seem to mind. Her father had shown up on time to drive her to all her physical therapy appointments, which were nothing like the relaxing hot stone massages she and Jeff had on vacations. Instead, these visits required Sarah to remain calm as the therapist released tight fascia near the scar and broke up adhesions that had formed under her arm. Sometimes, it felt like her flesh was ripping apart during the session, but the therapist assured her it wasn't, so Sarah trusted that everything was fine.

They pulled into the parking lot of the café where they'd been eating after every visit—a soup and sandwich shop Heather found and suggested that Norman try. Her daughter was good at pretending she wasn't orchestrating things behind the scenes when she was a master at doing just that. Heather's maneuvering seemed so effortless they almost went unnoticed. But Sarah knew her daughter better than anyone else. Fixing the relationship between her and Norman was a top priority for her.

"Do we order the usual or go rogue?" Norman asked after they stepped into the café.

Sarah and her father usually split a turkey sandwich. "Let's go rogue," she replied. "I'm in the mood for soup."

Norman also opted for soup, which came with a freshly baked roll. They found a table and sat down, and shortly afterward, a young woman arrived with their food.

Norman reached for his spoon and asked, "How many more visits do you think you'll need before your arm is one hundred percent?"

"I get twenty on our plan, so I hope it's better before I run out of those."

As Sarah buttered her bread, she thought of how much the insurance company had paid for her care and was grateful, as there was no way she could afford the bills herself.

"Make sure you do the home exercises," her father said.

Sarah dug into her soup. "I do them every day."

Having Norman remind her to follow the home physical therapy routine was odd. These interactions with her father were too new, making them feel foreign and stand out. On the other hand, when her mother gave advice, it seemed natural, like a gentle nudge from an older, wiser person she trusted. Sarah guessed it would take time to feel that way about her dad.

***

At Dr. Zimmerman's suggestion, Sarah restarted immunotherapy to prevent a cancer recurrence while going to physical therapy. Unfortunately, the additional treatments caused severe joint pain, so her oncologist stopped immunotherapy indefinitely because the side effects outweighed the benefits of the drug.

Sarah regained full range of motion in her arm when she finished physical therapy. However, the chest wall was still numb, as were her armpit and the underside of her upper arm. The therapist said it could improve, but there were no guarantees the areas would feel as they had before the surgery. She also recommended a compression sleeve, which would be necessary for air travel because she had underarm lymph nodes removed. If Sarah didn't wear the sleeve on the plane, there was a chance her arm could swell to twice its size and possibly stay that way.

Sarah made a note to ask about the sleeve at next week's breast-fitting appointment. Most women wore a lightweight puff to replace the missing breast after surgery, but Sarah had skipped that step since she worked from home, preferring to finish PT first, then get the prosthetic breast and bras when she was able to put on her favorite tops. Although the uneven look was awkward, it was temporary, and she could disguise the issue when she went outside by wearing her down-filled coat. But spring was coming, and Sarah would be out and about soon. She hoped that the people at the medical supply store would be able to make her look like her old self.

Heather came with Sarah to the fitting appointment. As they entered the building, Sarah glanced around, noting the place had a warm, welcoming vibe. A redheaded woman sitting at the front desk greeted them. Once Sarah said her name, the lady smiled and took them to a private room resembling an upscale lingerie boudoir.

"Your fitter will be right in. Make yourself comfortable," she said.

Heather and Sarah removed their coats and set them on the bench before eyeing the offerings hanging on the wall: beautiful bras in stylish colors and camisole tops with built-in pockets for the prosthetic breast. They even had bathing suits.

"These bras look way better than I thought they would," Heather said.

"Agreed." Sarah reached out to touch one of them. "And they're buttery soft."

Sarah's concern about how the bras would look and feel abated after seeing that they were indistinguishable from bras at popular lingerie stores. She and Heather walked around the room, checking out everything they had, and then the fitter came in and introduced herself.

"Every fitter here is a breast cancer survivor, so we understand how you're feeling right now," the woman said.

Sarah hadn't known that before making the appointment. But, now that she did, she felt she could trust this woman completely.

The fitter smiled at Sarah. "We're going to have fun. First, I'm going to measure you so we can find a silicone breast that best matches the one you have. Then I'll have you try on a bunch of bras to see which ones you like. Afterward, we'll look at leisure forms and get you a compression sleeve."

Sarah nodded. It was a lot of new information all at once.

The woman measured Sarah before leaving and returning with a nude bra and two breast options. She had Sarah try each of them. Instead of just seeing how they looked in the bra and comparing them to her remaining breast, she had Sarah put on the fitted tee shirt she had worn to see how each looked under clothes.

"I like the second one," Heather said. "It looks just like your real breast in that top."

Sarah and the fitter had the same opinion. Now that Sarah had found her new breast, she tried a bunch of bras and ended up with two nude ones, two black, and one that was a soft rose.

The fitter put the selected bras and prosthetic breast on her desk before turning to Sarah. "Before we choose a leisure form, I want to give you a tip." The woman leaned forward and said, "Be careful what necklines you choose from now on. See what I mean?"

Sarah looked down the fitter's V-neck shirt and saw the concave chest wall and full, pocketed bra.

She stood up straight, adding, "No one knows when it's a crewneck or turtleneck, but low-cut tops like mine or tops that show cleavage don't work because there's no cleavage on the other side."

"That makes sense," Sarah said, realizing for the first time that she'd have to go through her closet and donate tops she could no longer use. Sarah shrugged it off. As a middle-aged woman, she rarely showed cleavage anymore, anyway.

The fitter left and returned with two leisure forms and a black camisole top. She handed one of the forms to Sarah. "These are filled with quick-drying beads."

Sarah gently squeezed the form and felt the beads move. "It's light. Much lighter than the silicone breast."

"It's great with swimsuits, workout tops, or when you want shape but don't want to wear your normal form."

Sarah tried both leisure forms with the pocketed black cami top, which the fitter said was great for summer or perfect under cardigans. Sarah leaned forward and looked at her reflection in the mirror. The top's design did a great job hiding the scar, and the cami clung to her just right.

"Definitely get the cami," Heather said.

Sarah followed Heather's suggestion and added the cami to her pile, and then she was fitted for the compression sleeve and told how to use it.

The fitter put all the items into a shopping bag and handed it to Sarah. "I've included care instructions for everything. But if you have any questions, give me a call."

"I will," Sarah said. "Thanks for all your help."

As she and Heather got into the car, Heather said, "What a positive experience."

"I know. It was more like a shopping excursion than a medical visit."

"Even better that insurance paid for everything," Heather mentioned.

Sarah couldn't agree more.

***

During the week, Sarah went through her closet and eliminated tops that wouldn't work, and then she and Heather went shopping for new crewneck tees and blouses with higher necklines.

Sarah wore one of her new tops the day she met Nancy for lunch. They chose a French restaurant. Not too fancy of a place, but fancy enough to feel special.

"You look great," Nancy told her after they were seated at a bistro table.

Sarah smiled at her friend. "So do you."

The warm glow of the restaurant lighting was a welcome change from the fluorescent bulbs at the cancer center, and the French love song emanating from the speakers sounded way better than the constant beeping of the chemo machine.

Sarah unfolded the white cloth napkin and laid it across her lap. "How's your family doing?"

"My son is always studying. It seems like he's been becoming a doctor forever, but he'll get there eventually." Nancy smiled, then added, "My sister is still living with me. We've been having a lot of fun, making up for lost time."

Their waiter brought glasses of water and said he'd be back after they had a chance to look at the menu.

"How's your family doing?" Nancy asked.

"They're doing well. They're happy that things have finally settled down."

Both women studied the menu, bouncing options off each other before making a selection and each ordering a glass of wine.

When the waiter brought their drinks, Nancy reached for hers and asked, "Is your brother still dating Dr. Zimmerman?"

"Yes, he is. I just talked to him yesterday, and he was all, 'Rebecca this and Rebecca that.' I know that's her first name, but it throws me every time."

After Nancy took a sip of wine, she asked, "Have you seen them together yet?"

"Not yet," Sarah said. "But everyone's getting together for Easter, so she might be there. If so, I'll try to remember to call her by her first name."

Nancy chuckled. Only she could understand how difficult that may be to do. She took another sip of wine and asked, "How are things with your dad?"

"It's going oddly well." Sarah set her wine glass on the table, trying to think of the best way to explain. "He started acting like I always wanted him to act after I stopped caring what he did."

Nancy nodded. Then the waiter showed up with their salads.

They chatted about recent movies they'd watched as they ate, and when the main courses arrived, Nancy finally asked, "How are you feeling?"

Sarah had been avoiding that topic as she didn't want to sour the mood with talk of health. But since Nancy asked, she wanted to be honest. "I'm happy to be alive, but I don't feel like my old self." She sighed. "This pixie cut isn't my style, but it's better than being bald. And the prosthetic breast looks great. I mean, I can't tell the difference when I look in the mirror." She paused, then admitted, "But I don't feel like myself. I don't feel attractive anymore."

"You look beautiful to me," Nancy said. "And I'll bet your husband thinks you look beautiful too."

Nancy and Sarah exchanged a look that said everything without saying a word. Her friend knew how she felt because she was going through the same thing. Nancy wore an amazing wig as her hair grew out. Sarah chose to live with the awkward hair growth phases as they came. Both wore pocketed bras with breast forms. It was what they had decided to do, and they could learn to live with the decision or get reconstruction at a later date.

"How are you doing?" Sarah asked.

"I've been feeling everything you described, but overall, I'm in a different place."

Sarah had never asked about her prognosis, but for some reason, doing so seemed appropriate now. "Did you get the pCR?"

"Not this time." Nancy held her gaze, wearing a genuine smile. "But I'm enjoying every moment of my life," Nancy said, digging into her food. "God has a plan for us all, and today, he wants me to have fun with you."

Sarah had no idea how Nancy could be so happy as she faced what was to come, but she smiled back at her friend. They would continue to have fun despite the chance that one day, Nancy could be gone.

We're all here for as long as we're meant to be here, Nancy had said in an article Sarah read. That could be true. Sarah didn't know for sure.

If there was a God, Sarah hoped He was planning a long, happy life for Sarah, surrounded by loved ones and good health. But, if her life was meant to be shorter, she wished for the power Nancy had to enjoy it all the way to the end.

Chapter 37

Sarah looked out the window as the plane landed in Phoenix, Arizona. It was the first vacation she and Jeff had taken in a long time, and they both looked forward to staying at the luxury resort in Sedona, Arizona, where they planned to swim, hike, and eat lots of Mexican food.

As they rode the shuttle to the rental car area, Sarah removed her compression sleeve and stashed it in her purse. Having it on her arm made her feel uncomfortable, but thankfully, she only had to wear it on the plane. Although it was mid-October, the temperature in Phoenix was ninety-five degrees. It was a dry heat but still too warm for Sarah, who preferred the eighty-degree days, and fifty-degree nights Sedona had this time of year.

Jeff turned to her after they hopped into the rental car. "It's about two hours until we get to Sedona. Do you want to head there now or grab a bite to eat?"

Sarah wasn't hungry yet but didn't want to starve Jeff. "I'll leave it up to you."

Jeff decided to drive to their destination and get food after they arrived. Before they left, he stopped at a convenience store and bought two bottled waters, as he'd heard they should always have water with them in the desert.

Sarah's phone vibrated as they got back into the car. Her father had left a voicemail message. "Have a great time!" Norman said. "Don't forget to take pictures."

She'd been doing that since she received the photo album. Slowly but surely, she was filling the pages of the book. The most recent picture was from Linda's birthday party. Sarah, Jeff, Heather, Caleb, and Mike sat next to each other on the gray sectional sofa, smiling as Norman asked them to say cheese.

Sarah gazed at the mountains as they headed north. It had been almost a year since treatment ended and only a few months since she had the chemotherapy port removed. She didn't have the energy she had before having cancer, but she no longer slept all the time and finally felt well enough to enjoy a trip like this.

The hotel website said the pool was heated so people could swim at night. One reviewer claimed she had gone swimming in January after it snowed. She said the pool was so warm that steam rose from the top of the water and that she was only cold when she got out to put on the hotel robe. Sarah wondered how they could afford to keep a large pool that hot before realizing that's why they charged a ridiculous amount of money to stay there. It was so people could have experiences like those.

As they got closer to Sedona, the scenery changed. The mountains went from tan to rust, and the cactus trees were replaced with juniper and Pinon pine. Sarah perked up as they drove down the town's main drag, her eyes taking in the little shops and restaurants surrounded by breathtaking red rocks. Most of the hotels were off the highway, but theirs was a bit further away, tucked into Boynton Canyon.

Jeff turned onto the road that took them to where they were staying. Mansions dotted the side of it, the homes spaced far enough apart to be close to their neighbor but not too close.

"I'm already digging this place," Jeff commented as he glanced around.

"Me too," Sarah said. "I may never want to leave."

They grinned at each other and, shortly afterward, pulled up to the resort entrance, where a security guard greeted them with a smile. Once they told him who they were, he explained how to find the main lobby, and they went there and checked in. Next, someone took their bags and asked them to hop on a golf cart before whisking them to their room.

Sarah's eyes widened as the young man opened the door to their casita and set their luggage off to the side. She'd stayed at some lovely places, but nothing compared to this. The room had a king bed, TV, and a sitting room with a sofa and kiva fireplace. She and Jeff entered the bathroom and saw the deep soaking tub, separate shower, and double sinks, all in top-of-the-line finishes.

"Yeah, we're not leaving," Jeff joked. "We'll try all this stuff out soon. But first, let's eat."

They walked to the main lobby and checked out the restaurant. Once they saw carnitas tacos on the menu, they ordered those with prickly pear margaritas since it was a local specialty. Everything was next-level delicious, making Sarah wish they had this kind of Mexican food at home. But, since they didn't, she would eat it every day she was here, firmly believing that vacation calories didn't count.

Between air travel, car travel, and tequila, it had been a long day, so Sarah and Jeff returned to their casita and quickly fell asleep in their comfy bed.

Sarah woke before Jeff did, feeling well-rested. She quietly padded to the patio door and pulled the curtain aside. The sun's morning rays lit up the panoramic red rock mountains, making them glow with warmth. A tall spire in the distance caught Sarah's eye. She was staring at it when Jeff appeared behind her and wrapped his arms around her waist.

"Morning," he said.

Sarah turned to face him. "Morning," she replied before giving him a kiss.

He pulled away and asked, "Do you want to go hiking or swimming after breakfast?"

"Swimming," Sarah replied.

Sarah had a fruit smoothie for breakfast so she wouldn't look bloated in her new swimsuit. Finding one she liked had been difficult as most mastectomy swimsuits were matronly, and although Sarah was middle-aged, she still wanted to look good. Thankfully, Nancy recommended an online store with stylish mastectomy swimwear, and Sarah found a purple floral one-piece with a fun boho vibe.

She put it on after they returned to the room, then examined herself in the mirror. The underarms were a bit higher than her old suit, which was a great way to hide any scars, and there was shirring at the bust where cleavage would usually show. All and all, it didn't look much different than regular one-piece suits. Only a trained eye could tell them apart.

Jeff held her hand on the way to the pool, seeming to sense that she was self-conscious about wearing the swimsuit in public for the first time. He grabbed two towels from the stack available to guests and set them on the padded seat in one of the empty cabanas.

"We should probably use sunblock," Jeff said as he removed his tee shirt.

Sarah pulled the bottle out of her bag and squirted some into the palm of her hand as Jeff positioned himself so she could easily reach his back. When Sarah finished putting it on him, he turned toward her, took the bottle, and squirted some into his hand so he could apply it to his arms and legs.

Jeff looked at Sarah afterward. "I should put some on you too."

Sarah hesitated before pulling the sheer purple swimsuit cover-up over her head. It provided a modicum of modesty as she walked through the resort, but she was at the pool now, and it was time.

Jeff rubbed sunblock onto her back. She put some on the rest of her exposed skin when he finished. Afterward, they sat back and took in the view of the pool surrounded by red mountains. It was jaw-droppingly gorgeous. Sarah took a picture with her phone but knew the photo wouldn't do the place justice as sometimes you just had to be somewhere to understand how awesome it was.

"I'm going in," Jeff said. He looked at Sarah. "You coming?"

Sarah surveyed the other people at the pool. To the left, a family of four munched on chips and guacamole. To the right, an older woman with a floppy hat was reading a book.

Sarah stood. She watched Jeff head to the shallow area and climb down the steps. He glanced back at her, and she began walking toward him, taking measured breaths. She almost stopped to ensure the others were still doing what they had been doing before she rose but chose not to, telling herself they were busy with their lives and had no reason to stare at her.

Once she entered the pool and was up to her neck, she eyed the other people and learned they were doing the same thing they had been doing. She was just another woman on vacation with her spouse.

Jeff began swimming to the other end of the pool. Sarah stayed next to him, matching his stride. They rested their arms on the edge and faced each other, then Jeff came closer and kissed her on the lips. He put his arm around her waist and rubbed her back as they stared at the mountains, then they swam to the middle of the pool, where Sarah playfully splashed him. Smiling, Jeff splashed her back.

At that moment, Sarah finally became a woman on vacation with her spouse. She forgot she was wearing a mastectomy swimsuit and had a good time. They stayed by the pool most of the day, ordering chicken tacos and margaritas for lunch, and then retired to their room for a much-needed nap.

That evening, Sarah showered and put on the black nightie she had altered. Although there were beautiful lace pocketed bras, bralettes, camisoles, and stylish swimwear for people like her, there didn't seem to be any mastectomy lingerie. Maybe she was supposed to wear one of the bras and underwear for date night, but that bored Sarah because she wore those every day. With some needle and thread, she added fabric to the back of the left side of the nightie, creating a pocket to hold the lightweight form she'd bought to use just for times like this.

Sarah applied lip gloss and found Jeff waiting for her in bed with the fireplace crackling nearby. She strutted toward him seductively, the way she had before getting sick.

Jeff pulled her into his arms and kissed her passionately. With more passion than he had in years. His lips trailed down her neck as his hands explored her body, then he slipped the right shoulder strap of her nightie off and began kissing her breast. Thankfully, the left strap stayed in place, so the form-filled nightgown covered her scar. In the old days, the nightie would've come off by now. Now, she had to navigate having sex partially clothed.

As Jeff pulled her onto his lap, he slipped off the left strap of her nightie. Sarah was about to protest but didn't get a chance because Jeff started kissing her scar. The chest wall was still numb from surgery, but she could feel his soft lips repeatedly touching her skin. The action caused a swell of emotion so powerful it made her body tremble and brought tears to her eyes. Then, Jeff looked up at her, and a moment later, their lips crashed together with an intensity Sarah had never experienced before.

She was still thinking about it as she tied the laces of her gym shoes the following day. It was the best sex they'd had in decades, which didn't make sense as this was the worst she'd looked in all that time. Maybe it was because they were on vacation at a fancy resort. Or maybe it was the margaritas. It was also possible that Jeff loved her more now because of what they'd been through together, and her appearance was secondary to how he felt.

Sarah donned her baseball cap and grabbed her water bottle, ready to go on a hike. She put her cell phone in her pocket even though reception was iffy in the canyon. She may not be able to make a call, but she could take pictures.

They walked to the concierge and asked the man what hikes were nearby.

"There's the Boynton Canyon trail, which is longer, and the Vista trail, which is a half-mile hike to the vortex." The man pointed to the spire. "It's right up there by Kachina Woman."

"Kachina Woman?" Jeff asked.

The concierge clarified. "That tall, thin rock formation is called Kachina Woman. Native Americans believe she guards the sacred place."

Jeff eyed Sarah. "Which trail do you prefer?"

Sarah gazed at the spire, feeling pulled in that

direction. "Let's try the Vista trail and check out the vortex."

They located the trail entrance. Jeff led the way through the red rocks and trees, their footfalls the only sound on the red sandy path. It occurred to Sarah that there were bears and bobcats here. Even mountain lions. One could appear out of nowhere, and she or Jeff could die.

We're all here for as long as we're meant to be here, Nancy had said.

Sarah accepted the risk as she continued, reminding herself she had no control. The path grew a bit more challenging as they went upward. They had to climb several rock steps and pay attention to their footing as they did it to make sure they didn't trip and fall.

Jeff stopped to take a drink of water afterward. Sarah did the same. They were used to walking on paved streets and could walk for miles at home, but the changing elevation and terrain made it harder here. She and Jeff had to take a short break to catch their breath.

A juniper tree with twisted branches caught Sarah's eye, and she asked Jeff to take a picture of her standing next to it. He took a few, and then she took a picture of Jeff next to the same tree.

They continued upward, and Sarah heard Native American music in the distance. Jeff pointed to a man sitting high on the rocks, playing the flute. His serene song floated through the canyon, giving what was already a special place a truly magical feel.

The soulful music made Sarah reflect on her cancer

journey. It brought her a new friend, made her and Jeff grow closer, and the person who cured her of the disease ended up being the right woman for Mike. Heather had a grandfather she adored, and Sarah and Norman had a good relationship for the first time in fifty years.

She and Jeff reached Kachina Woman. The view of the canyon from this vantage point was the most beautiful thing Sarah had ever seen.

As Jeff laced his fingers around hers, she remembered all those trips to the hospital. Initially, the hour-long journey each way had seemed the only negative aspect of choosing that cancer center. But now, she realized what a positive role the train played in her life. It had been more than a mode of transportation. It was an agent of transformation—a healing train.

The End

Thanks for reading *The HealingTrain.*

I hope you enjoyed it.

Your FREE book is waiting.

The Rescue is the heartwarming story of the dog that cheated death and transformed a woman's life.

Get your free copy at the link below.

To get your free copy, just join my readers' group here:

kimcano.com/the-rescue-giveaway-lp

Books by Kim Cano

Novels:

A Widow Redefined

On The Inside

Eighty and Out

His Secret Life

When the Time Is Right

The Healing Train

Novelette:

The Rescue

Short Story Collection:

For Animal Lovers

About the Author

Kim Cano is the author of six women's fiction novels: *A Widow Redefined*, *On The Inside*, *Eighty and Out*, *His Secret Life*, *When the Time Is Right*, and *The Healing Train*. Kim has also written a short story collection called *For Animal Lovers*. 10% of the sale price of that book is donated to the ASPCA® to help homeless pets.

Kim wrote a contemporary romance called *My Dream Man* under the pen name Marie Solka.

Kim lives in the Chicago suburbs with her husband and cat.

Visit her website for a free book and learn of new releases: www.kimcano.com

Find Kim Online:

Website: www.kimcano.com

On Twitter: twitter.com/KimCano2

Facebook Fan Page:
facebook.com/pages/Kim-Cano/401511463198088

Goodreads:
goodreads.com/author/show/5895829.Kim_Cano

Acknowledgements

I want to thank Dr. Gradishar and the Northwestern Medicine Prentice Women's Hospital team for their hard work saving my life. I would also like to thank my family for taking care of me during my cancer battle. Everyone did something, but I would like to mention my mom, who dropped everything and rushed to Illinois from Florida. She stayed here until I was cancer-free. She cooked, cleaned, and took me to all my chemo sessions downtown. That was a lot of train rides! Thankfully, my husband worked from home during my illness. By day, he was an IT manager. At night, he would wash mountains of veggies and make green juice, then assure me everything would be okay. After my surgery, my husband's nurse cousin took care of me in her home. She took a week off work, emptied my surgical drains, cooked me breakfast, lunch, and dinner, and ensured we only watched feel-good films.

While I was sick, I worried about my book business. I didn't have the energy to market my books, but I got lucky because a hotshot book marketer named Melissa Storm from Novel Publicity took me on as a client. She and her team doubled my book sales. I appreciate all their help and cannot recommend their services enough.

Lastly, I would like to thank my friends who went out of their way to check on me. Some of you had already won your own cancer battle and gave me hope.

I don't want to forget my cat, Oliver. He is always by my side and is the best medicine of all.

Made in United States
North Haven, CT
21 May 2024

52753863R10176